Without Chance

By Christopher Bailey

Published by Phase Publishing, LLC

Without Chance

Starjumper Legacy:
The Crystal Key

Coming Soon:
The Vanishing Sun
The Plague of Dawn

Without Chance

Christopher Bailey

Phase Publishing, LLC
Seattle

Text copyright © 2014 by Christopher Bailey
Cover art copyright © 2014 by Phase Publishing, LLC

Cover art by Tugboat Design
http://www.tugboatdesign.net

Phase Publishing, LLC first paperback edition
July 2014

ISBN 978-0-9899734-3-4
Library of Congress Control Number 2014910630
Cataloging-in-Publication Data on file.

For everyone who has ever been
condemned for loving another.

And for my Angel.
Without you, I wouldn't have a Chance.

CONTENTS

CONTENTS

Prologue

The Dream

It was always the same. All I could feel was pain and heat. Pain from the bruise on my forehead that I was sure was just developing. Pain from the fire that was slowly, but tangibly, rising all around. Locked in a steel prison, burning alive as I peered through a tiny glass window, screaming noiselessly for someone to help me.

No one would help me. The face outside the tiny window was grotesque. It was a devil, I know it was a devil, but it wore a cheap rubber mask to make itself look human. I'm not sure which human it was supposed to look like, but he wasn't pretty.

Underneath the mask, the face was all wrong. It bulged in the wrong places, a sharp red chin peered out from beneath the rubber. Two small horns had pierced the mask, protruding from the forehead of the garish face. Fierce, yellow eyes seemed to burn into me, their glee at my anguish evident.

As quickly as it had appeared, the horrible face was gone. Moments later, a new face appeared. The heat was rising. I was still screaming, but I couldn't even hear myself anymore. Everything was silent.

I pounded on the door, but no noise came back to me. Even the flames licking all around brought nothing to dispel the cacophonous silence. As the new face appeared, time seemed to slow. I shouted my pleas for help.

The face drew close. This face was human, though I could not distinguish the features exactly. It was a nice face though, warm and pleasant, though the expression on it was sad.

Surrounding the image outside the glass was a halo of wispy light, like a backlit silhouette. The light was golden, and seemed to shine not from the face, but from somewhere deeper. It trailed off the face in my window like iridescent steam. As the face stopped just before the window, it spoke. I couldn't hear the words. I couldn't hear anything. But I knew what the voice said, as it echoed in my mind.

"I'm sorry, Ryan. I can't help you." Then the claws came, breaking through the form in my window as though my regretful visitor was made of nothing more substantial than the wispy light surrounding it. The pleasant face broke apart like smoke in a breeze, glowing faintly for a moment before it was gone.

The devil in the human mask reappeared. He

was laughing. I couldn't hear it. I could feel it, grating against my bones as the flames consumed the tattered remains of my flesh. I silently screamed again, and the dream broke.

I sat bolt upright, startled awake by a bump in the road. It never seemed to matter when or where I had that dream, I always woke up at the same point; just before the fire devoured the last of me. I didn't understand how that worked.

I rubbed my eyes, and ran my hands through my longish hair. My dad kept telling me I should cut it. It didn't even reach my shoulders, so I didn't know what the big deal was. Besides, I took care of it. It was nothing special, just the sort of dirty blonde that half the kids I know had, just the slightest hint of an outward curl at the tips. My dad beside me spoke, pulling me more fully into the waking world.

"You okay Sport?" he asked me. I hated when he called me that.

"I'm fine. And I'm not five," I retorted.

He glanced over at me. I got my hair and looks from him, which is to say he's about as average as I am. Although I got my blue eyes from my mother, thank God. My father's eyes were a dull, listless gray. They used to be a lot brighter, before mom died. He sighed and nodded.

"Sorry Ryan," was all he said. He couldn't get it through his head that I was fourteen, not five. He still called me Sport, still kept trying to tousle my hair.

He even asked me if I wanted to go to the zoo last month. What he was thinking, I have no idea. Lions, and tigers, and bears? Yeah, right. Just give me my mp3 player and my game console, and leave me alone. Was that too much to ask?

Apparently it was. Not only would he not leave me alone, but he went and uprooted me in the middle of the school year, taking me away from all of my friends, my baseball team, my home, even my mother's grave. He basically robbed me of my entire life. He said it was all for his job, but personally I thought he just couldn't stand being where everything reminded him of her.

She'd died a year ago. Cancer, pretty common these days, but she hadn't beaten it like some people did. We'd spent two years before she finally died watching her wither and rot in her own body, and not a thing any of us could do about it. Nothing had been the same after that. Dad barely spoke to me, and when he did he treated me like I should still be playing Cops and Robbers with my kindergarten playgroup. Everyone we talked to was constantly telling us how sorry they were, as if they actually gave a damn.

To top it off, we moved from Phoenix to some backwater redneck town called Turnbridge. This place was so far off the map I couldn't even find it when I looked. Dad said it wasn't that small, had fifty thousand people. Please, anything less than a cool half million and you're kidding yourself.

We had actually come into town yesterday, and moved all our stuff into a barn that they apparently call a house in this part of the country. It was okay, I guess, but Dad said we'd be without internet for at least two months while he saves up enough money at his new job in the local hospital to pay to have lines run out to our place.

I'm not kidding, we actually were going to have to pay someone to have internet lines run out to our place. What kind of civilized town doesn't have lines for internet and cable run to every property already? I could answer that fairly simply. This town wasn't civilized.

"You ready?" he asked, again breaking me out of my thoughts. We were pulling up in front of the school.

"Are you kidding? I can't believe it takes half an hour to get to school," I grumbled at him. "And I can't believe you're making me go to school on a Thursday, one day after moving to this dump. Can't cut a guy a bit of a break? Couldn't we have taken the week to settle in? It's not like I'll be behind or anything. They probably teach the three R's; reading, writing, and roping. Half the town probably has the same last name. Bunch of inbred, dumbass hicks."

"Ryan!" my father snapped, giving me his warning look. He hated it when I swore. I didn't care though, he didn't intimidate me. He was too broken to do anything about it since Mom died anyway.

I glanced out the window at the school. The place looked about like the rest of the town. It was old, rundown, and shabby. Definitely not up to my standards. As the car pulled to a stop I grabbed my bag from the floor in front of me and jumped out.

"I love…" my dad began before I slammed the door on him. How could a guy be expected to build a decent rep in a new town with his father shouting that kind of thing across the school grounds? Fortunately, nobody seemed to have noticed.

The kids were a bit more fashionably dressed than I'd have expected, only about five years behind the current styles by my estimation, though there were definitely more cowboy boots and hats than I was comfortable with. It wasn't the universal standard, but they were clearly widely accepted out here.

As I walked toward the front doors of the school, backpack slung over one shoulder, I actively avoided the stares being directed my way. I was obviously unfamiliar, and clearly not from around here.

I didn't blame them. I'd have stared too, if one of these yokels had wandered into my school back home. That didn't make me any less resentful though. This was probably one of those towns where everyone knew everyone, and was nose-deep in everyone else's business. I took a deep breath. This was going to be a long day.

Chapter One
Chance Meeting

I looked immediately for the office, since I had to check in and pick up my class schedule. It wasn't hard to find, first door to the right as soon as I walked in. It was open, and I could see the receptionist's desk.

Heading through the door I was greeted by a portly, though friendly-looking woman behind a desk. She wore a floral print dress, and had her hair tied up behind her head. Unfortunately that made her round face rounder, but at least she looked nice enough even if she did look like she belonged in an old sitcom.

Her greeting consisted of holding one hand up to forestall my speaking as she talked into a telephone that had to be at least a few decades old. I mean, the thing still had a rotary dial. I'd seen those before, in movies.

I looked at her desk. Tidy, but a little cluttered. She had a picture on one side, showing herself, a man only slightly less round than she was, and a chubby-cheeked infant. A whole round family, I thought to myself. They looked happy. I remembered what that was like. I sighed and looked away from the picture.

She spoke for a moment to whoever was on the other end, hung up, and turned to me with a warm smile. I found myself liking her, despite my unpleasant mood that morning.

"Good morning, sir," she said. I liked the way she called me sir. It implied that she intended to treat me like a person, rather than a child. I smiled back. Maybe this town wasn't a total loss.

"Good morning," I replied. "My name is Ryan Jacobs. I start school here today and need to pick up my class schedule." Her smile broadened.

"That's jus' wonderful!" she exclaimed, her accent showing through. I found I liked her accent too. It was soft and charming, rather than the cowboy movie accent I was expecting. "The good Lord knows we can benefit from a polite new student. We jus' got your transcripts on Monday. You're a pretty good student already, but there's a bit of room for improvement in your social sciences scores." She winked at me. "Don't worry though, we all struggle with something. Mr. James teaches in that department, and he's wonderful. We'll get that C to an A in no time with him."

She handed me a few slips of paper. I looked down and flipped quickly through them. One was a copy of school rules. Blah, blah, blah, same as every other school. The next sheet was my class schedule. I had algebra first. It should be illegal to schedule math classes first thing in the morning. Woodshop next though, so that was cool. I skimmed over the rest. Nothing riveting.

The third sheet was a school map. The school was bigger than it looked, I realized. I was suddenly very grateful for the map as I regarded the many turns of the surprisingly long hallways. The school must extend pretty far back from the road, though it didn't look it, driving up.

"I'm Mrs. Bradley," she told me. I looked back up at her. "Anything you need, or if you have any questions at all, you jus' come to me, okay? I'll be right here." I smiled at her again.

"Thank you. I'll definitely do that," I told her honestly before turning and heading into the press of students in the hallway outside the office. I paused just outside the doors to track down classroom 3C on the map.

The lights flickered slightly overhead. Wow, maybe rundown was the right description for this place, I thought in annoyance. I had just found the C hallway when someone bumped into me, causing me to drop my papers.

"Sorry," sneered a voice as it moved past. I looked up into the face of what I instinctively recognized as the popular kid in the school.

This was given away both by the confidence in his walk, the unpleasant smile on his face, and the group of his fellow students that moved with him, laughing as he chuckled at me. The moron wore a great big cowboy hat as if it were a sign announcing his coolness. Clearly he misread the sign, I thought.

He turned and kept walking, his entourage in close at his heels. Only one of the girls in the group kept looking my way. Long blonde hair, very pretty. The kind of girl most guys fawned over. She gave me an apologetic smile before they rounded a corner and moved out of sight. You could have stopped and helped, I thought bitterly, or even said something to the jerk.

As I picked up my papers and stood, I felt eyes on me. You know that creepy, hairs standing up on the back of your neck kind of feeling when you're being stared at? This wasn't like that at all. Just sort of an awareness that someone's eyes were on me. I looked up, tossing my head slightly to shake my hair back.

He was standing beside the top of the stairs, leaning up against the railing as the other kids streamed past him. He was so still, it was like watching water rush past a rock sticking up out of a river. Movement churned all around him, but there was only perfect stillness within him.

There was something sad, something bright, and something else I couldn't identify in his eyes. He was also watching me. Intensely, though not unpleasantly. He was just very focused, and clearly not embarrassed to be caught watching someone.

As I looked up at him, he tilted his head slightly to one side curiously. Might as well start trying to rebuild now, I thought. I gave him a half-smile and a nod before looking back down to pick up the last of my papers. When I stood back up, he was gone.

I followed the map to my algebra class, walked into the room, and stopped. Good ol' Mr. Popularity was sitting there, on the far side of the room. Great, as if math weren't painful enough. Guys like that always got me riled up. Just that stupid, arrogant smile, the way they just assume all attention is on them… I can't stand that.

"You may seat yourself there, Mr. Jacobs," came a voice behind me. I looked up at the tall man now beside me, and followed his gesture to an empty seat toward the back. I nodded and moved that way. The man moved into the room, taking a seat behind the desk up front. Enter the teacher.

He was older and wore thick glasses, but stood quite straight and in a manner I could only describe as "proper". I glanced at the propped-open door. Mr. Allen, the nameplate read. Just as I moved into my seat, I heard someone across the room whisper sharply to me.

"Hey! City boy!" came the harsh sound. I looked up. Mr. Popular was looking at me. He leaned slightly forward and mouthed clearly "My… school…"

I looked away, barely suppressing an eye-roll. This guy was way too full of himself. I might have to figure out a way to take him down a peg.

I wasn't sure how though. I wasn't big, not a great fighter, and didn't have any friends to back me up. This guy was obviously bigger, older, and stronger than I was. Hell, he probably rode bulls in his spare time. Maybe a rodeo champ. That's probably why he was so popular out here. He also had a lot of friends, if his groupies this morning were any indication. Definitely not to be handled lightly.

"Mr. Porter," the teacher said from the front of the room. All eyes turned his way. "Kind of you to greet the new student, but I'd appreciate it if we kept social hour out of my algebra class. Am I understood?"

"Yes, sir," the hick, apparently last named Porter, said. Why did so many teachers feel the need to address kids by their last names?

The rest of the hour was as I expected. I wasn't behind at all, they were almost exactly where I'd left off at my old school. It was dull, but manageable.

I made it out the door at the end of the hour before Porter could catch up and make a nuisance of himself, and headed deeper into the press of students pouring out of the classrooms. I wasn't a coward or anything, I just preferred to avoid trouble when I could. At least until I knew I had the upper hand.

Each class was similar, not too far from where I'd left off, though in woodshop I was going to have to start the semester's project from scratch. The others were at least a week ahead. I had a good idea what I was doing though, so it wouldn't be too hard to catch up. A free period or two in here and I'd have it all wrapped up.

When I made it to lunch though, I couldn't help but take a few deep breaths. So far, I was halfway through my day, and had been spoken to only by teachers, secretaries, and one complete ass. I got a lot of stares of course, and quite a few whispered conversations among people across the room as they pointed at me, but that was about it. Lovely.

I got my food, and looked around for a place to sit. The lights were flickering in here too. Not enough to be really obvious, just enough to be kind of annoying. That kind of thing could give a guy a migraine.

I felt the eyes on me again. Following the feeling, I saw the same kid who'd been watching me this morning sitting at a table with a couple of girls. He was watching me unashamedly again, so again I gave him a casual smile and a nod. He blinked, then slowly smiled. It wasn't a creepy slow smile, it was warm and seemed genuine, tinged with pleased surprised.

Taking this as an invitation, I moved his way. The girls looked up as I approached. I was sitting down when one of the girls noticed and gave me a dirty look.

"Umm... I don't think so," the other said, eliciting a giggle from the other girl. "You do not seriously think you can sit with us, do you?" I looked to the boy, but he just watched me curiously. I clenched my jaw a few times.

"Apparently not," I said and stood, taking my tray with me. I moved to a back table that wasn't yet occupied and sat.

"Hey, can I sit here?" a voice behind me asked a moment later. I turned and looked up. The boy was watching me with that same intensity, but there was definite hope in his eyes at the question. I nodded.

"Sure, if you want."

"Thanks," he said, sliding into a seat across from me. "Sorry about those girls. Niceness isn't really their strong suit." I nodded again. His accent was subtle, just enough to let me know he had some local roots, but it was definitely there.

"That seems to be a common trend around here," I replied. He smiled at this.

"It's not so bad. Problem is, it's all the jerks who are most talkative. Those of us with better manners tend to be overlooked a lot." He looked down at his tray for a moment before looking back up. "I saw what Noah did this morning. I wish I'd gotten to you first. I could have warned you about him. The guy is a Grade A thug." I looked up at him.

"Noah? You mean Mr. Porter?" I asked, imitating my math teacher. The boy laughed, a bright, playful sound.

"You have Mr. Allen for Algebra, huh? I hate

it when they call you by your last name," he said. I grinned.

"Me too. I'm not my father, and I have a perfectly good first name," I said.

"Which is…?" he asked with a raised brow.

"Ryan," I replied, holding my hand out to him. He flinched back. I pulled my hand slowly back, not sure whether to be offended.

"Sorry, I just sort of have a thing about being touched," he said apologetically.

"Good to know," I said with a nod. I'd have to remember that. He looked embarrassed. "What's yours?" I asked, hoping to change the subject, since he looked definitely uncomfortable. I heard giggling and glanced up. Several people at nearby tables were watching us and whispering to each other, snickering at comments others were making.

"Chance," he said, bringing my eyes back to him.

"Really? That's different. Kind of cool though," I said. He smiled.

"I like it," he replied.

"What's with them?" I asked, gesturing with my fork at our audience. Chance glanced over his shoulder at them.

"Ah, don't mind them. It's not really considered acceptable to be seen with me," he replied, then hesitated. "Actually, I should have warned you about that, too. Talking to me is likely to make you very unpopular around here."

"That's okay," I replied. "I was never all that popular myself. Had a few friends back home, but that's all. Besides, nobody else here seems worth talking to at all."

"You only really need one good friend," Chance said. "Where are you from?"

"Phoenix," I replied.

"Arizona?" he asked. I nodded.

"Cool. Long way from home, huh? Move here with family?"

"Just my dad. He's all the family I've got. He works at the hospital." Chance made a face.

"I hate that place. Creeps me out," he said. I laughed.

"It's not that bad, as long as you can handle sick people,"

"Sick people I don't mind. It's the dead ones that freak me out."

"Makes sense," I said, making a mental note that Chance was apparently a fairly sensitive guy, and to take it easy with him. He definitely seemed nice though, even if he was fairly intense.

Despite his calm, and his casual manner, there was something almost frantic churning underneath. He seemed so excited that someone was actually hanging out with him. Poor guy really wasn't popular. He had been sitting with those girls though, so I wasn't sure what the real dynamic there was.

"Is the food always this bad?" I asked him, taking another bite of the macaroni and cheese.

"No," Chance said. "Normally you can't even tell it's food." I couldn't help it, I burst out laughing. After several more bites of the mediocre meal, I switched my attention back to Chance.

"How about you? Did you move here?"

"Born and raised, I'm embarrassed to say," he said. I chuckled.

"At least you didn't get absorbed into the hick culture," I told him, gesturing at his wardrobe. He wore a light gray t-shirt with dark gray edging, a pair of blue jeans, and a pair of worn, comfortable-looking sneakers. Not high fashion, but not out of the loop, either. Casual was totally acceptable.

I wasn't too far off that mark myself, though I had a name brand logo on my blue shirt, and my shoes were definitely newer. I wasn't prone to top fashion either, but I did prefer to stay within bounds of acceptability. He smiled.

"Yeah, I never got into the whole rodeo thing," he said, toying with the food on his plate. "Part of why I was never all that popular, I guess."

"You were sitting with those girls, though," I pointed out. He glanced their way before looking back at me.

"Nah, they just don't care that I'm there. They never talk to me or anything though. It's just an easy empty seat." I found I was having a bit of trouble figuring out why he wasn't popular.

He was good looking, definitely good looking enough to gain some popularity. He was nice, which admittedly hurt his chances at school-wide fame, but he certainly seemed cool enough. Just a casual kind of guy. Certainly nothing that would contribute to the school-wide shunning he kept implying.

"Well, keep sitting with me and I suspect we'll never have to worry about anyone sitting at our table," I told him, gesturing around. Every table in the place was full, except ours. We had our own private table in the back corner, and everyone else seemed to be actively avoiding it.

I suspected I'd just effectively assassinated my chances of gaining a group of friends by befriending Chance, but he was right. You only needed one good one. Chance glanced around at the stares and snickers, and sighed.

"Yeah, as long as you don't mind joining me in my outcast status, we're all set back here."

"Sounds like a plan," I told him with a smile, and finished the last of my lunch. "Gotta go, English time." I said. He nodded, and gave me a wave as I moved off.

This place definitely had a weird social system, I thought. The big dumb hick was the star, and the casually cool guys like Chance and myself were totally shut out. Could be worse though, I told myself. At least it looks like I've got someone to hang with.

Chapter Two
The Bible Thumper

The rest of the day was no different. I was ignored by most students, snickered at by a few, and I wasn't far behind in any of my classes. Two of them I was even ahead in. Chance and I didn't have any classes together I was disappointed to learn, so I didn't see him again until my dad came to pick me up.

My dad had been so thrilled that he'd worked out a work schedule that allowed him to both drop me off and pick me up. Unfortunately, it meant he was working six six-hour days every week. He seemed to think it was worth it though.

I had just climbed into the passenger side of my dad's green sedan when I spotted Chance by the school doors. I smiled and gave him a wave. He waved back, and grinned.

"New friend?" my dad asked. I nodded.

"Yeah, he's cool." I said casually. There was

something about him that I really liked, but it certainly wasn't acceptable to say something like that to your father.

"Glad to hear it," he replied. "So your first day wasn't too bad after all."

"Could have been worse. Met the school bully though," I told him. He looked over at me, concerned.

"Everything okay?" he asked. I nodded.

"Yeah, I've got it," I said, a little annoyed that he was prying before I reminded myself that I'd brought it up.

"Okay. Let me know if he becomes a problem, all right?"

"I said I've got it, Dad."

He nodded, and began the long drive home. We didn't speak the rest of the drive. We usually didn't. In fact, that conversation was the longest one we'd had in several months.

We pulled up in front of our little two bedroom rambler, gravel driveway crunching under the tires. At least it was shady, I thought. There were a lot more trees here than in Arizona. Good lawn, too. Enough space for some flag football, assuming I ever got enough friends to get a game going over here. I was beginning to think that was unlikely. Dad said this was 'prime horse country', whatever that meant.

I went straight to my bedroom, tossing my backpack on the bed and digging out my homework. Most of my stuff was still packed, but getting homework out of the way early was something I'd learned from my mom. Homework first, chores second, play third.

Might seem like a lame setup, but trust me, getting it all done and out of the way first thing always leaves me a lot more free time. I'm not sure how it always works out that way, but it does. Besides, it always made my mom happy when she'd come home from work and I'd already have homework and chores done. It never took that long when you just did it.

It also meant that my dad never had to come talk to me to make sure I was getting it done. He'd long ago learned I'd get it done quickly and first thing on my own, so he left me alone most of the time which is what I wanted anyway.

My dad left me alone again today as I sat in my big bean bag chair doing my algebra, and listening to my mp3 player. He used to complain that it was so loud that even with my headphones in he could hear it in the other room and how could I study with that racket, but it never bothered me. It helped me focus. He'd stopped talking to me about that, too.

He didn't come get me until it was time for dinner. By then I'd finished my algebra, my English, half of next week's Spanish, and had made a serious dent in my unpacking. I was just hanging up my old team jacket in the small closet when my dad came in.

"Hey Sport, dinner's ready," I turned my most biting glare his way. "Sorry. Ryan, dinner's ready." I turned away, but not before I caught the look in his eyes. Like a beaten puppy, I always thought. Hard to respect a man that broken, I thought to myself.

I went into the kitchen and sat at the small table across from him. He didn't talk to me. He'd fixed spaghetti, his favorite. I had to admit he did a good job of it. Maybe he'd be okay with it if I had Chance come over sometime. He probably would. He'd just be glad I wasn't a total shut-in again.

I had a phase right after Mom died where I wouldn't talk to anyone. It had gone on so long that he'd sent me to a shrink. I finally realized I was going to be a total head-case if I didn't sort myself out, if only from listening to that idiot with the degree telling me that he understood me, over and over again.

And look at me now, a genuine social butterfly, I thought wryly. I did the dishes, finished unpacking, and went to bed, all without saying another word to my father. What was the point?

The next morning went by in similar fashion; long drive to school, tolerable classes, and lunch with Chance. The more I talked to him, the more I liked him. His sense of humor always got me laughing, and he had just as little respect for the idiocies of the public school social hierarchy as I did.

There was something I noticed about him though. I was beginning to suspect he was from a really poor, probably broken family. He had dodged the few questions I'd ventured about his family, and he was wearing the same clothes he had worn the day before. Nearly finished with lunch, I decided to ask him.

"Can I ask you something personal?" I asked. His eyes snapped up to mine, that guarded look entering his eyes that seemed to show up when I tried asking him questions about himself.

"I guess," he replied cautiously, rolling a forkful of peas around on his lunch tray.

"It's just that you've got on the same shirt you had yesterday…" I hedged. Chance glanced down at his shirt, then back up at me. He looked really uncomfortable, so I continued. "I'm not judging, you don't smell or anything, I just wondered about it. Your favorite shirt or something?" He looked down at the shirt for a long while, then back up at me.

"It's the only one I have," he finally admitted. He wouldn't meet my eyes.

"That's cool," I reassured him. "I was just wondering about it. Like I said, no judging here." He nodded but didn't say anything, or look back up to meet my eyes. "Sorry man, I didn't mean to upset you." He shook his head dismissively.

"No, it's fine," he replied, finally looking back into my eyes.

His eyes were so intense, I thought for the hundredth time that week. Most people talk about striking blue, or piercing gray, or vibrant green eyes. I'd never heard anyone talk about the depth of a pair of really dark brown eyes. When Chance looked at me, I felt as if I were the absolute focus of his undivided attention. You'd think that would be disconcerting, but I found I really liked it.

He ran a hand through his dark brown hair, or rather over it, since his hair was cut really short. Not buzz-cut short, but close. That seemed to be the style out here. I opened my mouth to change the subject, but was interrupted.

"Howdy, city boy," I suppressed a groan as Noah Porter approached, two of his brain-dead lackeys at his side. All three were grinning like idiots. I'd managed to completely avoid him all morning. Oh well, I thought. It had to happen sooner or later. This school wasn't that big.

"Hello. Can I help you?" I asked him in as polite a tone as I could force. He came right up behind Chance, who had to lean far to the side to avoid touching him as the rodeo king leaned down over the table toward me.

"I'm more interested in helpin' you, city boy. You a good Christian?" he said. This took me one hundred percent off guard. That was undoubtedly the most random question I had ever heard.

"Wait, what?" I asked, dumbfounded.

"I thought it was a simple question," he sneered. "Are you… a good… Christian?" I couldn't believe he was actually asking me this. The big, dumb, hick was apparently also a missionary. The Lord works in mysterious ways, it seemed.

"Umm, no," I replied, unsure how to answer. Noah's expression darkened.

"See city boy, that's why I'm concerned. How d'you expect to avoid burnin' in Hell if y'ain't a good Christian?" I looked to Chance for help. To my surprise, he was actually suppressing laughter!

"Hate to break it to you man, but if I'm not Christian, I don't believe in Hell either," I told him.

Chance was about to bust trying to hold it in, despite his leaning far to the side, continuing to avoid touching Noah. I don't know if it was those stupid flickering lights or if it was just Noah, but I found I was suddenly developing a headache.

"That ain't gonna save you," Noah said, leaning just a bit closer. My eye was caught by the glint of flickering fluorescent light on gold at his neck. A small golden crucifix hung there. Wow, this guy really was nuts. "God hates sinners. If I were you, I'd seriously think about going to church on Sunday. For your own good."

With that, he and his somber-looking buddies walked off. No sooner had Noah and his buddies walked away then Chance burst into laughter. Not light, casual laughter, but riotous, gut-busting laughter. He was folded over the table he was laughing so hard.

"What the hell was that?" I asked him, though I couldn't prevent the smile from sneaking through at his obvious amusement.

"No..." he gasped between breaths, "...that

wasn't Hell... your afterlife is!" he finished with another burst of laughter.

"I'm glad you think it's funny," I said wryly, though I was unable to keep my smile from turning into a grin. Chance was a lot of fun to watch like this. "Seriously man, I have never had some jerk come up to me and ask if I was a Christian before. How weird is that? I thought Christians were supposed to be all 'love thy neighbor' and stuff!" Chance was regaining his composure, though slowly.

"Sorry to tell you this, but being a Christian doesn't make you Christ-like, man," he said. "No matter how much some people think it does. That's the problem with Noah though. He totally thinks he's in the right picking on people like that, as long as he thinks they're going to Hell. Bible says non-Christians burn, right? Why not give them a little taste of their eternal torment before they go?" He chuckled again, and wiped at his eyes, which were in danger of actually shedding tears over his bout of laughter.

"Bible says a lot of things," I retorted. I'd had an interesting conversation with my Uncle Liam once on the subject, though I'd never been a church-goer myself. "Besides, if I'm going to Hell because the Bible says all non-Christians burn, wouldn't he go to Hell for eating shellfish and pork? Or wearing poly-cotton blend t-shirts?" I remembered my uncle joking about that. Chance laughed again.

"Yeah, I guess you're right," he said. "Hell

sure must be crowded. Don't worry though Ryan, I'll save you a seat. Right by the fire." He tossed a playful wink my way and I laughed.

"Your t-shirt is poly-cotton too?" I asked teasingly. He laughed.

"Probably. But when I go to Hell, it won't be for wearing poly-cotton t-shirts," he said with a smirk, "I have much more interesting things to burn for."

"Ladies and gentlemen, a professional sinner. Right here folks, step right up!" I said dramatically. "Honestly Chance, what could you possibly have done to warrant the fire and brimstone treatment?" Chance's gaze slipped away from mine.

"Can we change the subject?" he asked. I realized I'd stumbled onto dangerous territory here, and quickly obliged him. I made a mental note to be careful around that subject.

"Yeah, actually I have to go anyway," I told him. "Class starts soon. Besides, if I eat any more of this... whatever it is, I might die. Like literally die. I wonder if the hospital here has a good poison control center. What is this, anyway?" He leaned over to look at my tray and smiled, though it still wasn't a full smile.

"That would be either the chicken pot pie, or the fish taco. Could go either way." he said, looking up at me. I tried, I honestly did. I tried to give him a stern look. I couldn't hold it though. I laughed. His grin broadened and he turned back to his food.

As I stood and walked away, I couldn't help

but wonder what it was about my friend Chance. He was obviously poor, obviously some trouble on the home front, had a weird thing about being touched, and apparently actually did think he was Hell-bound, though for what I couldn't imagine. The guy was a distinct mystery. I couldn't figure him out. Oddly, I liked that about him. It gave me something to think about.

"Freak," I heard someone mutter as I passed. I looked their way, but everyone was turned away from me so I couldn't tell who had said it. I kept walking.

I made it through my last couple of classes, eager for the bell. I'd only been in school for two days this week, but after the move and the drama I was really tired and was aching for a weekend. On my way toward the door amid the rush of students clamoring to escape, I saw Chance leaning up against a set of lockers near the front of the school. He saw me and smiled.

"Hey Ryan," he said.

"Hey," I replied. "What's up?"

"Listen, I just wanted to tell you to have a good weekend. Things have gotten a lot cooler around here since you showed up. I'm glad you came."

I looked at him a long moment. That was a bit more emotionally expressive than was normally acceptable for two fourteen year old guys, especially two who had only recently become friends, but I'd already figured out that Chance had a different set of rules he played by. Finally I nodded.

"Yeah, it is nice to see this school wasn't completely overrun by the inbred hicks," I replied with a half-smile. He chuckled.

"Not completely, but close," he replied.

"Hey, give me your number so I can call you this weekend. Maybe we can hang out," I said, pulling out my cell. I knew right away I'd said the wrong thing again when his smile dropped. He shook his head and looked down.

"Don't have a phone. Besides, I'm sort of grounded. I can't really go anywhere anyway."

"Oh," I replied, mentally kicking myself for sounding like a complete idiot. "Sorry man, what did you do?" Another wrong question. Even in the flickering hallway lighting, I could tell he was even more upset.

"I don't really want to talk about it," he replied, not looking over at me. "Have a good weekend though. I'll see you Monday morning." He turned and walked into the crowd.

"Stupid," I muttered at myself shaking my head, and went out to meet my dad. Chance might be an interesting mystery, but it definitely was going to take some caution to keep from hurting him.

Chapter Three
Secret Mission

I thought about him all weekend as I sat around playing video games. Saturday was okay, since my dad worked all day, but Sunday seemed to drag. He seemed to want to do something together, but he didn't seem willing to bring it up, so he didn't say anything. Neither did I. Two guys, living in the same house, sitting in the same room for fourteen hours, neither saying anything. Awkward. I'd love to say that was unusual, but welcome to my Sundays.

I wished he and I had some common ground, but we liked literally none of the same things. The only thing we had any common interest in was baseball. Only he loved to watch it, and I loved to play it. I couldn't stand watching someone else play. What was the point? He liked to do jigsaw puzzles and I liked first-person shooters. He liked going to the park for a jog, I liked watching horror movies. We had nothing.

I was excited for Monday morning, and was up before my dad came to wake me, a fact which really surprised him. I was already mostly dressed when he opened my bedroom door.

I finished pulling on my shirt and almost laughed at the expression on his face. I'm usually sprawled out across the entire bed, blankets doing their best to tie me into knots when he came in each morning to wake me for school. He used to tease me about it. Not for a long time though.

"Already up, I see," he said, trying to mask his surprise. "That's great! I have breakfast ready when you're up for it." I nodded.

"Thanks."

Breakfast in silence, the drive to school in silence. Already this was getting tedious. I decided to throw him a bone when he dropped me off, just to shake things up. Just before I climbed out of the car, I looked over at him.

"See ya later," I told him. He actually smiled, again with a hint of surprise on his face.

"Three o'clock on the dot," he replied. I gave him a small smile back, and closed the door. There. That ought to make his day.

"Ryan!" I looked up to find Chance sitting on the low stone wall that ran along the front of the school, separating the walkway from the flowerbeds. I grinned at him.

"Hey!" I replied, heading over and sitting

beside him. "What's up?"

"That your dad?" he asked, gesturing in the general direction of my dad's sedan.

"Yeah, that's him." Chance nodded at my reply. I looked over at my dad, who was leaning over to look at me through the side window. His smile had disappeared. I couldn't quite pinpoint his expression before he sat back and drove off, but it wasn't a happy one. Weird.

"You guys aren't very close, huh?" he asked. I looked over at him, confused.

"What do you mean?" I asked, not sure whether I should be offended or not. He shrugged.

"You guys weren't talking when you pulled up. Then you turned, said one thing to him, and he looked surprised. I pay attention."

"Yeah, we don't talk much," I replied.

"I don't with my dad either," he said to my own surprise.

"You guys aren't close either?" I asked, genuinely curious to finally get something personal out of him.

"No. We had a huge fight a couple of years ago. He won't even come to see me now." Ah, separated parents and a father that wouldn't even visit his son. That explained a few things.

"That sucks, man," I said with all the eloquence I could muster. "How about your mom?"

"Oh, she talks to me sometimes," he said

casually. I could tell this subject was painful for him though. "She's always so sad though. Sometimes it's hard to listen to it. She used to be so happy." Boy, that sounded familiar.

"What happened?" I asked.

"It was my fault. Same problem with my dad, actually. It was my fault."

"You can't just say you're sorry?"

"I wish I could. It's too late for that, though. You just can't fix some things, Ryan." He looked over at me, expression somber, eyes deep and haunted. I nodded and reached over, patting his hand consolingly. He flinched back, but too late. My hand touched his an instant before he jerked back.

A ripple of emotions crossed his face, starting with shock, moving into horror, then turning to one of simple confusion. It was morbidly fascinating, like watching the monster in a horror movie slowly change shape.

"Oh my God, I'm so sorry Chance," I said, a pit in my stomach at the thought of so careless a mistake. I didn't know what it was with him and touching, but I knew he didn't like it. "I totally forgot about the touching thing. I'm really sorry. Are you okay?" He was rubbing his hand where I'd touched him, his expression confused, and surprised.

"I…" he stammered, "I think so. It's okay. With you, I mean." He very slowly reached his hand out toward mine, gently touching the back of it. I kept very still, fascinated by the expressions on his face, though a bit uncomfortable at the way he touched my hand.

His fingertips stroked my skin, I could feel the warmth of him. I got an odd, subtle rush from the contact. He looked up at me, expression filled with wonder. "It's okay with you. I don't know why you're different, but I think it's okay for you to touch me. It doesn't hurt at all." I opened my mouth to respond, but the school bell rang. I looked toward the school, then back to him. I gave him a smile.

"Don't worry. Just in case, I won't make a habit of it," I told him. He looked up abruptly.

"I kind of hope you do," he said, looking a little embarrassed. Not quite sure what to make of that, I pulled my hand gently out from under his and smiled.

"See you at lunch," I said, and headed toward the doors. He was still sitting there when I went inside, slowly rubbing his hand where I'd touched him.

I really wished now that I knew what his deal was. I mean, I was curious before, but now it was driving me absolutely crazy. He'd said it hurt him when other people touched him. Why didn't it hurt him when I touched him? Why did it hurt when others did? I couldn't help but wonder if he'd been abused. That would explain a few things too.

In the fifth grade, a kid in my class had gone completely insane and tried to stab a teacher with a pair of scissors. They found out later that he'd been severely abused by his step-mother. The teacher had touched him in just the wrong way to set off a complete fit.

Nothing inappropriate, she had just patted his shoulder when she went to stand up from where she'd been leaning over his desk to help him with something, and he'd snapped. That kind of thing could really mess up a kid's head. It must have been pretty bad for Chance to find any touch actually painful, though.

I spent my whole Algebra hour thinking about what he'd said, "I kind of hope you do". Did he mean he hoped I'd touch him more? I guess if nobody else was able to touch him without it causing him issues, he'd probably be pretty starved for comfortable contact. I really didn't want to freak him out though, and I was afraid that it might hurt him the next time. I didn't understand what the source of the problem was, so I was reluctant to really mess with it.

I also didn't know how I felt about it. It was weird, how gently he'd touched my hand. Guys didn't do that. Punched, shoved, wrestled, whatever, but they didn't touch each other like that. Despite that, I'd liked it. Maybe I was the one starved for comfortable contact, I thought to myself.

I made it through algebra without getting called on, which is a good thing since I would likely have given the ever-popular response of "Huh?" if I'd been asked to answer anything.

As I was making my way out of class, I felt a

light shove behind me. Not too hard, but it didn't feel friendly, either.

"I didn't see you in church this weekend, city boy." Oh, great. I'd been so distracted that I hadn't made it into the crowd before Noah caught up with me.

"No, I did my praying at home in circle with my coven, thanks," I retorted. He scowled, and shoved me again. He was rapidly backing me up into the lockers across from the classroom. This wasn't going to be good.

"Oh, funny," he said. Two of his sidekicks had materialized next to him as well. This wasn't getting any better. I should watch my mouth.

"What's with you, anyway?" I demanded, feeling aggressive now that I was cornered. "I thought the whole point of this country was that I could worship whenever, wherever, however, or even if I wanted to. You're Christian, that's cool. I'm not, leave it alone."

"I'm just tryin' ta help you," he growled.

"I thought conversion by the sword went out with the Crusades," I said. Another shove, and I slammed into the lockers. That one hurt. I think one of the combination locks hit my shoulder blade.

"We'll save yer souls by any means necessary, or you're gonna burn," Noah said, lifting his clenched fist.

"Gentlemen!" Mr. Allen called sharply from

across the hall. Noah lowered his fist, slowly.

"That was your last friendly warning, Jacobs," he whispered and turned, walking away. That was a friendly warning? This was going to get ugly fast. Less than a week in town and I'm already about to be burned at the stake by the Turnbridge Inquisition.

What kind of nutcase thought that converting someone to a religion that preached peace by using violence and threats was a good idea? I had to wonder if his whole church was like that. If so, it was definitely more of a cult than a church. Scary stuff. I couldn't wait until lunch.

Walking into the lunchroom, I saw Chance already at our table, waiting for me. I waved, got my food, and headed over.

"Hey Ryan," he said. "Listen, I wanted to apologize for this morning. I got a bit intense. It's just... been a long time." I nodded.

"No problem, man. I'm sorry I slipped up," I replied as I sat down across from him.

"No, I'm glad you did. I didn't think anyone would ever be able to touch me again."

"So it hurts you when other people touch you? That's a bit... different." I took a bite of the questionable-looking hamburger.

"I know, right? But yeah, it's painful. Almost like electric shock, you know?"

"That bad?"

"Yeah."

"What caused it?" I knew I was pushing things, prying in like this, but this was the first time he'd really opened up about himself and I was dying of curiosity. He hesitated.

"It's complicated," he responded, fiddling with a limp french fry. "I wasn't born that way or anything. It just sort of happened one day. I can't really explain it." I could tell he was shutting down, so I just nodded.

"That's okay. We don't have to get into it," I replied, taking another bite.

"Thanks," he replied. "Hey, I also wanted to tell you that it's okay if you touch me. It seems like it's fine when you do it, and I kind of needed that." I looked up at him. He looked back, intense brown eyes seeming to draw mine in.

"Well, I mean if I don't know the cause, or why it's okay when I do, I don't want to, you know, mess with things," I replied honestly. He shook his head.

"No, I kind of want you to,"

"You said that," I told him, a little uncomfortable.

"I just mean that I don't know why you can, but the fact is that you can. If that changes, we'll know it pretty quickly." He shrugged. "I mean, if you're not okay with it I understand. Guys aren't really much for touching, so it's cool. It's just… it's okay if you want to. You don't have to, or anything". He wouldn't meet my eyes all of a sudden. I felt really bad for him. He looked so uncomfortable talking about this. Not that I could blame him, I was feeling a bit awkward myself.

"How about we just keep it relaxed," I told him. "I'll just pretend you don't have a problem. If I happen to touch you, it happens. Otherwise, we won't sweat it. I just don't want it to get weird if we over-think it, you know?" He looked very relieved.

"Totally. Thanks, Ryan." I just nodded and dug into my fries. I wondered if they used actual potatoes in these things. I rather doubted it.

I really liked Chance. I felt really bad for him, he obviously had a lot of issues to deal with. The poor guy was still wearing his lonely gray shirt too. Probably the same jeans too, now that I thought about it. I wondered how he'd feel if I offered him some of mine. I had plenty for my needs. Some people got weird about what they considered charity though, and Chance was touchy already. The cheap fluorescent lights were flickering again. Man that was getting annoying.

"By the way," he said, bringing me back to the conversation, "I have kind of an offer for you." That piqued my curiosity.

"Really? What kind of offer?" I asked.

"I've been working on sort of a project for a while I was hoping you might be willing to help me out with." His smile had returned, and this time it looked mischievous. Now he really had my attention.

"Sure, if I can. What's the project?"

"I'm trying to solve a murder," he said, his eyes sparkling, but sharply focused on my reaction. I laughed.

"Uh huh," I replied.

"I'm serious," he said with a light laugh of his own.

"Next you'll be telling me you invented peanut butter," I told him with a grin.

"Nah, just jelly," he teased. "I really am serious though. Two years ago, a kid here was killed. Cooked to death right in the big walk-in oven in the cafeteria that baked that hamburger bun you're munching down on." I almost choked. He laughed.

"Are you kidding me?" I snapped, though his timing couldn't have been better. I had just put the last bite of burger into my mouth.

"Not one bit," Chance said. "His name was Dominic Hale. They said it was a suicide, that he'd turned the oven up max and locked himself inside it." I realized he was actually serious under his teasing, playful expression.

"You're really mean it," I said in awe. "You don't think it was a suicide?"

"Not for a second," he replied adamantly. "I knew the guy. Nice kid. He was definitely picked on, but I really knew him. He never in a million years would have killed himself. He was too stubborn for that. Problem is, I've never been able to get anyone else to listen to me."

"So you've been trying to solve your friend's murder for two years?" I asked incredulously. Chance nodded. "Sounds to me like you're the stubborn one." He grinned at that. I mulled over the idea of someone baking to death in the oven that had just baked my lunch. I was suddenly a little queasy.

"You've got that right. So anyway, I need someone to help me do some online research."

"You can't do that yourself in the library?" I asked. He shook his head.

"No, computers and I don't really get along. Should just be point and click, right?" he asked. I nodded. "Nope. They do things they shouldn't when I start messing with them. I have no idea how. Some of us just aren't computer people. So, you up for it?"

"Yeah, that's cool," I told him, excited despite my slightly upset stomach. I wished he hadn't told me about this right during lunch, though. "How about tomorrow after fourth period? I have a free period then. Supposed to be studying for a history exam next week, but I've got that down pretty solid for a change. Whose class are you in then?" Chance frowned and hesitated a moment before answering.

"Hmm, I can get out of it, don't worry about it. I'll meet you in the library tomorrow after fourth then."

"Sounds cool. As for me, I think I need to go throw up a hamburger bun," I stood and Chance laughed.

"Sorry Ryan. You have to admit it was funny though."

"Yeah, but just wait. I'll get you back for it." I clapped him on the shoulder as I walked past him on the way out of the cafeteria. He smiled up at me, with an intensity that was unusual even for him, laced with gratitude that eased a bit of my discomfort. I smiled back and left the cafeteria.

Chapter Four

Strangers in the Night

Pain and heat. Pain from the bruise on my forehead that I was sure was just developing. Pain from the fire that was slowly, but tangibly, rising all around. Locked in the steel prison, burning alive as I peered through the tiny glass window, screaming noiselessly for someone to help me.

No one would help me. The devil was outside again, his smiling human mask a mockery to the species. The horns still protruded from the mask's forehead. The fierce, yellow eyes seemed to burn into me, their glee at my anguish evident. The mask changed; I recognized who it was meant to be now.

It looked as though Noah Porter's face had been torn from his skull and placed over the face of the monster hiding behind it. I could see blood lining the edge of the mask. This one wasn't rubber, it really was Noah Porter's face, torn from his skull and worn as a mask by the servants of Hell he so actively seemed to pursue. A long, forked tongue darted between Noah's bloody lips.

As quickly as it had appeared, the horrible face was gone. Moments later, a new face appeared. The heat was rising. I was still screaming, but I couldn't even hear myself anymore. Everything was silent. I pounded on the door, but no noise came back to me. Even the flames licking all around brought nothing to dispel the cacophonous silence. As the new face appeared, time seemed to slow. I shouted my pleas for help.

The new face drew close. This face was the same as before, indistinguishable, surrounded by the halo of wispy light. It still trailed off the face in the window like iridescent steam. As the face stopped just before the window, it spoke. I couldn't hear the words. I couldn't hear anything. But I knew what the voice said, echoing inside my mind.

"I'm sorry, Ryan. I can't help you," is what it said. The voice belonged to Chance. For the briefest of instants, his impossibly deep brown eyes glistened clearly with unshed tears from the otherwise indistinguishable face.

Then the claws came, breaking through the form in my window as though my regretful visitor was made of nothing more substantial than the wispy light surrounding it. The pleasant face broke apart like smoke in a breeze, glowing faintly for a moment before it was gone. The devil wearing Noah's face reappeared. He was laughing. I couldn't hear it. I could feel it, grating against my bones as the flames consumed the tattered remains of my flesh. I silently screamed again, and the dream broke.

I sat bolt upright in bed. It was still dark outside. A glance at my alarm clock told me it was just past three thirty. I dropped back onto my pillow, mildly disgusted to feel the dampness there. From the way my skin felt, I'd been sweating pretty intensely.

I got out of bed, and went into the bathroom. The cold air brushed across my sweat-covered skin like a winter breeze, though it was only early fall. The leaves hadn't even fully changed yet. I was going to have to start wearing more than just boxers to bed. I turned on the pale yellow light.

It was pointless to turn on the hot water; it always took at least ten minutes to get even lukewarm so I just turned the knob for the cold water.

Splashing the icy water on my face was biting, shocking me into a clearer state of mind and pushing the nightmare further from my perceived reality. I looked at myself in the mirror. My eyes looked heavy, my hair damp and listless. Not my best look. I sighed and wet my hands again, running them through my hair. It would take a bit more work before school, I knew.

The dream had come at least once a month for close to two years now. I had never told anyone about it. It had never changed before. It had never come so soon after the last one either.

The devil wore Noah's face this time. I didn't understand. Noah was obnoxious, and a bully, but he wasn't evil. At least I didn't think so. And the voice… Chance's voice. The face still wasn't his, though the eyes had become his in the last moments. Chance's voice had seemed so sad, so full of regret.

It was too early to think about this. I'd be a wreck if I didn't get a bit more sleep. Assuming I could fall back to sleep. I shut off the water, turned off the light, and went back to my room. Passing my window, something caught my eye. In front of the house, across the large yard, a truck was parked.

That wasn't an unusual sight in Turnbridge, three quarters of the population owned trucks, but it was unusual in front of my house. Our nearest neighbors were within sight, barely, across a field lying between the two houses. There was no reason for anyone to be parked here. I moved closer to the window.

I looked at the truck for a full minute before I realized there was someone in it. The figure had been leaned back against the seat, sitting as still as a corpse. There was no light other than from the moon, which gave precious little. If the figure hadn't moved, I wouldn't have known they were there at all. Abruptly, the truck pulled away, tires crunching on the gravel on the side of the road. It didn't turn its lights on.

I felt a chill. How long had that truck been there? Could have been there all night, for all I knew, watching the house. The driver might not have stayed in the truck the whole time either. I was shivering now and only partly from the cold. I remembered Chance's words at lunch yesterday.

Someone had killed a kid by shoving him into an oven. I suddenly couldn't get the image of my body folded and broken shoved into the oven in our kitchen out of my head.

True, Chance had said that murder had taken place two years ago, but who knew what had triggered the killer into that level of violence? And right after the dream... It was too much for me to cope with at three thirty in the morning.

I watched out the window for almost an hour, some part of me convinced that the truck and its driver would reappear. The man, or woman, would get out, break into the house, and spend the rest of the night taking their time in murdering me and my dad.

I struggled over whether I should tell my dad or not. I doubted he'd do much more than look outside, tell me he didn't see anything, and then tell me to go back to bed and not worry about it.

Finally, sleep started to come for me again. My eyes hurt. I made my way back to my bed, flipped over my pillow, and closed my eyes. Thankfully, the dream didn't come again. I woke up to my dad's voice.

"Ryan? Better get up or you won't have time

for breakfast." I rolled over and groaned. My head hurt, just badly enough to be annoying. I was groggy; my last few hours of sleep hadn't been very deep or restful. My father wisely took this for acknowledgement and left the room.

After a few more minutes trying to reorient myself to the waking world, I rolled out of bed and went for a quick shower. I couldn't get Chance out of my mind. It had occurred to me sometime during my first few waking minutes that if I were being watched or followed, Chance might be too. I found myself desperate to get to school and make sure he was okay.

I dressed quickly and hurried into the kitchen, shoveling down a bowl of cereal so fast I couldn't even have told you what kind it was. My father watched me hurry around calmly, though he did gather his own things so he could be ready when I was. I probably should have thanked him, but I didn't.

We hurried to the car, and pulled out of the long driveway onto the road, heading into town. We drove for almost ten minutes before he broke the silence.

"Everything okay, Ryan?" he asked.

"I'm fine," I told him.

"You're in a big rush this morning."

"Yeah."

"Someone you're in a hurry to see?" he looked at me sidelong for a moment before looking back at the road.

"Chance," I replied. He glanced at me again. I avoided looking at him.

"That your friend?"

"Yeah."

"The one you were talking to when I dropped you off yesterday?"

"Yeah, why?" I scowled at him. I was getting annoyed by the questions. I don't know why my father talking to me irritated me so much, but it never failed to get me riled up.

He looked at me again for a long moment. He looked concerned, but he just shook his head and stayed silent. Neither of us said another word.

I'd been considering telling him about the truck outside, and why I was concerned for Chance, but I couldn't bring myself to confide in him. And now I was angry with him for being nosy.

We pulled up in front of the school. I didn't see Chance. I practically leapt out of the car, grabbed my backpack, and raced to the front doors of the school. I was so focused on my goal that I bumped into someone as I pushed through the crowd. In a hurry I may have been, but my mother's heavy training in manners took a reflexive hand in my actions and I immediately stopped.

"I'm really sorry, I'm just..." I stopped as the girl I'd bumped into picked her backpack off the ground and looked up at me. It was the girl I'd seen my first day with Noah and his groupies. She looked angry.

"You tryin' to get back at me for Noah bumpin' into you last week?" she asked with a scowl. Her drawl was similar, though more delicate than Noah's. More like Mrs. Bradley in the office, I thought. It was a very soothing accent, I was beginning to realize. I'd never thought so before, hearing that twang in country singers' voices and in cowboy movies. It sure wasn't soothing when I heard it from Noah. This was different though, less sharp.

"No," I hurried to explain. "I really am sorry. I was just in a hurry, and I wasn't watching where I was going. I'm really sorry. Are you okay?" She considered me for a moment, before apparently deciding that I was genuinely apologetic.

"I'm fine," she replied. "Just keep an eye out for me next time, okay?" She said that last with a bit of a smile. I couldn't help giving her a smile back.

"I will, thanks."

"Weren't you in a hurry?" she asked, a little bit coyly. I mentally kicked myself. I really was in a hurry, but I was so shocked at someone other than Chance being nice to me that it had caught me completely off guard.

"Yeah, I really am," I said in a rush, starting to back away. "Hey, I'll catch you later though, okay?" She nodded, still smiling. It occurred to me that I didn't even know her name. I raced through the doors.

"Mr. Jacobs," a voice called. I stopped, biting back a curse. I turned. It was Mrs. Bradley.

"Yes, ma'am?" I replied. She smiled at me.

"Principal Avery wants t' have a word with you after your third hour, jus' before lunch," she told me. She was wearing another flower-print dress. It was different, but similar to the one she'd worn before. At least she looked pretty good in them. Not everyone could pull that look off. "If you could jus' hop on over here before goin' t' the cafeteria that would be fine." I nodded.

"Yeah, I will. Thanks!" I said, moving back into the crowd before it occurred to me to wonder what the principal wanted. I couldn't imagine what it could be. I hadn't broken any rules or anything, so I couldn't be in trouble. Well, I'd worry about it later. For now, I needed to find Chance.

He wasn't in the main hallway, and hadn't been outside. I was starting to get really worried. I didn't see him up by the rail at the top of the stairs either. I hurried to the cafeteria. I ran in, and looked around. A few tables were occupied by a handful of early students, sitting and talking or getting some last-minute homework done. I didn't see Chance though.

I turned around to check somewhere else, maybe the library, and stopped. Chance was standing in the doorway, leaning in the frame as casual as could be. He grinned at me.

"Looking for someone in particular?" he said.

"Chance!" I jumped forward and grabbed him before I could stop myself. I pulled him in and hugged him. He only hesitated a moment before his own arms wrapped tightly around me. He held me like he'd never hugged anyone before in his entire life, or thought he never would again.

After a long few seconds, I let him go and shoved him backward, feigning anger, though I really was a bit annoyed he hadn't been around out front when I got here like he had been the day before.

"Where were you? I was worried!" I told him. His eyes shone brighter than usual as he smiled at me, but he tilted his head slightly and his brows came down.

"Not that I mind, it's nice to know you care, but why exactly were you worried?" he asked. I looked around. A couple of the nearer students were watching us; some of them sidelong, others very directly.

"Come on," I told him, taking his shoulder in one hand and steering him out into the hallway. Once in a less conspicuous location, I continued. "Someone was at my place last night." He looked at me curiously.

"So?" he asked. I rolled my eyes.

"So… we don't know anyone out here, we live out in the middle of nowhere, and this guy didn't come visit us, he parked out in the middle of the street in front of my place in the middle of the night, and just sat there."

"That's… creepy," Chance replied after a moment as it sank in.

"I know, right?" I said. "I woke up in the

middle of the night and he was just sitting out there in his truck. I think he saw me watching him, because only a minute or two later he took off, no lights. Anyway, I got to thinking that maybe this is about that kid you were telling me about. What was his name, David something?"

"Dominic," Chance told me. "I don't know how it could be related though. You didn't even know about him until I told you yesterday. How could someone else have figured out that you're in on the case and started stalking you because of it already?" He had a point.

"I guess you're right. I was just a little... I don't know, a little freaked out by the idea. And then seeing the guy in front of my place last night. Anyway, I just thought that if they were after me, they might be after you, and then when I didn't see you out front this morning..." The way he was looking at me caused me to trail off. "What?" I asked.

"Nothing, just... been a long time since anyone was worried about me," he replied with a soft smile. Something about his eyes pulled at me. I couldn't quite place it. Something... I shook myself to clear my thoughts.

"Don't make too big a deal out of it," I told him as casually as I could manage. "Who else am I going to get to talk to me out here in Hickville?"

"Good point," he replied, but he was still smiling at me.

"Although I did have a nice chat with a girl out front," Chance's smile slipped.

"Which girl?" he asked.

"Blonde, pretty, hangs with Noah sometimes," I told him. He stared at me.

"Jennifer? Are you kidding me?" I just nodded. "Ryan she's…" He stopped.

"She's what?" I asked. Chance didn't answer for a long enough that I repeated the question. "She's what, Chance?"

"She's Noah's."

"What? She can't be with that preachy punk," I insisted. Chance shrugged.

"Has been for years, man."

"Why on Earth would she be with him? She seems so nice," I protested.

"She is," Chance assured me, "…as long as you're one of them."

A couple of kids passed by us in the hallway, snickering and pointing. I'd almost gotten to where I didn't notice anymore. They had sort of become a part of the background, like the lights flickering overhead. Chance's issues had really put him outside the social network, and me too for being friends with him.

"One of the hellfire groupies, you mean? That's ridiculous," I argued. Chance shrugged.

"Suit yourself," he said, sounding a little sullen. "If you're into her, give it a shot and see where it gets you." The look he was giving me was a little bit concerned, but held a bit of a challenging edge to it.

I almost made a snappy remark about it, but I paused. He looked a little bit upset by this line of conversation, and he'd brought up a valid point.

I thought about it, and I realized I wasn't actually interested in Jennifer. She was pretty and all, but I wasn't really attracted to her. I liked that she was nice to me, but that was about it. And if she would stop once she realized I didn't belong to their little crazy cult then there wasn't any interest in interacting with her at all.

"No, not really," I told Chance honestly. "She was just nice. Nobody else has been nice to me since I got here except you. Well, and Mrs. Bradley, but I doubt she'd want to hang out." Chance laughed. "Speaking of which, she told me this morning that the principal wants to talk to me. Any idea what that's about?

"Not a clue." Chance shrugged. "Didn't get yourself in trouble while I wasn't looking, did you?"

"Nah, any trouble I get into, you're sure to be involved in." I heard the bell and sighed. "Gotta go."

"Yep. See you at lunch," he said, turning and heading off toward his own class.

Chapter Five

Confrontations

I realized halfway through my first class that I'd completely forgotten in my rush to see if Chance was okay to put my homework in my backpack. I was able to convince my teacher to let me bring it in the next morning, but it bothered me.

I was never a straight-A student, but I was diligent, and worked hard at all of my subjects. I almost always held at least above average grades in every class. I'd never failed to turn in a homework assignment, at least not in years.

I was still inwardly grumbling about it when I made it into the lunchroom. The lights were always flickering in here. Did they ever intend to get anyone in to fix that? It made my brain itch.

Chance was at our usual table, having gotten there ahead of me as usual. His third hour teachers must let them out a little early every time. He already had his food, but waited patiently for me to join him before he picked up his fork.

"Hey Ryan," he said as I approached, though he was frowning.

"What's up?" I asked as I sat across from him.

"As much as I hate to do this to you…" he began. I frowned too, wondering what he could mean. "…weren't you supposed to go talk to Principal Avery?"

"Damn it!" I cursed. "You're right. I completely forgot. Man, this has not been my day." He gave me a sympathetic smile as I stood and raced back out into the halls, heading for the office. When I entered, Mrs. Bradley smiled.

"Good afternoon," she said warmly. There was something different in her eyes now though. Maybe it had been there this morning. I hadn't been paying as much attention. Was it sympathy? What was going on?

"Hello, Mrs. Bradley. Is he ready for me?" I asked. She nodded, and gestured me back toward the principal's office. I thanked her and moved through the doorway. I froze before I'd taken a single step inside. My dad was seated in one of the two chairs across from the principal's desk.

"Dad…" I said, stunned.

"Hi Ryan," was all he said.

"Come in please, Mr. Jacobs," Principal Avery told me. I looked his way. I'd seen him in the halls, though I'd never spoken to him.

He was a solid man. Not fat, but distinctly barrel-shaped. His huge, square jaw, and thick moustache made me think he'd have made a decent character in a western film. He wore a three-piece suit, but he definitely looked like he'd be more comfortable in Wranglers and a Stetson, which only added to my mental image of the cowboy movie character. I entered the room, not noticing as Mrs. Bradley closed the door behind me. I sat beside my father.

"What are you doing here?" I asked him.

"I asked him to come, Mr. Jacobs," Principal Avery said.

"Why?" I asked pointedly.

"There've been some troubling rumors circling the school about you, Mr. Jacobs," he replied.

"Like what?" I asked, genuinely surprised. I knew I wasn't well liked, thanks to my friendship with Chance, but I didn't really care. Didn't know there were rumors going around though. I should have assumed as much, I just hadn't really thought about it. Besides, it was weird that the principal cared, and that he'd called my dad about it.

"We're concerned about your friendship with Chance," my dad said. I looked at him in shock.

"What? Why?" I realized I wasn't sounding all that intelligent, but I was genuinely baffled.

"We don't think your friendship with Chance is entirely… healthy," my dad replied. Before I could reply to that, Principal Avery spoke.

"We don't feel it's our place to interfere with anyone's friendships…"

"Then don't!" I interrupted, suddenly hotly angry. My stress from the emotional roller coaster since waking up from the dream last night all became very focused.

"It's not that simple, Mr. Jacobs. You are clearly under some false ideas about your friend. He's not…"

"I couldn't care less what you guys think of him!" I snapped back, my voice rising. "That kid has been nothing but nice to me since the first day I got here, and not one damned other person has even made the effort!" I knew that wasn't technically true, Jennifer had tried to be nice to me, but I was too angry to correct myself.

"Ryan," my dad spoke in his 'let's-all-calm-down' tone of voice, which only made me more furious, "we're just concerned for you. That's all. Whether you realize it or not, Chance is…"

"I can't believe you would turn on me like this!" I shouted at my dad, standing up from the chair. "The whole time we were getting ready to move to this dump, you were telling me 'Oh, it'll be fine Ryan, you'll make plenty of new friends,' but I haven't. I've made one. Just one. He's a better friend than I've ever had, and now you're not happy with who I choose to be friends with? You can mind your own damned business!" I turned on the principal, in a full fury.

"As for you, everyone in this school has it out for Chance, including you! What kind of principal doesn't want to help every student in his school? Do you know the kind of bullying that goes on in this place? Do you know what your star pupils are doing? Bunch of psycho cultists in this Hell-hole!

"Are they the ones being dragged back here for a chat with their parents?" I continued. Principal Avery was getting angry, but he didn't say anything. I kept on. "Hell no! You have to waste everyone's time just because you don't like someone making friends with the least popular kid in the school! You really like the status quo staying right where it is, don't you!

"I won't listen to you bad-mouth my best friend," I snapped at the principal, leaning over the desk to pointing my finger at him as if I intended to spear him with it, then turned back to my dad, "...and I won't listen to you telling me who I can be friends with! You've never even met him; you don't know what the Hell you're talking about! Let me know if you guys ever want to have a conversation with me without slamming someone I care about who isn't even here to defend himself." I turned to the door, practically ripping it open, and stormed out.

"Ryan!"

"Mr. Jacobs!" I heard the two calling me in chorus. Mrs. Bradley looked up at me, concern on her face. She opened her mouth, but I stormed right past her, and she closed it again. Once out of the office, I broke into a run.

I went out the back door of the school, out onto the field. I'd seen a good spot to sit and collect my thoughts the couple of times I'd been out here.

I didn't spend much time out on the yard here, it was mostly for the kids to shoot some hoops or play soccer during their free periods. Nobody wanted me around, so I hadn't had any real reason to be out here.

I slipped down behind a tool shed not far from the outer fence, nestled back in a corner. I wasn't visible from the school here, and could compose myself in peace.

I was seething. What kind of parent condemned their kid's friends without meeting them, or knowing anything at all about them? Chance wouldn't get me into trouble. He didn't do drugs or drink or anything stupid like that. He wasn't a bad influence, he was a genuinely nice kid. I couldn't figure out what they saw wrong with him.

I'd been out there for at least an hour when I heard footsteps. They were approaching slowly, like the person wasn't sure where they were going, or that they wanted to take their time to get there. Probably someone looking for me, I thought.

Then the footsteps stopped, perhaps a dozen feet on the other side of the shed. I waited for several minutes, and was just about to poke my head out and see what was going on when a voice spoke.

"I don't know why I came here today," the voice said softly. It was almost a whisper, clearly not intended to carry far. I could only hear it because it was echoing between the school wall and the tool shed. It was definitely a woman's voice though. "I just wanted someplace quiet to get all this out. Your father says it's pointless to try and talk to you, but I have to try. I can't give up."

"Don't give up, Mom. Please don't give up on me," a second voice sounded. I recognized it with surprise as Chance's voice. I hadn't heard him walk up.

"I won't give up," she said, "no matter what your father says. I think he feels guilty, because of the fight. He won't come see you because he feels guilty. He doesn't blame you, please believe that."

"Yes, he does," Chance replied. "You heard what he said to me, what he called me. He wanted me gone from his life. He said it himself. I…"

"Your father loves you. I love you. The whole thing was my fault. I should have told him,"

"No, Mom!" Chance protested. I could hear the strain in his voice. "It isn't your fault! Please don't…"

"He's just shut down completely," she interrupted. "He won't open up to me, won't talk to anyone about it. I know he thinks about you every day though."

"I just wish you would…" Chance began, but she cut him off again.

"I think about you every day, too. Nothing's been the same since that fight. We used to laugh so much. Remember when we took that trip to the Junction?" She laughed, but it broke and became a sob.

I could hear the tears in her voice. I wanted to be somewhere else, shouldn't be involved in this, but I couldn't leave without them seeing me, and this also shouldn't be interrupted. The emotions in their voices pained me. I was almost to the point of tears myself, and I didn't even understand what had happened.

"Mom…" Chance started, but I heard the tears in his voice too.

"We won't ever have that again," she said, crying more freely now. "Some things you just can't fix." I recognized the words. Chance had said them to me yesterday. Now I knew where he got them. "Just remember, even if he never comes to see you, never even says goodbye, he really does love you."

"I love you, Mom," Chance whispered, his voice cracking.

"I love you, baby. Happy birthday," she whispered. I heard footsteps moving away again.

"Bye Mom," Chance said. I heard him sniffle, and had to bite my tongue to keep from crying too. It wasn't fair to him for me to have heard all of that and have me keep it from him. You didn't lie to friends.

I stood slowly and moved out from behind the shed. Chance spotted me, sniffed sharply and wiped his hands over his eyes, pointlessly trying to cover up the fact that he'd been crying. I understood.

"Hey," I said softly.

"Hey," he replied, voice soft and sad.

"I'm sorry Chance, I didn't mean to overhear," I told him sincerely. "I was back there trying to get myself back in check after my meeting with Principal Avery and my dad, and…"

"It's cool," he replied. "If anyone had to overhear that, I'm glad it was you." I nodded.

"Your business, I won't ask what that was all about," I told him.

"Thanks," was all he said. He definitely wasn't ready to talk about it yet.

"You okay?" I asked him. He nodded, but I could see his lip quiver slightly as he suppressed breaking into tears again.

I couldn't have stopped myself from my next movement. It was as inevitable as gravity bringing the rain down. Seeing him hurt, eyes full of that much pain and loss, it was more than I could take. I stepped forward and put my arms around him.

His arms wrapped around me and he clung to me like I was his only anchor in the storm of emotions raging through him. He cried, sobs seeming torn from his body as he buried his face in my shoulder. He cried like he'd been holding it in for far too long.

I knew what that felt like, too. How anyone could hate this poor, wounded soul I'll never understand. He was so loving, so open. Nobody was like that anymore. Maybe nobody ever had been. My own emotions overcame me, connecting with his on a level I didn't understand, and I cried with him. For him. For both of us.

Chapter Six

First Confession

I don't know how long I held him there. I didn't care, either. I was there for as long as he needed me. And, I realized, I needed him too. I hadn't cried since my mother died. When at last he had cried himself out, we held each other for a while longer. Eventually, he pulled away, wiping at his eyes.

"I'm sorry, Ryan," he said, his voice rough.

"No," I replied, my own voice raspy. "It's cool. Just don't go spreading it around, okay? They hate me enough here as it is." He smiled softly, reaching up one hand to wipe at the tears on my own cheek.

"Trust me, I won't breathe a word of it to anyone. Wouldn't be good for my reputation, either," he gave me a rueful smile. I looked away, remembering the meeting with my dad and the principal. He noticed the look and frowned. "What?"

"I don't want to tell you. You've got a lot on your mind already," I told him. His frown darkened.

"It's obviously bothering you, Ryan. Tell me," he insisted.

"It's just…" I wasn't sure how to begin. "My meeting with the principal. He called my dad." Chance stared steadily at me, so I continued. "It was about you."

"What did they tell you?" he asked in a carefully controlled tone. He looked worried, but maybe a little bit resigned, too.

"That I shouldn't be friends with you," I started hesitantly, but as I spoke, my anger trickled back in. "I think they think you're some kind of bad influence or something. I have no idea where they got that. My dad even said my relationship with you isn't healthy. As if he'd know, we've been friends not even a week and he's never even met you."

"Only a week," Chance said, as if to himself. He noticed me looking at him and smiled. "Just feels like I've known you forever, you know?" I smiled and nodded. I did know. I'd never felt this close to anyone, and I had known him for only a few days, and two of those days were the weekend where I hadn't seen him at all. Then something occurred to me.

"When I told you it was about you, you didn't say what about, you didn't ask what for, you asked what they told me," I said, though not harshly. Never harshly to Chance. He flinched as if I'd raised a hand.

After a moment, he sighed.

"There are a lot of important things you don't know about me yet, Ryan," he said with a solemnity rare in his usually smiling features. "Things I can't tell you. Things it's not really safe for you to know."

I stared into his unfathomable eyes, searching. All I saw was his sincerity, and his concern for me. No guile, no deception, just sincerity and concern. Finally, I nodded.

"Okay," I replied. He blinked.

"Okay?" he asked in surprise.

"Yeah. Okay. I trust you," I told him. His eyes seemed to grow even deeper as he smiled slowly. He reached up, and with the tips of his fingers tucked an errant strand of hair back behind my ear. It was a remarkably gentle gesture, I thought. I was okay with it though. I kind of liked it. He seemed to come to a conclusion at that moment.

"There is one big thing I can tell you, which is why a lot of the students here hate me," he said. "Only thing is, I'm afraid you'll hate me for it, too."

"Chance, the one thing I can never do is hate you," I told him. I hadn't realized it was absolutely true until I said it, but it was. "If you're ready to share, just spit it out."

"I'm… not really normal," he began seriously. I knew he was leading into something, but I decided he needed to be lightened up a little.

"Not telling me anything new there," I said.

"Shut up, this is hard for me!" he said, though not angrily. He even smiled slightly. He took a deep breath before continuing. "Ryan, I'm gay." I blinked, trying to process this.

"Like, limp-wristed, light in the loafers gay?" I asked, parroting mocking phrases I'd heard tossed about back in Phoenix. Chance frowned at me.

"Keep talking like that and I might have to kick your ass, Ryan." I wondered briefly if he could, and decided it was probably best not to risk it. A kid like Chance probably fought dirty. Besides, I hadn't intended to offend him, I was just trying to process this new information. It didn't really surprise me. In fact I was a little surprised I hadn't realized it already. I had already noted how sensitive the guy was.

"Sorry," I said honestly. "I've just never really known anyone who was gay. Not personally anyway. I mean, there were some in my school, but that was it. I wasn't friends with any of them or anything."

"Well, now you are," he replied. "The question is, now that you know, what are you going to do about it?"

"Nothing, I guess," I answered. "I mean, it doesn't really bother me. It's a little different, but it doesn't really make you any different from who you were thirty seconds ago." He smiled again.

"You're okay with it?"

"Sure. Why wouldn't I be? Who you're into doesn't affect me at all." I said. He looked away, quickly. "Jesus, Chance. Are you telling me that you're into me?" He looked back reluctantly, as though his eyes were being drawn back to mine against his will.

"Kind of, yeah," he confessed. Before I could reply, he burst out defensively, "but can you blame me? I mean, you're such a great looking guy, and you're sweet and funny, and…" he looked down again and he continued in a subdued tone, "and you see me for me. How could I not be into that?" He looked so vulnerable in that instant, I couldn't bear it. I had to turn it into a joke just to break the ache I felt building. I sort of puffed up my chest and put on my best arrogant face.

"Well, I guess I am pretty irresistible," I told him.

"Damned right you are," he said with a grin. I was glad to see my joke had eased a bit of his tension. He seemed so relieved that I wasn't freaking out over his revelation.

"Seriously though," I knew I had to caution him, "don't think that because I'm okay with you being gay and having a crush on me means that I'm interested, okay? I'm not into guys." He was nodding before I finished.

"It's cool, it's cool," he assured me. "I wasn't going to make a move or anything. I'm not really in a position right now to have a boyfriend even if by some miracle you were into me too."

I thought that last felt a bit like him throwing

up a wall to shield himself from the fact that I'd just told him I wasn't interested. I wasn't about to ruin that. His attraction aside, he was still my best friend, and I wasn't about to see him hurt any more than I absolutely had to.

"Cool, we're good then," I said. He nodded, glancing at the sun.

"Hey, what time is it?" he asked. I glanced at my watch.

"Oh man, we've totally missed fourth hour. You gonna to be in trouble?"

"No way. It's my birthday, I can do what I want," he grinned.

"That's right! I heard your mom say that!" I exclaimed. "Why didn't you tell me? I'd have gotten you a present!" He made a face.

"Please don't. I'm not really into the whole birthday thing anyway. They're kind of a downer at my place. As you can see," he gestured in the direction his mother had gone with a sad expression.

"Well, happy birthday anyway. I still wish you'd told me." I said. I really wished he had. Birthdays were supposed to be happy. The exchange between Chance and his mother had been anything but. He smiled.

"Thanks, Ryan."

"Hey, how old does that make you?" I asked him. He gave me an odd grin.

"Fourteen."

"Really?" I was surprised. "I thought you were already my age. I didn't know I was older than you." He shrugged.

"Not by much, I don't think. Just a few months," he said. I nodded.

"Yeah."

"Hey, are you going to be in trouble for missing class?" he asked me. I laughed.

"If I am, it won't be anything added onto the trouble I'm already in for cussing out my dad and the principal," I told him. He stared in shock.

"You... you did what?" he asked, completely unable to believe it.

"They were all over you," I protested. "I'm not putting up with that." Chance stared another few seconds, then laughed. Hard. I loved it when he did that. You just couldn't help but laugh with him when he went off that way.

"Ryan, you are something else. You're the only person I know who would stand up to Principal Avery and his own father to back up a guy he barely knows," he said, still chuckling as he put his arm around my shoulder and steered me back toward the school. "Best friend ever, seriously. Come on man, let's go raid the library for information. If you're still up for it," he added as he paused to look at me.

He was very close. I was suddenly very aware of the combined facts that he was gay, attracted to me, and now approximately two inches from my face. I gave him a light shove as a playful protest, to cover up my moving him a bit further away.

"Oh please, I probably just got myself suspended backing you up. Let's go do some digging," I said, keeping my tone light.

He smiled, but I could see in his eyes that he was aware of why I'd really moved him back, and was a little hurt. I'd have to be careful about tattoo, I told myself as we moved back into the school.

Chapter Seven

Quiet in the Library

The library wasn't crowded, though a few kids were around. Chance pointed me to the computers, and I moved toward the back tables that held them. Sitting down, Chance sat in the seat beside me, carefully not touching the computers, I noticed. I hid my grin from him. He sure was paranoid about this computer thing.

"Okay, what do we need to look for?" I asked him.

"Newspaper articles. December 14th, two years ago," he replied. "We want anything that mentions the name Dominic Hale."

"Got it," I said as I started typing. It took me a minute to find the right search engine for this through the school's internet provider. They had the internet on this system pretty restricted.

"So what's with your interest in this kid?" I

asked him as I typed.

"I knew him," Chance replied. I remembered him saying that before. "Pretty well, actually. Everybody said it was a suicide. Even the cops said so. I have two problems with this. First, like I said I knew Dominic and he would never have killed himself. He was depressed a lot, sure, and was picked on all the time, but he was a tough kid. He wouldn't have given up like that." I nodded. That made sense to me.

"And second," he continued, "who kills themselves by cooking themselves in an oven? I mean really, there have got to be easier, less painful ways to go." I gave him a half-smile.

"You have a point," I answered, "I can definitely think of a few easier ways to do that." Chance looked at me sharply and I laughed.

"Don't worry, I can't die yet," I told him, "I haven't even had my first kiss." His sharp look suddenly became a flirtatious grin.

"I can help with that, you know."

"Easy there, tiger," I laughed. "I don't swing that way, remember?"

"I don't know, if you're not into a girl as hot as Jennifer, there may be hope for me yet," he retorted. I made a face at him.

"Shh!" came the stern whisper of the librarian. Chance and I looked at each other and snickered quietly.

"Yeah, keep it down," Chance whispered. I

was about to reply, but something caught my attention.

"Wait, here we go," I said as the incredibly slow internet search came back with a hit. Wow, this school needed a lot more than just light rewiring. This was dial-up slow. "We have one here from the county paper. Let's see what we've got." I loaded it up and began reading from the article.

"'Turnbridge Tragedy'. Catchy headline," I joked. Chance's eyes were locked on the page though, so I continued. "Fourteen year old Dominic Hale was found dead Thursday morning by Turnbridge Middle School cafeteria workers, after having turned on and then locked himself into the school's large bread oven.

"According to school authorities, Dominic was a normally happy boy, though he had recently become depressed after having attempted to come out to his parents. Picked on by his peers for his sexual orientation, he had sought the counsel of a local minister, who has regretfully admitted that his attempts to console the boy had been unsuccessful...'" I tapered off and looked at Chance. "He was gay, too." I said. Chance nodded.

"Yeah. His parents didn't take it well. It was pretty hard on him," he replied.

"Is that how you knew him?" I asked, unsure if I should be more specific and ask if they'd been together. Chance shook his head though.

"No, I knew him before either of us knew we were gay." I nodded, but I watched him closely.

"That's why you want to find out what really happened," I realized out loud. Chance looked at me.

"What do you mean?"

"People think he killed himself because he was depressed, caused by his being gay and not being accepted for it by the other kids, or his parents," I reasoned, "but you think he was murdered." Another realization hit me. "You think he was murdered because he was gay." Chance took a deep breath and nodded.

"Yeah, I do," he answered simply. "And I think I know who did it." I gaped at him.

"What? Why haven't you told someone?"

"It wouldn't matter. I can't prove it was him. Yet." He looked very pointedly at me at the last word. I waited. So did he.

"Well?" I demanded. "Who was it?"

"Noah Porter."

"What?" I was more surprised than I should have been, I think.

"Think about it, Ryan. He's a bully, he's always roughing people up for their 'sins', wears that stupid crucifix all the time. The guy's a psycho," Chance said, as if I needed to be told that. "Those fanatics are already really hard on homosexuality. Can you imagine what he would do if he got his hands on someone openly gay? I could totally see him trying to do his 'God' a favor and start their hellfire burning a little ahead of schedule."

I thought about it. Noah was a bully. I didn't think he was a killer, though. It was a huge step from pushing someone around and pushing someone into a heated oven.

"I don't know man, that seems a bit extreme, even for him," I argued. Chance just shrugged dismissively.

"You asked what I thought. There it is," he said. I nodded.

"Wouldn't he be after you then, if that was his deal?" I asked him. "Everyone knows you're gay, right? Why does he leave you alone?" He nodded.

"Yeah, but he doesn't really have a choice with me. It's complicated," he replied with a note of finality. I knew right away I wasn't getting any more out of him than that.

"Okay then, so how do you prove it?" I asked. He sighed.

"I don't know. I need to find some clue I've missed. Something I can use as evidence."

"After two years? I would think most of the evidence would be long gone by now."

"Probably," he admitted. "But I can't stop trying. I owe it to Dominic. I know he didn't kill himself. Let's try another article." A few more clicks and I'd found the local Turnbridge newspaper, and located their article on the subject. The computer screen flickered slightly.

"Man, aren't they ever going to get that fixed?"

I complained. "They need to rewire this whole dump."
Chance smiled sidelong at me.

"Yeah, they do. They won't though. Costs too much."

"That sucks," I said. "What are they going to do when the wiring goes out altogether? The whole school could burn down." Chance looked thoughtful.

"That might not be a bad thing," he retorted. I laughed and shoved him. He laughed too.

"Shh!" came the sharp, insistent whisper of the librarian. Chance and I smothered our laughter as best we could.

"Okay, this one's local," I said as I regained my focus, "'Middle-schooler Dominic Hale was found dead Thursday in the cafeteria of Turnbridge Middle School, in what police are calling a tragic suicide. Known to be a troubled youth, Dominic Hale was openly gay and had recently had a falling out with his parents. His teachers described him as being habitually depressed and bullied, and prone to bouts of dark rage. His mother tells a different story, however.

"'Dominic was a sweet boy, always so bright and eager to help. It was only recently that things got bad, and he realized he was gay. His father and I had a hard time with it, it's against our faith, and he fell into depression. He wouldn't commit suicide though, no matter what they say. He was always so determined to make something of himself, to prove to everyone that who he liked didn't matter.'

"'According to police, there was nobody else in the school at the time except the janitor, who has been proven to be on the phone talking with his out-of-state brother at the time. There was no evidence of struggle, and police have no reason to suspect foul play…'" I stopped again.

"Man, this kid must have had it rough," I said softly, imaging being in his position.

"Yeah, it wasn't easy for him."

"At least he had you though," I replied. Chance shook his head however.

"No, I wasn't as supportive and positive for him as I should have been. I was still so naïve about everything," he said sadly. I reached over and patted his arm.

"I'm sure you did the best you could. Kid as depressed as that, there's not much you can do."

"He did not kill himself," Chance glared at me.

"I didn't say he did," I protested. "I'm just saying that whatever happened, the kid had it rough, and you couldn't really have done much to help him out." Chance looked at me for a moment, then sighed.

"Yeah, I guess. Nothing like regrets, though. Do any of those articles talk about the oven itsel…" Chance trailed off, and I looked at him curiously. "It's awfully quiet in here."

"Duh, it's a library," I laughed.

"No, I mean really quiet. Listen." I did. He was right, it had gone completely still. No rustling of papers, no turning of pages, no sound of shuffling feet or pencils scratching.

"That's weird," I whispered as softly as I could. Chance nodded. We looked around, but from our vantage point, we couldn't see most of the rest of the library. We didn't see anyone around though. I started to stand up to go see what was going on.

"Ryan!" Chance suddenly shouted, shoving me sideways, hard. I went down in surprise, just as the huge rack of books behind us crashed over onto the desk. The heavy shelving unit slammed into the table, the top of it striking the computer monitors, which exploded in a shower of glass. Books crashed down all over me, several hitting hard enough to bruise.

I looked frantically for Chance, and spotted him underneath the long table.

"You okay?" I asked, looking around.

"I'm fine! What happened?" he asked. His push had dropped me in the triangular space created when the bookshelf had struck the table.

The table had held, leaving me under a pile of books, in a tent made of table and shelves. I rolled under the table and out the other side, jumping up. I couldn't see anyone in the entire library. Even the librarian was gone. At her desk was her "At Lunch, Be Back Soon" sign. Chance moved up beside me, also looking around.

"Check this out," I said, spotting something at a nearby table. It was a black backpack, sitting open beside the table just on the other side of the fallen bookshelf. Nobody was sitting there, however.

On the table in front of the empty chair was a Bible. On the front cover, embossed in gold, was the name Noah J. Porter. Chance and I looked at the Bible, then to each other.

"Still think my theory about Noah is so far-fetched?" he asked. I looked back at the Bible, then back to the fallen shelf and destroyed computers. I was no longer so sure.

Chance and I both ran into the hallway and looked around. Nobody in the halls either. Not too surprising, class was in session for those without a free period, but it still felt eerie. We moved down the hallway.

We'd just rounded the corner into the B hallway of the school when we spotted Noah. He and four of his friends had a girl pinned up against the lockers about twenty feet down the hall. They were pretty focused on her, and hadn't noticed us yet.

"You know what God did to your people, right?" Noah was asking. I found myself moving forward involuntarily, angrily.

"Ryan…" Chance warned.

"What do you mean 'my people'?" the obviously frightened girl asked. By her tone, she couldn't decide whether to be more terrified or confused by this.

"All you God damned homos," Noah replied

with a sneer. "Killed ever' one of you fags in Sodom and Gomorrah, then sent 'em all to Hell. God hates you people. I hate you people. Every God-fearing Christian hates you people. Why don't you kill yerself and save God the trouble?"

"Leave me alone," the girl said, though her voice lacked any real force.

"Maybe just something to remind you of your place," Noah said, lifting his fist as two of his buddies grabbed her arms and pinned her to the lockers. I'd been moving forward slowly the whole time, but I suddenly found myself running.

"Ryan, don't!" Chance yelled behind me. I wasn't listening. Noah's friends standing behind him backed up in surprise at my sudden, rapid appearance. Noah didn't notice, primed to hit the girl.

I hit him broadside at a full sprint. I jumped right before I hit him, so I'd hit him high. He was completely unprepared and went over sideways without any resistance at all.

We went down hard, my elbow slamming into the ground hard enough to send a jolt clear up to my shoulder. I ignored it, I was already swinging. I caught him hard across his left cheek, whipping his head to the side. His arms came up to shield his face, but he didn't need to. His four friends had gotten over their surprise quickly and were hauling me off of him, despite my flailing wildly.

I was never really a fighter. My initial

successful assault on Noah had been born of pure outrage, not of any skill. It took the four only seconds to have me completely restrained, and slammed back up against the lockers. I looked around wildly. The girl was halfway down the hall, running as fast as she could.

Where was Chance? There, standing back at the end of the hallway, unmoved from where I'd left him. He stood, watching me with a mixture of panic and shock.

"Chance!" I yelled to him. He didn't move, frozen in place.

"Yer demon boyfriend ain't gonna help you," Noah said darkly as he stood and slowly, menacingly, approached me. A small, bright trickle of blood came from a cut on his cheek where I'd hit him. I got some measure of satisfaction from that. Really, it was the little things that brought you comfort when you were about to die.

"I think you need to seriously reconsider your opinion of evil," I told him. I looked back to Chance, still standing at the end of the hall, watching. He looked terrified. I couldn't believe he wasn't coming to help me, or at least running to get someone to help me.

"I think you need to seriously reconsider yours," he replied. "Relations with the Devil is even worse than relations with other men."

"What the Hell are you even talking about?" I demanded.

"You know what I'm talking about," he

sneered.

"God damn it, would you assholes let me go?" I growled at the four boys holding me hard up against the metal of the lockers. The lights overhead were sputtering so badly it was beginning to give the hallway a surreal appearance.

I was absolutely unprepared for Noah's fist slamming into my gut. The breath exploded out of me, and simply refused to come back in. My entire abdomen felt like it was trying to cave in on itself. I frantically tried to suck in air, but my lungs refused to work.

"Do NOT take the Lord's name in vain!" Noah yelled.

I managed to turn my eyes up toward him from my position curled over my stomach. At some point, the four boys had let go of me, and I'd dropped to the floor. I didn't remember that happening, though. I managed to take a shaky, ragged breath. Then Noah kicked me in the side.

Oddly, this hurt less than the punch. Maybe he'd numbed my abdomen already with the first blow. The inability to breath was becoming excruciating though. Noah leaned down over me.

"Listen, you devil-worshipping piece of trash, ain't nothing waiting for you but Hell. I tried to help you, I really did. You jus' can't help evil. You can't cure evil. All you can do is let it be judged. Don't worry, city boy. You will be judged. When God's hands come for you, then you'll know. Then you'll see. Soon enough," Noah finished with a dark smile, "soon enough you'll burn."

He and his minions turned and walked away down the hallway, leaving me gasping for air on the floor. They had left the hallway before Chance came over to me, slowly.

"Ryan?" he asked hesitantly. I turned my eyes away from him. "Ryan, are you okay?"

"Do I look okay to you?" I croaked, still cradling my stomach, each breath a painful effort in willpower. My voice was barely audible.

"I'm so sorry," he said, laying a hand gently on my shoulder. I pulled away.

"I thought friends were supposed to have your back," I spat, bitterly. He was quiet for a long moment.

"I couldn't help you," he whispered. "I tried to warn you."

"What, so they could have just pounded on that poor girl, instead of me?" I growled as I looked his way. His deep brown eyes were wet with tears.

"You couldn't help her, and I couldn't help you." he said. "All you did was buy her a little time. Noah will catch up to her later, when you're not around to be a substitute punching bag. Now Noah really hates you, and you're going to have to deal with that."

"Yeah, alone apparently," I said, clenching my eyes shut as I focused on slow, steady breathing.

"Ryan, you don't..." he started.

"Go away," I said softly. He heard me though. I didn't look up for several seconds. When I did, he was gone.

Chapter Eight
Suspended

I had been back in class for about twenty minutes when I was paged over the school's crackling intercom.

"Ryan Jacobs, report to the principal's office immediately."

The snickers and whispers that erupted in the room at this point suddenly struck me as bearing an eerie resemblance to a pack of hyenas in the dark.

"Ryan? You may go," the teacher instructed.

I sighed, then winced at the pain in my stomach as I stood. I headed to the office. Not much else I could do at this point. As I walked into the main office, Mrs. Bradley looked up from her desk. She didn't smile this time, just shook her head softly and pointed at the office door. I went where she directed me.

My father was there again. Or maybe still, I

didn't know if he'd actually ever left. It had only been a few hours, though it sure felt like a lot longer than that. Maybe he and Principal Avery had been 'discussing' me ever since. I moved to the chair beside my father and eased myself into it.

"Mr. Jacobs," Principal Avery sighed. "In a single afternoon, you have disrespected your principal and father, ditched class, vandalized the library resulting in thousands of dollars of damage to our computers and shelving, and assaulted one of your fellow students. This behavior is completely unacceptable."

"I did not vandalize the library! Someone pushed the shelves…" I protested, but my father interrupted.

"Ryan, don't," he said softly. "There were witnesses."

"What?" I asked incredulously.

"Your father has talked me out of having you expelled, but you will be suspended for the remainder of the week," Principal Avery said coldly. "I am going to tell you this as clearly as possible, Mr. Jacobs. Next Monday, if you do not feel you are capable of conducting yourself in an acceptable manner, you are not welcome back here."

I looked at him in shock. He actually believed all of this was my fault. I looked to my father for support, and found none. He stared at me, eyes showing again how broken he was.

I looked back to Principal Avery. His expression was cool and collected, but his eyes burned hotly. As angry as he apparently was with me despite his controlled tone, I had to wonder if I would soon be treated the same way Chance was, with everyone hating me and just shutting me out. After a moment I realized I didn't care. If Chance talked to me, I didn't need anyone else to.

"Go and get your things, Ryan. We're going home," he said. I stood slowly, painfully, and left the office.

I looked at Mrs. Bradley as I passed, but she carefully focused on the paperwork in front of her. You too, I thought? Great. Turned on and abandoned by the only people I had left.

My father believed I was a violent delinquent, the principal thought I should be expelled, the usually friendly secretary wouldn't even look at me, and my best friend in the world had abandoned me to be beaten up by the school bully. He hadn't even gone for help. To top it off, some crazy religious fanatic was apparently now trying to kill me. It was amazing just how much life could actually suck. As if my mother dying wasn't enough for one guy to have to cope with.

I stormed through the halls, lost in my dark thoughts. Grabbing my things from my locker, I didn't even bother with my textbook from the class I'd been called out of. It didn't really matter at this point. I made it almost out of the school when a voice stopped me.

"Ryan…" the voice said. I didn't turn. I knew it was Chance. "Ryan, I'm really sorry. Those guys terrify me. I mean, Noah is the one who…"

"Save it Chance," I snapped, not turning. "I can't be friends with someone I can't trust."

"I told you, I can't help," he protested, sounding hurt and defeated.

"You could have gone for help," I said, as I finally turned around. The halls were empty, the lights flickering absently. "Don't you ever go to class?"

"Only when I have to," he said with a small, half-hearted smile. I shook my head.

"Go to class, Chance. At least you still can."

"What do you mean?" His confused expression was almost as painful as his wounded one.

"I got suspended. I can't come back until Monday."

"Ryan, you have to come back!" he protested, a panicked look coming into his eyes.

"I can't. That's what suspension means," I told him bitterly. "Go to class, Chance. You'll be fine. I'm the one Noah's trying to kill, not you. You'll be fine." I realized I was trying to reassure myself as much as him. I shoved the feeling back down and turned away, heading for the doors.

"Ryan," Chance said behind me. I stopped again, but resolutely refused to face him. "Be careful, okay?"

I didn't respond, I just walked away.

My father had the car out front and waiting. I climbed in and buckled my seat belt, not saying anything. He was quiet for a few minutes before he spoke.

"What happened to you, Ryan?" he asked. I didn't respond. "You were always so bright, so happy, so quick to laugh and make jokes. You were always so friendly. Ever since your mom got sick, all of that has disappeared. It was bad enough back in Phoenix, but since we got here you've..." he looked over at me. "I'm worried, Ryan. There's something really not right with you lately."

"Not right with me?" I snapped. "There's something completely jacked up about this entire town! Haven't you seen it?"

"This town isn't the problem, Ryan," he argued. "Everyone can see it but you. You've gone from being a great, happy student with lots of friends to being this brooding, sullen kid who's not doing well in class, is damaging school property, attacking other students, and has only one friend who is..."

"You leave Chance out of this!" I said as threateningly as I could. "And that library incident was not my fault!"

"Oh, so just the attacking students part is?" he asked sharply.

"That psycho and his four brain-dead partners were about to beat up on a girl!" I yelled. "You're damned right I attacked him! All because she likes other girls? What the Hell is wrong with everyone?" My father looked at me, a little surprised, then his face went steely again.

"I can't trust you, Ryan. You said you didn't vandalize the library, but there were witnesses! Five different students came in to report it!"

"Let me guess, the same five who claimed I attacked them?" I retorted. He didn't respond. I knew I was right. "Awfully convenient Noah's backpack and Bible were on the table right behind the shelves that just about crushed us."

"Ryan, this is getting out of hand. You need to get yourself under control. I've made an appointment with a counselor at the hospital for you this weekend."

"Awesome, now you think I'm crazy."

"You're not crazy Ryan," he argued. "You're just upset. Maybe about your mother, maybe about something else," he glanced sidelong at me, "but whatever it is, you need to talk to someone about it. Someone trained to handle this kind of thing."

"Yeah, kid's having a hard time. Instead of listening to him, let's send him to the nuthouse. It's easier for everyone that way," I said bitterly. My sarcasm was not appreciated.

"Ryan it isn't a nuthouse, and I'm not sending you there. We're just going to go in on Saturday and talk to someone about what's bothering you."

"What's bothering me is that nobody, not even

the people who are supposed to care, seem to give a damn," I said. "It probably wouldn't concern you at all to know that I think someone is trying to hurt me, and that with me gone all week, nobody is going to be around to look out for Chance in case whoever it is decides go after him."

I realized that the thought of nobody being there to back up Chance if something happened really bothered me, despite my resentment at him not having come to my own aid. He was terrified of Noah, after all. He really was convinced that the guy was a psychotic murderer.

Considering what happened in the library, and in the halls after, that thought didn't seem at all out of place anymore. I couldn't blame him too much for not wanting to charge in against a killer and his four minions. I would have, though, for Chance. My dad looked over at me, and then back to the road.

"Doctor Sadler told me paranoia might be one of the symptoms," he said almost to himself.

"Symptoms? Are you kidding me? You really do think I'm crazy!" I shouted at him.

"Can you blame me after everything that's been going on?" he snapped back.

"Everything that's been going on? Like the library and the fight? I told you Dad, that Noah kid is a serious problem! I'm not doing anything but trying to protect myself and Chance!"

"I'm not concerned about Chance, Ryan!" my

father yelled back. "I'm concerned about you! You haven't been right since your mother died! I thought moving out here would help, but it was like lighting the fuse! You've completely lost control of yourself, and I can't think what to do to help! We're going Saturday to see Doctor Sadler, and I don't want to hear another word about any of this!" I glared at him, furious at his lack of faith and belief in me.

"Shouldn't be a problem," I muttered, "you haven't heard anything that I've said in years anyway." He looked at me, and I could tell I'd hurt him. He looked away and didn't say another word.

We got home, and I went to my bedroom, closing the door behind me. I hooked up my mp3 player to my speakers, and turned up the hardest rock I had in my collection loud enough that I probably wouldn't have heard my dad even if he were shouting right outside my door. Just the way I preferred it at that moment.

I spent my afternoon and evening locked in my room, lying on my bed, staring at the ceiling as I listened to my music. Thoughts came and went, most without real form or direction. I was trying hard not to think too much. I ate dinner at the table with my father, neither of us saying a word. I went to bed and slept dreamlessly, to my great relief.

As the next day passed, I couldn't stop thinking about Chance. Yeah, he'd left me high and dry when I'd stepped in to help that girl, but the more I thought about it, the look on his face told it all. He wasn't just afraid of being hurt by Noah. He really thought Noah was a killer and was terrified by the idea of making him mad.

I couldn't really blame him for freezing up like that, especially after the guy had just tried to crush us with the bookshelves. That was a lot of stress for a guy to deal with. Add to that his mother's visit to the school, and that it was his unhappy birthday...

That thought hit me hard as I realized I'd totally shut him out after the Noah incident. Chance was probably crushed, losing his only friend on his birthday. The more I thought about it, the worse I felt for reacting like that.

It really was stupid of me to jump in and help that girl against five guys, all bigger than I was. Although being honest with myself I knew full well I'd do it again if given the chance for a retake. Whatever Chance said, I'd given the girl the opportunity to get away. I was glad she'd taken it.

After his talk with his mother, getting almost crushed to death by the shelves, during which I now realized he'd saved my life, watching his best friend get pounded on and unable to do anything about it, then rejected by that same friend all on his birthday... I had to figure out a way to make it up to him.

I spent the next two days trying to figure out something I could do for him. While reading that evening, I finally came up with something. I'd have to get my dad to let me go to a store in town when we went for my appointment Saturday, but I could manage it I thought. I just had to cooperate well enough on Saturday for him to want to do me a favor.

Thursday afternoon, I was dozing lightly in the crispness of the afternoon out on our small porch when I had a nightmare. Not the nightmare, I hadn't had that one since Chance's voice had appeared in it. This one was different.

I was in the library at school. The fallen shelving had been replaced, and brackets installed to bolt it to the floor. To prevent another "accident", I assumed. All the shelving units had been bolted down.

Everything was slightly hazy, though still carried a realness unusual in my normal dreams. The computers had been removed from the back table, but new ones had not yet been put in their place. The table was empty, showing damage where the heavy bookcase had connected with it. Had the table been any less solid itself, the table might have collapsed as well. As I slowly turned, I heard voices.

"Hell awaits you, girl. Your sins will be purged in the fires of eternal damnation. Let your judgment come." I couldn't make out the voice, it too was hazy. In the dim, misty vision, I couldn't see the source of the voice, either. Moving slowly, like through a thick soup, I walked, curving around shelves and peering down rows of books.

"I never hurt anyone," another voice

responded. This one was a young girl. It sounded familiar.

"Your sins are unforgivable! God's justice will be your reward."

I rounded the last set of shelves and spotted the maintenance closet in the back of the library. Inside the small closet stood a girl on a tall stool. Her hands were behind her back, and a long electrical cord was wrapped around her neck, the other end tied to a pipe on the ceiling. She was crying softly.

In front of her stood a man. No, I realized, not a man. As the figure turned, I recognized the devil. My devil. The one wearing Noah's face like a Halloween mask. The mask-face saw me, and slowly grinned, revealing long, jagged teeth behind the bloody lips.

Still looking at me, the devil reached out behind itself and grabbed the stool. I silently shouted out my protest, and the devil laughed, the horrible sound resonating in my bones.

With a mocking abruptness and a tilt of its gruesome head, it yanked the stool out from under the girl. She dropped fast, hitting the end of her cord with a jerk, feet kicking well out of reach of the floor.

I screamed, and jerked awake as my whole body convulsed, trying to move forward to help the girl. The reality of the dream was so thick in my thoughts that I had my cell phone out and in my hand, dialing 9-1-1 before I knew what I was doing.

"9-1-1, what's your emergency?" came the

calm woman's voice on the other end. I tried to speak, but I had trouble getting my words out.

"Closet..." I coughed, almost feeling as though the cord were around my own neck. "Turnbridge Middle, library. Closet. Help her!"

"I'm sorry sir, do you mean Turnbridge Middle School?" the dispatcher asked. I hung up the phone in horror as full wakefulness reached me. I'd just made a 9-1-1 call based on a dream. I had to be completely out of my mind. Maybe my father was right.

I wondered if they had the technology to trace my cell number. I was really hoping that Turnbridge was back-country enough that they didn't even have caller id, let alone phone tracing abilities.

After the first hour passed, I relaxed. If they were going to come after me for prank calling 9-1-1, they would have done so by now, I reasoned. A few hours later, my dad came home. He saw me sitting still on the porch lost in thought and slowed as he approached from the car.

"Hi Ryan," he said.

"Hey," I replied.

"I had a surprise visit today at work," he said, sitting down in the chair beside me.

"Yeah?"

"Yeah. About an hour ago, a bunch of people came racing into the ER. I was doing an inventory check in the department, so watched the whole group of them come in," he said. I looked over at him, unsure where this was going.

"Intense," I said.

"They had a little girl with them, Ryan. A girl from your school," he said, watching me closely. I felt my heart leap up into my throat. "Poor girl had been hung by an extension cord in a closet at your school."

"Is she okay?" I whispered, my heart in my throat. I wasn't sure if I should be afraid or relieved.

"Sort of," he answered. "She was resuscitated, but her windpipe is badly damaged, and she won't wake up. Doctors are afraid she might have brain damage from oxygen deprivation. She might not wake up. But she's alive, so the doctor is hopeful."

"Thank God," I said. "I'm glad she's alive."

"Well that's the interesting thing, Ryan. Along with the paramedics came a couple of police officers. They were looking for me." I realized in horror that the cell phone I used wasn't in my name. It was in my dad's.

"What did they want?" I asked, trying to feign a casual attitude. I failed miserably, my hands shaking and my voice cracking.

"To know how I knew she was in trouble there," he said. "They were very interested in knowing how I knew that at that precise moment, a little girl at my son's middle school was committing suicide in the maintenance closet of the school library." I looked at my hands, and willed them to stop shaking. The dream was real. How could that be? How had I seen it? What the hell was going on?

"What did you tell them?" I asked.

"I told them that my son had made the call, and he was a student there. I told them that I assumed you had known the girl, and maybe knew she was planning something."

"I did know her, sort of," I said. "I just met her on Monday. She was the girl those boys were trying to beat on." He looked at me for a long time. I couldn't read his expression.

"Do you think she was picked on enough to want to kill herself?" he asked me.

"She didn't try to kill herself, Dad," I snapped. "Somebody tied her hands behind her back, put her on a stool, and hung her up there, then pulled the stool out from under her."

"How could you possibly know that, Ryan?" he demanded, sounding exasperated. He also sounded confused, and a little bit scared. I decided to try something different. I decided to open up to him a little. Just a little.

"I…" I took a deep breath. I couldn't look at him while I said this. "I dreamt about it. I could see the whole thing. He pulled the stool, and she fell. I woke up, and called 9-1-1."

"You saved that girl's life, Ryan," he said softly. "She would have been there maybe for hours before someone found her. If you hadn't called when you did, she wouldn't have made it. But Ryan, people don't dream about other people's murders."

"I think I do," I whispered back.

"Have you had any others like that?" he asked.

My recurring nightmare flashed in my mind, but I shook my head. No reason to freak him out even more by telling him I've dreamt my own murder. I've dreamt about my own murder, I realized, and apparently my dreams of death were real. My hands began to shake again.

"Does..." he hesitated. "Does Chance tell you about these things?"

"No," I answered. "I don't think he has dreams like that, either. I doubt he'd believe me if I told him. He's a little obsessed about a murder that happened in that school two years ago, but nothing recent. That one looked like a suicide too, but Chance doesn't think it was. With everything going on, I'm starting to think he might be right."

It occurred to me that my dream of burning in that oven might not actually be me. Maybe I was dreaming about Dominic Hale's death. Except the voice telling me it couldn't help called me by name.

My father looked away, repeatedly flexing and relaxing his jaw like he does when he's really upset about something. He didn't speak for several minutes.

"Who was it that tried to kill the girl in your dream?" he asked. I was hoping he wouldn't ask that, though I knew he would.

"In my dream, it looked like a devil," I told

him. He took a long, slow breath, and was quiet for another minute.

"Ryan, I think we need to tell Doctor Sadler about this," he finally said. I sighed. He still thought I was crazy.

"Okay, Dad." He looked back at me.

"Okay?"

"I said okay," I replied tiredly. He nodded, patted me on the leg, and stood to go inside. "Hey Dad?" He stopped.

"Yeah Spo... Ryan?" Nice save, Dad. I appreciated that he tried though.

"Can we stop at a store when we go into town on Saturday?"

"Sure, what for?"

"I just need a couple of supplies for a project," I said. At his expression, I quickly clarified. "I want to make a present for someone." He considered, then nodded.

"Yeah, I don't see why not."

"Thanks," I said as he went inside.

I sighed again. Well, I'd tried. Nobody could say I hadn't tried. He was polite about it, but my father obviously thought I was crazy. He wasn't going to be any real help. I was more convinced than ever that Chance was in trouble.

Dominic had been gay, and murdered in such a way as to look like suicide. This girl, whatever her name was, was also gay and someone had tried to do the same to her. Chance was gay, and someone had tried to crush him with a bookshelf, which would probably have looked like an accident had it succeeded. I desperately wished I had some way to get in touch with Chance.

I got up, and went inside. Nothing I could do until Monday, but that didn't stop me from worrying.

Chapter Nine
The Amazing Headshrinker

We drove into town without speaking again on Saturday after my dad got home from work. We passed by the school, and I watched it the whole way past, a part of me wildly hoping to see Chance. It was Saturday though, nobody was around.

The hospital my dad worked in served four towns, Turnbridge being the largest which was more than a little sad. It was a fairly large hospital though, easily the biggest building anywhere in Turnbridge. We parked, and I followed my dad inside.

We took an elevator to the third floor, apparently devoted to mental health. I refrained from commenting on the fact that this town needed an entire hospital floor devoted to the whackos, mostly because I myself was there for good ol' American head-shrinking, as they say.

The office we were heading toward was

halfway down the first hallway, not far in. There was a big waiting area, and several doors leading off the big triangular lobby. A positively ancient woman sat behind a desk, and a few people sat in the waiting chairs. My father walked right up to the desk and addressed the woman.

"Ryan Jacobs here to see Doctor Sadler," he said loudly. I winced. As if the whole school thinking I was crazy wasn't bad enough. Let's just announce it to the whole town, shall we?

"Please have a seat, Mr. Jacobs. The doctor will be with you momentarily," the woman replied, with no traces of the local accent.

I had already gone to sit down. My father sat beside me for only a minute or two when one of the office doors opened, and a middle-aged woman with curly reddish-brown hair poked her head out.

"Mr. Jacobs?" she said. My dad and I stood, but she pointed to my father. "Just you first, please. I'll be with you in a few more minutes, Ryan."

She smiled at me as she said it, but the obvious message was that she wanted my dad's take on things before talking to me, which to me meant she was already going to favor his word over mine. I disliked her already, but I sat back down. I was halfway through a Popular Mechanics magazine that was almost eleven years old when someone sat down beside me.

"Hey Ryan," a girl's voice said. I looked up. It was Jennifer. She smiled at me.

"Hey. Jennifer, right?" I said casually, though I was more than a little surprised to see her. Her smile brightened at my recognition.

"That's right! Rumors sure get around, if we both know each other's names without havin' been prop'rly introduced," she said in her soft accent.

"Yeah, they must," I said bitterly. "Which is why I'm surprised you're talking to me."

"Well, I did hear about th' library, and your fight with Noah. Don't worry though, I know Noah an' I don't doubt that he started it," she said, to my surprise. "The library shelves were probably an accident, though. He might be a bit rough 'round th' edges, but he wouldn't ever take it that far. And I sure don't think you pushed them over like Noah told everyone you did." I considered her for a moment. She seemed to be serious, so I smiled.

"Thanks," I told her. "That's… that means a lot."

"That's okay," she said, "a lot of nasty stuff goes 'round in those rumors. I know better than t' listen to 'em. Is it true about your friend, Chance?" I looked at her.

"What, that he's gay?" I asked. "Yeah, he doesn't make any show of hiding it or anything. He's cool with it. So am I, though I'm not gay myself," I hastened to add. She hesitated, and seemed about to say something, then changed her mind.

"Glad to hear that, though. It'd be a shame if a

good lookin' guy like you was gay," she said. I felt my cheeks getting hot.

"Wouldn't be that great a loss to womankind," I said jokingly. She smiled at me.

"I'd be more concerned 'bout the sin," she said. I froze. "The Bible says bein' gay ain't right." I glanced down. A small, golden crucifix hung around her neck.

"If you're going to start in on my friend Chance, you can get up and walk away right now. He's never hurt anyone and I don't know why everyone picks on him like they do, but I won't put up with it."

My words were careful and measured, trying hard to keep from sounding angry or threatening. She considered me for a moment, then shrugged.

"I wasn't gonna," she said. "I'm sure he can't help bein' that way. I'm just sayin' that I'm glad you don't have that problem is all." I nodded, but didn't respond. We were quiet for a minute before she spoke again.

"So what're you doin' up here?" she asked.

"Nothing," I replied defensively.

"You're up here for somethin'," she laughed. "Don't worry, we all are. My mama over there gets stress headaches, so th' doctor gives her prescriptions for tension reducers."

Jennifer gestured to a pretty blonde across the lobby who looked like she probably spent three hours every morning just doing her hair. No wonder she was stressed, I thought. That kind of hairspray load had to do things to a person's mind. I smiled.

"My dad is just worried, after the fighting and stuff at school. He wants me to talk to a counselor. He thinks it'll help to have someone to talk to. I already do though," I told her. "I talk to Chance about everything." She looked away.

"That's too bad," she said. I wasn't sure if she meant about Chance, or the doctor. "I hope th' doctor is nice for you though. Who knows, maybe she can help you out." She brightened suddenly. "Hey, why don't you come with me t' church tomorrow? I can introduce you t' a lot of really great folks. Maybe you can talk t' th' minister. He's a counselor, too. Went to college for it an' everythin'."

"Thanks, but I'm a bit touchy about the church subject lately. Maybe another time," I told her.

"Well, all right," she said, "but how 'bout I give you my number, and if you change yer mind you can give me a call. I'm sure my mama'd be happy t' come give you a lift. I think we live on th' same side of town."

"If you can call it that," I muttered, but pulled out my phone. She rattled off her digits, and I entered her into my contacts list. I realized it was the first local number I'd put in this phone since we moved here. I hadn't even programmed in my dad's work number.

"It'd be a no-pressure kinda thing, Ryan," she assured me. "Jus' come listen t' th' sermon, meet a few folks, and you don't ever have t' come again if you don't want to."

I thought about that. I had no interest in her church, it obviously bred nut-cases, though Jennifer seemed nice enough. What could be interesting though was listening to what kind of service was given each week, considering the mindset of the local church-goers. It might explain a lot about Noah and his mindless henchmen.

"Yeah, maybe I will," I said. "I'll talk to my dad about it." Her smile flashed. She really was pretty. I still was not attracted to her. I'm not sure why that bothered me, but it did.

"That's great!" she exclaimed. "You just give me a call tonight, and we'll work out th' details. You'll jus' love it, I know!"

A doctor poked her head out of another room and called a name. I missed it, but Jennifer's mom stood, and gestured to her daughter.

"Gotta go," she said. "Call me!" I nodded and smiled.

"I will."

"Mr. Jacobs?" I stood as Doctor Sadler poked her head out of her office, my father walking out.

As I passed him on my way in, he patted my shoulder. He probably intended it to be comforting or reassuring. I found it irritating and patronizing. She gestured me to a seat.

I sat, and was surprised at how comfortable

the odd-looking red chair was. I looked around the office. It was decorated mostly in soft red, gold, and wood tones. The lighting was soft and warm, and she had a small candle burning by her laptop computer on one side of the desk. It was a relaxing kind of space, I grudgingly admitted.

"Ryan, your father tells me you're having some difficulties in school," she started. She didn't continue, so I assumed she wanted a response.

"Sort of," I replied. She waited, so I continued. "Just problems with a bully, same kind of thing that hundreds of thousands of kids deal with every day."

"You think your problems aren't special?" she asked. I considered the dreams.

"No," I said simply.

"Your father tells me that you've been having dreams. Dreams about people dying."

"Not dreams, a dream," I falsely corrected. "Just the one about the girl from my school."

"I hear you saved her life with that phone call," Dr. Sadler said.

"I guess so. She's in a coma though. Won't wake up."

"It's still pretty soon after the accident," she said. "She may come around any moment."

"It wasn't an accident," I snapped. She consulted her yellow notepad.

"Ah yes, you said it was staged to look like a suicide," she said. By her tone I knew already she didn't believe me either. Not that I expected her to.

"That's right."

"How do you know that?"

"I saw it in my dream," I told her, watching the flickering light of the candle. It suddenly reminded me of the lights in the school. Chance's face flashed through my mind.

"But you were at home on suspension, not anywhere near the school at the time," she said, trying to coax me into something.

"That's where I do most of my dreaming, yes," I said. She smiled without much humor and glanced at her pad again.

"Your father says that in your dream, the killer was a devil," she said. Loudmouth, I thought angrily at my father.

"That's right," I told her. No point lying about that much. It was too late now anyway. She made a note on her pad.

"Do you suppose it might be possible that the devil killing the girl in your dream might simply be your mind's way of telling you she had devils within her?" she asked. I glared at her.

"Not you, too," I muttered.

"I beg your pardon?" she asked.

"Nothing," I said. A quick glance had told me she was not wearing the little golden crucifix I'd started to associate with the religious nuts around here.

"Do you suppose your dream was symbolic of

her struggles because of her being ridiculed for being gay?"

"Good timing and awfully accurate for symbolism," I said wryly. "And she wasn't just being ridiculed, she was being physically attacked by five boys at the school." Another glance at the notepad, and a few scribbled notes.

"And that's why you say you got into a fight with the boys?"

"Yes."

"Ryan, tell me about your mother," she said, suddenly switching topics. Where did that come from, I wondered?

"Why?" I asked, immediately defensive.

"Well, because a trauma like that can have lasting consequences, and bring up issues even years later," she told me. I'll bet she thought she was being clever, with responses like that. It wasn't buying her any points from me though.

"Let's leave my mother out of this, shall we?" I said darkly. She scribbled a few notes on her pad.

"If you prefer, we can save that until next week," she replied. Next week? My dad hadn't said this was going to be a recurring thing. "Tell me about your friend… Chance," she said, looking at the pad to find his name. And here we go, I thought.

"Chance is my best friend."

"Has he been your friend long?"

"Just since I started school here."

"He's gay, isn't he?" she asked casually. I couldn't keep my fists from tightening up.

"Not that it's really any of your business, but yes. I don't think he'd mind my telling you that." She wrote something on her pad.

"Does he mind you talking about other things?"

"Of course he does, he has his private life too. You wouldn't want me sharing all of your secrets would you?"

"No, no I suppose I wouldn't," she said dismissively, scribbling on the notepad again. "Does he tell you to do things?"

"No, he asks politely," I told her, trying to keep too much of an edge from slipping into my tone. More notes. "Come on, he's a good kid. All that in the library, and the fighting, that's all Noah."

"Is Noah your friend too?"

"Hell no," I said angrily. "He's the bully I mentioned. And the one who attacked the girl. And I think the one who tried to push the library shelves over on top of me." She was scribbling non-stop now. The scratching sound of her pen on the paper was starting to get to me.

"Ryan, do you believe in devils?"

"Of course not,"

"You know they're not real?"

"Yes."

"You know people can't dream about things

they don't know about, right?"

"Tell that to the girl whose life I saved," I retorted. She hadn't stopped writing.

"Ryan, I think I have a few things to discuss with your father before we end our time today. I'd like to speak with him at the end of each of our sessions, so he and I can make sure we're all on the same page."

Yeah right, I thought. She just wanted to run everything I said by him and get his input before telling him how screwed up in the head I was. I was nothing more than the lab rat here.

"Fine," I said, standing up.

"It was very nice to meet you, Ryan. I look forward to seeing you again next week."

I didn't respond, just walked out of the office and sat down as my father stood and walked back into her office. What a sham, I thought. Less than fifteen minutes with me and she thought she had me all worked out. What arrogance to even assume she had the slightest inkling of what my life was about. I returned to my archaic Popular Mechanics.

Yet another aspect of my life that just wasn't right, I thought bitterly. Someone's trying to kill me, and they put me in therapy for it. What a jacked up world.

Chapter Ten
The Sleeping Girl

As my father and I went down the hallway just off the elevator, I noticed the sign pointing to Emergency Care. I thought about the girl, and had an impulsive idea.

"Hey Dad?" I asked. He looked down at me. "Can we go see her?"

"Who?"

"The girl who was strangled," I said, trying not to add "Duh" to the end of that sentence. Who else would I be talking about? He considered, but stopped walking.

"Yeah, for a few minutes," he replied with a sigh. We turned down a side hallway, not toward Emergency Care. We went to another wing of the hospital and spoke to the woman behind the desk.

The woman looked like an Islander, her hair in dozens of tight, elaborate braids, and a mother-of-pearl necklace. I smiled at her. This woman reminded me of my fourth grade teacher. She was a great teacher.

"Oh hi, Mark," she said to my dad.

"Hi Simone," he said, smiling at her. "Listen, I know it's not visiting hours, but my son here goes to school with the attempted suicide patient. They're friends and he wanted to just step in really quickly and see her." My dad touched my arm as he said "attempted suicide" to keep me from protesting. This was not the place to argue that point. I kept quiet.

"Sure, Mark," she said, "go on in." I'd been right. She had the same accent Mrs. Torrey in the fourth grade had.

"Thank you ma'am," I told her with a smile. She smiled back at me.

"Sure thing, sweetie. Your friend Katie is down the hall in room 146. You two need anything, you just give me a shout," she said. My dad thanked her, and steered me past the desk and down the hall. Her name was Katie. I made a note to remember her name. I didn't really know her, but it felt important.

We walked in room 146, my dad knocking softly, then glancing through the small window in the door before turning the handle and opening it. He gestured me in first. I hesitated, but this had been my idea. I stepped inside.

Katie lay on the bed, silent and still. She was lying in that unconscious position the doctors always put people into in movies; body straight, lying flat on her back, legs straight and arms straight down by her sides. You know, the kind of position that nobody naturally sleeps in?

She had tubes and tape everywhere, holding in her IV, monitoring her heart-rate and respiration, even a long tube down her heavily-bandaged throat.

On either side of the bandage I could see telltale traces of vicious bruising. The tube was attached to a machine that gave a regular hissing pulse. Her brown hair had been neatly arranged, also not a natural look for someone lying in a bed. I moved closer.

Katie was alone in the room, kept company only by the hissing and beeping of the various machines. She looked terrible. I felt a lump form in my throat as I reached her bedside. I watched her sleep for a minute, then unconsciously reached my hand out and touched hers.

I half-expected a miraculous reaction, like she'd suddenly wake up, or reach out and take my hand, but nothing happened. Not even a flutter of her eyelids. I sighed heavily, and turned to go. I wasn't sure why I'd come down here to begin with.

"What are you two doing in my daughter's room?" a sharp, rough woman's voice sounded. The woman looked angry, but bore a resemblance to Katie that nobody could miss.

"I'm sorry ma'am," I said quickly. "I'm Ryan, Katie's friend from school. I just wanted to see her, to make sure she was doing okay. We didn't mean to bother you."

She looked at me hard, then at my dad. He gave her a reassuring smile, but said nothing. Something seemed to click in her thoughts and her eyes went back to me in surprise.

"Ryan?" I nodded. "Ryan Jacobs?" she asked. I nodded again. Next thing I knew, I was completely smothered in the woman's embrace, pressed firmly into her bosom.

I was pretty sure, though I might have been mistaken due to all sound coming through either her arms or her breasts to reach my ears, that she was repeatedly saying "Thank you, thank you, you saved my baby, thank you, thank you," or something along that line. It was difficult to be sure.

I didn't want to pull away. Rather, I very much wanted to pull away, but I didn't want to hurt this woman's feelings. When she finally let me go, I gasped in a breath as inconspicuously as possible. She held onto both of my arms with her hands and looked at me directly.

"Thank God for your phone call, son," she was saying. I thought the cops couldn't disclose things like that, but I was learning fast that nothing was really done normally out here. "My angel Katie would be dead now if it weren't for you! You're an absolute miracle!" I laughed uncomfortably, embarrassed.

"No ma'am, I just was lucky enough to be able

to help her out this time," I replied.

"Not just this time, if what she told me earlier this week is true. Not only did you save her life on Thursday, but you saved her from getting beat up by a bunch of bullies on Tuesday. She told me all about it." My dad's head snapped over to look at me directly. Oh sure, I thought. Now you believe I got in that fight to help someone. I pointedly ignored him.

"It wasn't right, the way they were treating her. I had to do something," I said. "Anyone else would have."

"No Ryan, no they wouldn't," she protested, "It wouldn't be the first time my little girl had been bullied, or the first time someone had come by while it was happening. It was the first time anyone bothered to help, though. It meant so much to her. She was talking about it all night. Her own personal hero, she said. Katie was so angry that you were the one who got into trouble over it."

I was becoming very uncomfortable with the effusive praise, but it was a nice change to hear someone talking about my actions in a positive light.

"I'm just glad I could help. Twice," I added with a smile. Katie's mom laughed, and moved her grip to either side of my face. Before I could react, she leaned in and kissed me briefly, full on the lips. Surprisingly, it wasn't unpleasant, or as smothering as her hug had been, but it was a little bit disconcerting being kissed by someone else's mother.

"You're an angel, Ryan. When my Katie wakes up, she'll want to thank you herself too," I looked back at Katie, unmoving on the bed.

"You think she will?" I asked softly.

"I know she will," Katie's mother said sincerely. "God wouldn't send you to save my daughter's life only to leave her like this forever."

"I don't believe in God," I said, "I'm not Christian."

Katie's mom laughed again. It was a nice sound, despite her voice being raw from recent crying.

"We're not Christian either. We're Jewish," she told me with a wink. I grinned at her and she patted my shoulder, finally releasing me completely. "I won't keep you Ryan. But thank you so much for being such a good friend to her."

"I don't really even know her," I corrected.

"You came to her rescue twice in one week, hun. Sounds like a good friend to me. You and your dad ever need anything, you just let us know, okay? I'll tell Katie you stopped by when she wakes up." I nodded, not sure what else to say.

"Goodbye," my father said, speaking for the first time since we'd come in. He was looking at Katie's mother a little oddly. She gave him a warm smile, and reached out to shake his hand.

"Thank you," she said to him. He nodded and smiled back, then turned and led me out of the room. Halfway down the hallway, I spoke.

"Wow, she was... enthusiastic."

"You saved her daughter's life. More than once, to hear her tell it," my dad said in a soft tone. I looked up at him. "I'd be enthusiastic too, if someone had done the same for you." He looked down and met my eyes. "I'm sorry I didn't believe you about the fight. Things have been... hard... on both of us lately." I nodded.

"I know. We'll make it," I reassured him. He smiled at that.

"As long as we stick together, right?" he said wryly.

"Yeah," I replied half-heartedly. He was quiet for a while before speaking again.

"Ryan, I want to make a deal with you."

"Is this one of those 'get gold stars all week and I'll buy you ice cream' kind of deals?" I asked with a smirk. He laughed.

"No, this is one of those 'you trust me, and I'll trust you' kind of deals," he replied.

"I'm listening," I said guardedly.

"I think the big problem we have is communication," he said as we walked outside. "You won't trust me enough to tell me things. And then when you do tell me things, I don't trust you enough to believe you. Do you see the problem?"

"Yeah," I agreed, still not sure where he was going with this.

"So here's the deal, Ryan; you promise to trust

me and open up to me about everything going on in your life that you can, and I promise to take you at your word unless given evidence otherwise." He looked over at me as we climbed into the car. I considered this.

My problem with my father, or what at least for the past three years had been my problem, was that he wouldn't listen to me. I spent two years before my mother died trying to talk to him, but he had completely shut me out so I had simply stopped trying.

It had made perfect sense to me. Still did, honestly. If someone consistently wouldn't listen to you, you stopped trying to talk to them. It was really that simple.

But here was something different. Not only was he promising to do his best to listen, he was promising to believe everything I said until given legitimate reason to do otherwise. There was definite potential for abuse of this deal on my end, and I'm sure he knew that, but I had no intention of messing this up.

Not necessarily because I wanted to rebuild my relationship with my father. There was a lot of scar tissue there to be overcome still, but I very much wanted to know, under the current circumstances of legitimate danger to myself and to Chance and obviously unknown others, that I had an adult who would trust me completely, and back me up if I needed him to.

"I think that's a good deal," I finally said, after we'd made it back onto the road heading home. He smiled over at me.

"Feel free to start now," he told me, an obvious hint. I thought for a long moment.

"Everything I've told you so far is completely true," I started. I looked at him, but he gave no reaction, he just sat there quietly. I could almost feel him listening though. It was interesting. "The incident in the library was not me or Chance. The fight was started because I jumped in to save Katie from that jerk Noah and his pals." I glanced over at him again to see how he was taking it so far. He wasn't showing any signs of rejection, but I could tell he was trying hard to keep open. "And Chance..." I paused. He looked over at me for a moment before looking back at the road.

"Chance?" he prompted.

"Chance is my best friend," I said simply. "He's the best friend I've ever had." My dad was quiet a long time. I looked over at him. After several moments, he nodded.

"Okay. That's good enough for me." He reached into his pocket and pulled out a slip of paper. He crumpled it up in his hand, then handed it to me.

I took it curiously, and opened it up. It was a prescription slip from Doctor Sadler for some drug called ziprasidone. I frowned and looked back up to him.

"She wants you to drug me?" I asked in

astonishment. He nodded.

"Doctor Sadler thinks it will help with your paranoia and delusions," he said.

"I'm not delusional!" I argued.

"Dreams," he said, glancing down at me. Oh, I thought. That. "That's our deal, though. You tell me everything is the way you say it is, then your dreams are not delusions, and your paranoia is justified. Until I see proof otherwise, that's what I'm going to believe. At this point I have pretty good evidence that your dream was dead on. Pardon the pun."

"Thank you, Dad," I told him sincerely. He really meant to take this seriously. That's all I'd wanted from him in the first place.

"So tell me about the murders," he said. I appreciated that he said murders, not suicides. He really was trying.

"Dominic Hale, two years ago. Also looked like a suicide. At least that's what the cops labeled it. I didn't dream that one or anything," I said when he glanced over at me. "That's just the one Chance wanted me to help him solve. We did some research on the internet and couldn't find anything."

"Nothing about the kid at all?" he asked.

"Oh, we found the articles about his death, they just all said it was a suicide. Even his own mother said he wouldn't have killed himself though. Chance says he knew him, and he says Dominic wouldn't have done it either," I told him. He looked thoughtful.

"But no evidence to the contrary?" he asked. I shook my head.

"Nothing."

"Interesting. Does Chance have a suspect?"

"He sure does. Care to guess who?" My dad thought about that for a minute.

"That kid who was beating on your friend back there?" he asked.

"Right on," I replied. "Noah Porter. He's the most popular kid in school which should just show you how seriously messed up this place is, has a bunch of jerks that follow him around helping him beat up girls and rough up anyone who stands up for themselves, and has it out for 'sinners'."

"What?" my dad asked in surprise, taken off guard by that last. I was glad I wasn't the only one.

"Sinners. You know, violators of Biblical law? Future flaming embers in the fires of Hell?" I said. He gave me a look.

"I know what sinners are, smart alec. This kid only bullies people he thinks are sinners?"

"That's right," I agreed. "He has a real thing against gays. Accused me of being Chance's boyfriend, said Chance was evil."

"Are you?" my father asked after a moment. I looked at him blankly.

"Am I what?" I asked, confused.

"Chance's boyfriend," he said simply. I couldn't help it, I laughed.

"No, Dad. Although he did tell me he was into me. I told him I wasn't interested, and he agreed to keep things on a friendship level."

My dad nodded. I expected him to look relieved, but he didn't seem to take it one way or the other. I found myself wondering what he'd have said if I had said Chance was my boyfriend.

"So Chance thinks that this Noah kid has killed one kid and tried for another one now?"

"I don't know, I haven't talked to Chance since the second one. I'm on suspension, remember?" My dad winced. "It would be one murder and two attempted though, if you count the bookshelves."

"Noah's your age? Wouldn't this Noah kid have been like twelve two years ago?" he asked.

"No, he's older than we are. I think he was in the same grade as Dominic Hale, so he'd be like sixteen now. I don't know why he's not in high school. Probably can't pass the eighth grade. And he's huge, it wouldn't be hard for him to do everything he'd have had to do to kill Dominic or try to kill Katie."

"Wait, this kid is sixteen, huge, and had five of his buddies with him, and you jumped into them by yourself?" My dad looked at me with evident astonishment and awe.

"Four of his buddies," I corrected, a little embarrassed. My dad whistled.

"Well, my boy certainly isn't a coward," he said to himself.

"I split his cheek pretty good too," I said with a note of pride. I couldn't help it. My dad laughed.

"Probably shouldn't be too proud of that Ryan, but I have to admit I am a little bit too. You shouldn't fight, but doing it to help someone who can't defend themselves? I can't really fault you for that. So what's your next move?" he asked.

"I don't know. I have to talk to Chance. We may try to set Noah up though, get him to confess on recording or something. If Katie wakes up, it gets a lot easier. She can just tell everyone who did it."

"That would be easier. A witness would help a lot," my dad said. "Okay, anything else you want to share?" I hesitated. Well, if he was going to go full into this deal, so should I. I told him about my nightmare.

Chapter Eleven
The Sermon

That evening, I took leave of my senses and called Jennifer to tell her I'd go with her to church. She was thrilled. The next morning, I was waiting on my porch in the only button-up shirt I owned. We weren't really dress-up kind of people, but Jennifer had said to dress nicely.

My father had taken my request to go to church with her a little bit bemusedly, unsure where this fit into my master plan. It really didn't, but I was hoping for some insight into Noah's mentality. If I understood him better, I might have a better chance. Know thine enemy, and all that. He'd agreed, so here I was waiting for Jennifer.

I wanted to have something good to tell Chance when I saw him the next day. The thought of seeing him gave me a little surge of excitement. I'd missed seeing him all week. That, and I was desperate to apologize for how I'd reacted after the fight.

My dad had gone in to work, to make up for the hours he'd missed while coming to my school the week before. I felt bad about that, though I didn't feel responsible for it. It wasn't necessary, and it wasn't my fault. I still felt bad it had been a problem for him though.

A red truck pulled up in front of the house. A brief image of a dark truck sitting in front of my house late at night flashed in my mind. I dismissed it quickly though. This truck was bigger, had raised exhaust pipes and a roll bar. This definitely was not the same truck. I stood and walked forward.

The passenger door opened, and Jennifer climbed out, dropping to the ground from the raised cab. She was wearing a white dress with a wide peach sash around the waist. Her blonde hair was pulled back in a half-ponytail and tied with a ribbon, and she wore white shoes that could only be described as dainty. I felt like I'd just stepped into a 1950's film. Don't get me wrong, she looked great, but it seemed very old-fashioned to me.

"Hi Ryan!" she called as she walked toward me. I smiled and waved.

"Hey Jennifer. You look great," I told her. She flushed and smiled.

"Thanks. This one's my favorite," she said, brushing an invisible speck from the soft, white fabric.

"I can see why."

"You ready?"

"As ready as I'll ever be," I said.

"Oh don't worry, it's not as bad as all that. You'll love it. Come on!" She took my hand, and led me to the truck.

The fancy-haired woman from the waiting room was inside waiting. This time, the style would have taken at least five hours and three cans of hairspray. The truck cab reeked of the stuff. I worried for a moment about whether I would asphyxiate before we reached the church.

"Hello," the woman said stiffly to me. She barely looked my way. Clearly she did not approve of her daughter's pet project.

"Good morning, ma'am," I said, determined to be as polite as possible. I helped Jennifer into the cab, then climbed up beside her. Hopefully Jennifer being in the middle would serve as a buffer between her mother and I.

"Why isn't your father coming?" Jennifer's mother asked.

"He had to go back to work. He normally has Sundays off, but had to make up some lost time this week. He said to thank you for him for taking me," I said. She just nodded. Jennifer smiled at me.

"Are you coming back to school Monday?" Jennifer asked.

"Yeah, Principal Avery said Monday," I replied. Her mother scowled my way.

"You've been out of school?" she asked.

"He got blamed for an accident in the library that wasn't his fault. Principal Avery suspended him. It really wasn't his fault though," Jennifer said, quickly jumping to my defense.

This really was getting interesting, and we hadn't even made it to the church yet. I quickly developed a dislike for her mother, but I liked Jennifer a lot. She had a sweet disposition, and a surprisingly witty sense of humor. She kept playing interference with her mother too, keeping her from being too hard on me. I got the impression that with each passing mile, her mother disliked me even more though.

The church was past the school apparently, and we came upon it along the north side, which gave me a clear view of the back field and the side of the school where I'd overheard Chance and his mother.

I found myself watching the school as we passed, thinking about Chance again. I hoped he understood that I'd just been angry and I didn't hate him. I didn't think it was possible for me to ever hate him. Something just felt right when he was around, as if something in the way he resonated harmonized with me. I couldn't hold back the guilt for speaking to him the way that I did.

I kept picturing him at the school in so many different places that I almost missed it when I really did see him. I almost came out of my seat. Of course, his location didn't help. He was sitting calmly, straddling the basket on the basketball hoop. He was just leaning back against the backboard.

How on earth had he even gotten up there? He was sitting very still, eyes closed and head back. Maybe he was sunbathing, I thought. Good sunlight from there. Not any different than it was eight feet lower down though, and he was still wearing the same jeans and gray t-shirt.

We passed slowly. Jennifer's mother was a very conservative driver. I took the opportunity to watch Chance as we moved by him. The sunlight seemed to warm his features, and he seemed to simply bask in it. Without warning, his eyes opened and he looked down, straight at me.

I saw his eyes go wide in surprise. I reached up and touched the window and gave him what I hoped was a warm smile. He watched me pass for a moment, then dropped down from the basketball hoop with impressive ease and ran. Not toward me, but away from me, across the yard and toward the far side nearer the school. My heart sank. I really had hurt him.

We reached the intersection by the school and Jennifer's mother turned left, across the front of the school. The moment we were past the school, I saw him again. He was hanging on the fence just past the school, watching for us. He saw me, and hesitantly, hopefully, held up a hand to wave.

I smiled again and waved back. The look of relief that washed across his face was palpable. I could only see him for another few seconds, eyes locked on one another. What passed between us in that two seconds couldn't have been spoken aloud in an hour.

"What are you doing?" Jennifer asked curiously. I leaned back into my seat. I couldn't see him anymore anyway.

"Nothing," I said, but I couldn't shake the smile.

"Excited to be going back to school tomorrow?" she asked, misinterpreting my smile after seeing the school.

"Yeah," I answered honestly. She smiled.

Turned out the church was only a few blocks past the school. It was a big stone construction and looked very traditional, right down to the large cross mounted at the apex of the roof. We parked, and I got out, helping Jennifer down. She smiled at me as she took my hand.

"Thank you," she said. I just smiled back and turned to follow her mother toward the building. We climbed the steps in front of the big double doors and entered. A pair of women in dresses stood by the doors, greeting everyone by name as they came in. They spotted me, and both got all excited. It was unnerving.

"Oh my goodness, what have we here?" the older of the two asked.

"We just love new faces!" the other exclaimed.

"Vanessa, who is this handsome young man?"

the older woman asked Jennifer's mother.

"This is Ryan Jacobs," Jennifer answered for her mother who seemed to want only to get inside and sit down. "He's my friend from school."

"That's wonderful!" the younger woman said dramatically. She reached forward and fussed with my hair for a moment. I assumed she was straightening it, but I wasn't paying that much attention to it. I was busy trying to keep from recoiling at being randomly touched by this woman. Why was it that so many older women felt that they had the right to grope, assault, and otherwise manhandle anyone under eighteen?

"My, you're such a handsome young man. Be careful Jennifer, this one might just steal you away!" The two women laughed like this was the funniest thing ever. Jennifer took it with a casual smile. I am sure I was blushing with embarrassment. Others had stopped behind us and were within easy earshot.

Jennifer took my hand and led me past the pair and into the church. The main doors led to a small lobby which looked like it had several side hallways, leading to who knows where, and then directly ahead were open doors into a big chapel.

It was massive, with dozens of long wooden benches all lined up neatly facing a big altar on a railed-off dais, in front of a massive sculpture of Christ on the cross.

Crosses hung everywhere in the décor, from the windows to the carvings on the pews. I was already uncomfortable. This wasn't looking like it was a very good idea after all. I was stuck though. Jennifer was my ride home.

I was led by the hand to what seemed a random seat selection, though Jennifer had seemed to know right where we were going. Maybe they sat here every week. Everyone seemed to know right where they were going, actually. It was a little creepy.

I watched as people filed in. I knew a few of them. A couple of the school's staff were there, including the principal. He probably had a golden cross around his neck too, I thought, always hidden by his suit and tie. He must have felt my eyes on him and he turned. He seemed surprised to see me, and gave me a long stare before turning his gaze forward again.

None of the others seemed to notice me, thankfully. I recognized several of Noah's pals too, but didn't see him. I was relieved, until the minister walked in from a side door toward the front of the chapel, his hand on Noah's shoulder.

"What's that about?" I asked Jennifer, leaning close to whisper. She followed my gaze.

"That's Reverend Porter," she said.

"Porter?" She nodded. Oh fantastic. Psycho fanatic boy was the minister's son. This really wasn't a good idea. Everyone settled and quieted as the minister stepped up onto the dais.

"Brothers and sisters," he began in an accent thick enough that I suspected it was being intentionally dramatized, "we have had a trag'dy this week. A young girl from th' nearby middle school has 'ttempted suicide." Murmurs circled the room. I grit my teeth. "What terr'ble times in which w' live, that a young child such as her could be brought ta such a tragic crossroads. How, ya might ask, can God allow such things ta come ta pass? How can He permit such horr'ble circumstances on a young child tha' she would be brought ta such inner turmoil?

"I answer ya simply, my friends. He does not. This child was not one'a his righteous. She was not one'a the pure. She was a homosexual." The murmurs grew angry. I was floored. A young girl was nearly murdered and here these people were agreeing that it was her own fault.

"God does not allow such things ta happen ta those who remain true ta th' faith, an' follow His word! He does not allow such things t' happen t' those who follow His law! He does not allow such things t' happen t' those o' us within his Holy Flock! What He does allow, is justice fer th' wicked!" A chorus of 'amen's ran around the room. I suddenly felt sick. Bad things happened to good people all the time. It wasn't some prejudiced God playing favorites.

"In His infinite wisdom, He allowed this abomination ta see th' evil within herself! He allowed this child'a th' Devil ta know in her heart'a hearts the impurities tha' tainted her soul! She could not bear ta look upon her true self an' so sought ta take her own life, fer evil cannot tolerate its own image!" Was this what had been preached here when Dominic had been killed?

"'Tis upon us, yea it is our duty, ta see such sinners shunned from th' Flock! It is our divine obligation ta show these sinners their evil! It is our right as His Most Holy ta purge our society! We cannot allow such abominations among our people!" More 'amen's and a few 'praise Jesus' circulated.

I was starting to feel light-headed, and definitely nauseated. I grabbed a book from the small rack built into the pew in front of me. It was a Bible. I didn't care. I opened it and started skimming, trying to find something, anything, to drown out the man on the dais. It was all 'so-and-so begat so-and-so' for paragraph after paragraph. I flipped further.

"We are at war, my brothers an' sisters! A war between th' powers o' Light an' th' powers o' Darkness! I am ashamed ta say it, but th' Darkness is winning! We cannot allow…"

I forcefully tuned him out again. I flipped to the back, and found a topical guide. Skimming the words and the number of references to verses for each, I paused when I came across one particular word; 'love'. The references took up almost two pages. So many verses about love. So very many.

"Fer God hates th' vile sinners! It is abomination!" I shut him out again. I looked up the word 'hate'. There were much fewer references. I began looking through the verses the topical guide referred me to.

Time and again, I came across verses about hate. Almost unfailingly, they were verses about men hating other men. Only once did I find one talking about what God hated, in Proverbs. Homosexuality was not on that list, it was interesting to note. In fact, only seven things were on that list, and two of them were the same thing.

First on that list was a proud look. I glanced around. I sure saw a lot of proud looks as the minister spewed his hatred from the dais.

The second was hands that shed innocent blood. Katie's hands had been about as innocent as they come as far as I could tell, and someone in this room had done exactly that. More so, the minister was calling for the congregation to take it upon themselves to do the same. Not in so many words, but he wasn't really dancing around it either.

The third was a lying tongue. He was up there talking about how a thirteen year old girl deserved to be hung by the neck in a maintenance closet for something she hadn't had anything to do with and that God hated her for it. From what I was seeing, that sounded like a pretty clear lie to me.

The fourth was a heart that devised wicked imaginations. That sounded exactly like the kinds of things Noah and his friends thought up to do to those they considered sinners. From the looks on the faces around me, I suspected many of them at that very moment were devising wicked imaginations of how to "purge the evil" from their community.

The fifth was feet that are swift to run to mischief. I'd seen a lot of that from Noah and his friends as well, from knocking over innocent strangers like he had the first day I'd come, to conspiring to get me in trouble for what he and his friends had done.

The sixth was a false witness that spoke lies. And we're back to the lying tongue issue. Again, most of what I heard now being shouted from the dais was being fairly plainly disproven by what I was reading just in this one section of this exhaustingly long book. I was no scholar, but even a quick look at this book seemed to show that these people had it all wrong.

The seventh was he that sows discord among brethren. He was up there telling people to interfere with the lives of innocent people, with intent to do them harm because they fit his definition of sinners. In pretty clear terms, I'd just read that there were only seven things their God hated, and all seven of them were being done, or being called for, right here.

I flipped back to love, eager for something a little brighter. I skimmed several passages. I saw "…let us love one another, for love is from God, and whoever loves has been born of God, and knows God". Another read "…love one another earnestly from a pure heart". Another was "Owe no one anything, except to love each other, for the one who loves another has fulfilled the law", and "…but God shows his love for us in that while we are still sinners, Christ died for us".

They kept going like this, verse after verse, stating clearly that God wants people to love each other. That last one even outright stated the God still loved sinners. That isn't what the minister was declaring, though. The venomous bile continued to pour from the minister's mouth. The congregation was enraptured. I was horrified.

I buried myself in verses about love and peace until people began to stand and move toward the altar. There were plenty of verses like that to choose from. Reverend Porter was giving them all something as they approached, which they ate. I didn't remember the word for that, but I understood it was common practice in most of Christianity.

I used the opportunity to sneak out the doors as Jennifer and her mother moved forward. I couldn't go far. I didn't know how long they'd be, and Jennifer and her mother were my only ride home.

I sat on the small lawn by the church for a long time, clearing my head. The warm sun, unseasonably warm I thought though I wasn't yet familiar with the climate here, helped clear my thoughts. A slight breeze made the warm air extremely comfortable. So comfortable in fact that I almost drifted off. I heard the church doors open and people began filing out, which brought me back around.

A few moments later, Jennifer and her mother came out. Her mother was speaking to her in a forceful tone, to judge from their body language. Jennifer nodded and looked around, spotting me quickly. She ran over to me.

"Ryan, what happened? You missed th' last half of th' service!" she exclaimed. I stared at her.

"I caught the first half. Judging from that, I didn't miss much in the second half," I said.

"You didn't enjoy th' sermon? You seemed so fascinated by th' Bible you were reading. I was hoping it had taken hold of you." she asked, looking a little hurt. I sighed, then stood and looked her in the eye.

"Jennifer, you're really nice. I think you're a very sweet person. But how can you follow a religion based on a guy who did nothing but preach love and peace, while being ministered to by a man doing nothing but throwing around hate?" By the time I finished saying this, she looked truly crushed. "Thank you for inviting me, it really was a very nice gesture, and it sure explained a lot about Noah. But please, don't ever talk to me about your God again. I want nothing to do with a God like that." I finished, gesturing with disgust at the church.

She looked about to cry. I felt terrible, but I was upset by what I had seen in there and I couldn't understand how she wasn't as horrified as I was.

"Let's get you home," was all she said. I nodded, and followed her to the truck.

Chapter Twelve

A Chat with Dad

The drive back to my house was quiet. I looked for Chance on the way back but I didn't see him, to my great disappointment.

Neither Jennifer nor her mother said a word to me the entire half-hour-long drive. I was okay with that, I wasn't in any mood to talk. The sermon, or the part of it that I'd actually caught, had fairly effectively ruined my mood.

The only upside to the trip was that now I completely understood Noah and his friends, and why they behaved the way they did. Apparently, they had God's direct commands to behave that way. There was nothing quite like having a divine endorsement to be an asshole. And in this case, a killer. I had no doubts anymore that Chance was right; Noah had killed Dominic, and had tried to kill Katie, and Chance.

The devil hiding beneath Noah's face was a

pretty clear representation of the evil that hid within him. He'd tried to kill Chance in the library, and me in the bargain. His backpack had been right on the other side of the fallen shelves.

A kid being raised under the constant onslaught of that kind of psychological pressure was bound to crack sooner or later. Noah becoming a complete psychotic killer wasn't at all unreasonable with hate like that being forced down his throat from birth by his father.

I thought for a while about Katie. I was so glad she'd survived, but I didn't have the same degree of hope for her waking up that her mother seemed to. At least her mother still had hope. That was important, I felt.

The closer buildings of town proper slowly faded into the more sparsely placed homes and farms of the outskirts as we headed to my own house. The sunlight filtering through the trees flickered across my eyes as we drove, the strobing light almost hypnotic.

I wondered how much time Chance spent at the school. With his home life, it was no wonder he didn't want to spend much time there, including some time on the weekends as well.

I only wondered why he chose the school for a moment. There wasn't anywhere better to go to in Turnbridge. No mall, no arcades, no bowling alleys or skating rinks, the town had literally nothing to do.

You either entertained yourself at home, or

you spent a lot of time just sitting around, which is exactly what it looked like Chance had been doing.

Maybe my dad could take me up to the school when he went to work next Sunday, so I could spend some time with Chance, I thought. Maybe he'd even show me his place and introduce me to his mother. I didn't have much hope on that one, though I thought it would be nice.

We pulled up in front of my house. I opened the door and climbed down. I hesitated before closing it though. I turned back to Jennifer, who was looking at me a bit sadly. Her mother was pointedly not looking my way.

"Thanks for inviting me, Jennifer. I'll see you at school tomorrow," I said. She nodded.

"'Bye, Ryan," was all she said. I closed the door. I wasn't up for being polite to her mother, too. Something about that woman really bothered me. Maybe she was too into that crazy church. That certainly seemed to give people an unpleasant vibe. That whole place had really freaked me out.

I walked into the house and headed for my room. I got rid of the button-up shirt as fast as I could, kicking off my shoes and flopping down on my bed.

Reaching over to the bedside table, I turned on my mp3 player still hooked up to the speakers and picked up the small bag containing the little packs of thread I'd picked up the day before after my father and I had left the hospital.

Pulling out the thread and a pair of scissors, I cut a length from each color. It was probably lame, but I wanted to do something for Chance, and I suspected this kind of thing would appeal to him. It was just something to help me apologize to him, and to let him know we were still friends. I was thinking of it as sort of a late birthday present.

I hadn't done these since the third grade, but I was pretty sure I could still make a friendship bracelet.

This definitely was not something I would ever do for any other boy my age, since I knew it wouldn't be at all appreciated, but I suspected Chance would really like the idea. He was very third grade in a lot of ways. I kind of liked that about him. Besides, he seemed just thrilled to have a friend. Anything I did for him would be enthusiastically well received, I was sure.

I tied knot after knot until my dad came home. The timing was pretty good, I had only a few dozen knots left when my father walked in. He came back, peeking into the room.

"Hey, Ryan," he said.

"Hey," I replied, "how was work?" He smiled in pleased surprise that I was inquiring about his day. He took it as an invitation, walked in and sat down on the edge of my bed.

"Good, thanks. Sundays are pretty slow over at the hospital, so I had time to check in on your friend Katie."

"I don't really know her," I reminded him,

though I was eager to hear how she was doing. He chuckled.

"Her mom sure thinks you're her friend," he replied. "Nice lady." Something about the way he said that made me consider him closely. After a moment, I spotted what I was looking for; that look in his eye to tell me he was hiding something.

"Nice lady, huh?" I asked. I got the impression he might be interested. I felt a sudden surge of betrayal of my mother. She had only died a year ago.

"Yeah, we had lunch together. She's got a lot of hope."

"You had lunch together?" I was starting to get angry. Had he forgotten about my mother already? He looked at me for a long moment.

"Just lunch. She needed the company," he said. "Her husband passed away three years ago in an accident."

"Convenient," I retorted.

"Ryan, I don't need to explain myself to you," he said, his tone becoming darker. "It was just lunch with a lady who needed a listening ear." He took a long breath. "I'm not looking for anything more than that right now." I was about to give him a harsh reply, but I stopped myself. We were both trying, I reminded myself. I just nodded and let it go.

"I'm sorry, I'm just a little off today. How's Katie?" I asked, changing the subject.

"Still asleep," he replied, his expression

softening again. "She's doing well enough that they are probably going to try letting her breathe on her own sometime this next week."

"That's good. No signs she might wake up?"

"Not yet. Her mother has hope though, like I said. She has a lot of faith, too." I made a face. He noticed. "What?"

"Just not a big fan of the whole faith idea right now," I said.

"Church with your girl didn't go well?"

"No. The whole fire and brimstone bit is ridiculous enough, but this church is really scary. The minister kept talking about God hating people, and helping 'purge the wicked'."

"What?" my dad asked, shocked.

"Oh, and get this; Noah?" My dad nodded that he remembered who I was talking about. "He's the minister's son."

"Wow," he said. "Well don't take your church visit today as reason for prejudice. There are some very nice Christians out there. Some very cruel ones as well. Just like any group of people, you'll find kind ones, unkind ones, and indifferent ones. Being Christian doesn't make a person good or bad all by itself." I smiled at that.

"Chance said almost the same thing. 'Being Christian doesn't make you Christ-like'." I quoted. My dad nodded.

"Sounds like Chance is a bright kid."

"He is," I replied. "Anyway, I think Noah's father, the minister, is what brought Noah to become the psycho he is now. That whole church is nuts. No way I'm ever going back there!"

"So no second date with Jennifer, huh?"

"Dad," I said in exasperation, "focus! Noah is the one we think killed Dominic and tried to kill Katie and Chance! I think it's because they were gay! The minister kept going on about how Katie had been driven to try to kill herself because of her guilt at her wickedness, but then he talked about it being the 'wrath of God' and 'purging evil from our community'. Don't you get it? He's been preaching this garbage for so long that his son is buying into it! Noah's gone all kinds of crazy, and now is killing the people his dad tells him are evil!"

"Ryan, don't you think you're being a bit extreme?" my dad asked. "The police said there was no sign of foul play. And you said they declared the other boy a suicide as well. You don't think they can tell the difference?"

"Obviously not!" I replied. "I saw it, Dad. The devil with Noah's face put her up there! And he's the same devil in the dream that kills me!" My dad's expression became more serious.

"Do you really think you're in danger?" he asked.

"I really do!" I exclaimed. "He's already tried to kill Chance in the library, and me along with him. I think Chance is a primary target, since Chance is openly gay too. He says Noah mostly leaves him alone, but who knows how long that will last, or what Noah thinks he can get away with if he's careful about it?"

"I think you might be over-reacting a bit Ryan," he said. "The bookshelves could have been an accident, the death of the boy two years ago might have been a suicide. Katie might have been attempting suicide, too. Being gay in a society like ours is a lot of stress and social pressure. The suicide rate among their people are pretty high."

"What do you mean 'their people'?" I asked in irritation. "You say that like they're a different breed." My father sighed.

"I just mean that among gays, the suicide rate is pretty high. It's just a lot of pressure and social rejection. I don't have anything against it myself."

"Would you feel differently if I was one of 'those people'?" I asked him. He looked at me curiously for a minute.

"No, I don't think so. Are you?"

"No, Dad," I rolled my eyes and exhaled slowly. "I'm sorry, I'm just getting really edgy about how gay people are treated. Especially around here. Even the principal doesn't seem to care about Chance because he's gay. I wonder if he was that way with Dominic, too." My dad gave me an odd sidelong glance.

"I wouldn't worry about that," he said.

"Principal Avery has his own reasons to be concerned about your friendship with Chance."

"The same concerns you have?"

"Honestly? Yes."

"Chance told me that there are things I don't know about him. He said he'd tell me when he could, but it wasn't the right time yet," I told him. My father looked concerned, but he nodded.

"Okay, for now I'll leave it alone then," he said. "Just know that when you find out the truth about him, I'll be here for you. Doctor Sadler said I shouldn't tell you just now anyway. Too much stress, she says."

"God Dad, you told her too?" I asked in annoyance.

"I kind of had to. Chance is a big concern for a lot of people," he replied.

"I'll be open with you, you believe me. That's the deal right?" I reminded. My dad took a deep breath and nodded.

"Yeah, that's the deal."

"Okay, then believe me when I tell you that you have nothing to worry about with Chance. He's not dangerous, he's not a bad influence, he's not ever going to hurt me." My dad regarded me silently, then nodded.

"Okay, I'll drop it," he said.

"Good. Now as long as we're talking about Chance already, can I invite him over next weekend?"

"I don't think that's a great idea. We should

give it some time before inviting him here."

"Why?" I asked, frustrated by the way everyone, my father included, seemed to view Chance as an undesirable element.

"You told me to drop it. Just believe me that I have my reasons," he said. I sighed heavily, but nodded.

"Fine," I said simply.

"I've got to go make dinner," he said after a pause. "How do you feel about chicken?"

"Works for me." My father nodded and stood, heading out of the room. I turned back to the last few knots, but didn't start back in on them.

He was doing pretty well, I thought. He was shutting up about things I wanted him to leave alone, and he wasn't condescending toward me every time I said something he didn't like. It was definite progress. The guy might not be a total lost cause after all.

I had to admit, it was nice having someone else I could talk to, even if I knew he didn't actually believe half of what I said despite his promise.

I supposed that I should have been really concerned about what this deep, dark secret about Chance was that everyone else seemed to know but that Chance wouldn't tell me, but I trusted him.

He said it wasn't safe for me to know yet, so I didn't pry. I was curious, sure, but it was his secret to share when he chose. It wasn't my father's, or Principal Avery's, or Doctor Sadler's. It was Chance's. When he decided it was time he'd tell me and that was that.

I looked down at the nearly-finished bracelet. I'd gone with dark blue for the base, should go well with his blue jeans and gray shirt, and had run a strip down the middle in alternating rainbow colors. I was hoping he'd appreciate the rainbow, and that it would show him that his being gay really didn't bother me.

The more I thought about it, the more I realized it really didn't bother me, despite my knowing he was attracted to me. It's not like he'd push anything past what I wanted.

All I had to do was say 'No thanks,' if he tried to actually hit on me, which I didn't think he would. I'd already told him where I stood. I started tying the last few knots to finish it off as I waited for dinner. I couldn't wait until morning to see him again.

Chapter Thirteen
Second Chance

The next morning on the way to school, my dad and I did something we hadn't done in years; we just chatted. Not about anything in particular, just idle chatter.

We talked about the baseball season next year, whether I wanted to try out for the local team; we talked about his new job and how much his boss drove him crazy but that he loved the work; we talked about my favorite classes in school. I'd almost forgotten that my dad was actually a pretty cool guy when he wasn't acting like a whipped puppy.

I opened the door and climbed out, already looking for Chance. I looked back in, smiled at my dad, and told him goodbye. He said he'd see me at three, and I closed the door. I was barely halfway to the doors of the school when Chance came around the corner from the field behind the school. He saw me and jogged over.

"Hi Chance," I started. "I'm so sorr…"

"How did you do it?" he asked me, an intense, excited look on his face.

"Do what?" I asked, confused by the seemingly random question. He rolled his eyes as if he thought I were being somewhat thick. He glanced around at the kids passing by, and took my hand, dragging me at a run into the school. I followed, as if I had a choice.

It was a bit strange, his hand in mine. His hand was warm, and fit mine very comfortably. I was more than a little disconcerted by the fact that it didn't really bother me that he was holding my hand as he led me through the school. It only bothered me that it didn't bother me. Shouldn't it?

He pulled me all the way down the hall into the cafeteria and to our back corner. The cafeteria had a few kids in it, sitting, talking, playing games on their phones, the usual scene in the mornings in here, but our corner was pretty empty and nobody was within easy earshot. Chance all but pushed me into my usual seat, and took his across from me.

"So?" he asked me eagerly.

"I wanted to tell you I was sorry Chance," I started, but he interrupted me again.

"Yeah, I saw your face in the truck when you passed yesterday. We're cool." He smiled warmly at me, and it struck me how much affection was in his eyes when he did so.

"We're… wait, really?" I asked. "I had this whole big apology planned…"

"No need," he told me, waving my apology away. "What I do need is to know how you did it."

"Did what?" I asked, completely flustered. This was not going at all as I'd planned. He sighed, took a long breath, and spoke very slowly as if to someone very young, or slow in the head.

"How did you know about Katie?" he asked me. I realized I hadn't talked to him yet about any of this. It had happened last week and some part of my mind just assumed if it didn't just barely happen, Chance must already know.

"Oh!" I said, laughing. "Sorry man, I didn't even think about it. I just sort of thought that since I knew, you'd know."

"All I know is that the rumors around here are going crazy!" he exclaimed. "Everyone knows it was you that called 9-1-1 and saved her life."

"How does everyone know?" I asked. "Isn't police department intel, you know, confidential or something?" Chance laughed.

"In a town like this? Are you kidding? Everyone in town knew by sundown the same day it happened."

"Great," I groaned, putting my head in my hands. As if my reputation weren't complicated enough.

"So how did you know?" he asked, even more insistently. I took a deep breath, then another, then looked up at him.

"I dreamt it," I told him. He didn't know about my dreams. So far, only my dad, and Doctor Sadler thanks to my dad, knew. He stared at me.

"You what?"

"Dreamt it. You know, I fell asleep, and pictures went through my head?" I was a bit uncomfortable with the astonishment on his face.

"You dreamt it."

"Yeah."

"That's… amazing," he said softly.

"I know."

"So you were just lying there, snoring away, and you dreamt about Katie being attacked?" I paused as something he said stood out to me. Hadn't everyone decided it was an attempted suicide?

"How did you know she was attacked?" I asked him slowly. He opened his mouth, then shut it again. He hesitated before he spoke.

"I just sort of assumed, you know, with everything that's been happening, and Katie coming out two weeks ago," he said, without much conviction. I frowned at him.

"No, you knew," I accused him. "How did you know?" He looked away. "Chance!" I said sharply. He flinched.

"I was kind of there," he admitted.

"What?!"

"I was there," he said, looking up to meet my gaze.

"Did you see it happen?" I asked him, a little confused. Maybe he could confirm that Noah had done it. He shook his head.

"No," he told me. I looked him in the eyes for several seconds before I believed him.

"Then how do you know she was attacked?"

"I heard her scream just before she dropped," he said. "And when I got back there, someone had just left through the other door. I didn't see who though."

"Why didn't you help her down?" I asked him, more confused by the moment. "Or call 9-1-1? She'd been up there for several minutes when the cops got there. That's what they said at the hospital."

"It's... hard to explain," he said. "Ryan, trust me when I tell you I would have if I could have. I did everything I possibly could to help her, but it wasn't enough. If you hadn't called the cops, she wouldn't have made it." Again, I stared intently into his eyes before I believed him. He saw it the moment my belief registered in my eyes, and relaxed.

"So you dreamt the whole thing?" he asked again. I nodded. "Did you see who did it?" Here came the tricky part, I thought.

"No," I replied. "Well, sort of. In my dream, it was some kind of big devil wearing a mask."

"Do you think it was just the killer in a mask?

Noah's pretty big," Chance said. I shook my head.

"No, I mean really a devil. Red skin, fiery eyes, forked tongue, black claws, the whole deal. It was wearing the mask."

"Creepy," he said with a shiver. "What kind of mask?"

"That's the really creepy part," I said. "It was Noah's face. Not like a rubber mask for Halloween, it was like the devil had actually cut Noah's face off and was wearing it."

"Dude, that's messed up," he said, leaning back in his chair. His expression was one of awe.

"I know," I replied quietly.

"Maybe you're really psychic," Chance said with a smile.

"Stop that," I told him, rolling my eyes. He laughed. I opened my mouth to say something, but was unpleasantly interrupted by the appearance of Noah and three of his friends.

"Hey freak," Noah said in an amiable tone.

"What do you want, Noah?" I asked, trying to keep my tone level.

"Still hangin' out with yer devil boyfriend, huh?" he said, glancing Chance's way, then looking away just as quickly. That was interesting. As afraid of Noah as Chance was, Noah seemed a bit nervous about Chance, too.

"What do you care?"

"They call that 'consortin' with th' Devil'."

"Woah, big word Noah," I said, not really caring that it might be the last thing I ever said. "Don't hurt yourself." Noah came forward fast, but stopped just short of me.

"I'm more interested in hurtin' you, freak."

"What is it with you?" I asked him, standing up. If he was going to pound on me, at least I might get a good shot in like last time. I could see the still-healing wound on his cheek. Besides, now I had witnesses. The other kids had all gotten very quiet and were watching us. With concern or eagerness I couldn't say, I was busy watching Noah.

"I jus' hate sinners," he said. "So do my boys. So do all good Christians."

"That's funny. I read that fat book at your church yesterday, and that's not what it said."

"Shoulda been listenin' to th' preacher, freak. You don't know how t' understand th' Holy Bible. That's what a preacher is there for," he told me with a hint of a snarl. "I think now I've gotta teach you a lesson."

"One of these days you're going to pick on someone when your boys aren't here to help you out. I only hope I'm there to see it. Nice cut, by the way." I told him, indicating the still-impressive wound on his cheek.

It had started yellowing as the bruising healed, and the cut had long since scabbed over. It looked disgusting though. I'd hurt him more than I'd thought.

I braced myself to start swinging. The bell rang. I flinched. I was gratified to see that Noah did, too.

"Ya got th' Devil's own luck, freak," Noah said. "Don't worry though. Sooner or later…" he left the thought unfinished, not that I had any doubt what he would have said if he'd chosen to complete the statement. He and his friends turned and walked away.

"'Ya got th' Devil's own luck'," Chance said, imitating Noah's drawl. I shoved him and he laughed.

"I have to get to class," I told him. "I'm just back from suspension, so I'd better not be late. Later."

"Later," he replied with a smile. I was halfway to class before I realized that his tangent about Katie had completely derailed my entire apology plan, which had included giving him the bracelet I still had in my pocket. I'd have to give it to him at lunch, I decided.

I walked into my algebra class, and nodded at Mr. Allen, who just gave me an annoyed stare. I looked across the room, and Noah was there, glaring at me. Such a cheerful fellow, I thought with annoyance.

I couldn't understand how someone could go through their everyday life with so much aggression and hostility in their minds all the time. It had to be exhausting. And probably uncomfortable, I thought.

I sat in my seat and dug through my bag for my book. A stack of papers dropped onto my desk. I looked up into Mr. Allen's serious expression.

"Your work for last week," he said. "I expect it, and this week's work, all completed and on my desk by the end of the week."

"Yes, sir," I replied. It was an intimidating stack, but I was pretty sure I could manage it. It's not like I had anything else taking up my time at home. I'd even finished every video game I had left during my suspension the week before. He walked to the front of the class and began the day's lecture.

After my first few classes, I was making my way to the cafeteria when I spotted Noah down the C hall. He didn't have any of his boys with him this time, but he was with Jennifer. The pair were pressed up against the locker, and it looked to me like he was trying to see how far down her throat he could shove his tongue.

Now I knew everyone had their own kissing style, not that I had much experience with such things aside from an unfortunate incident in the third grade and my recent encounter with Katie's mother, but what I saw going on down the hall looked like something out of a horror movie. Jennifer didn't look to be resisting, but she didn't seem too enthusiastic either.

I clenched my jaw tightly shut and walked away. It wasn't my business, she wasn't resisting him, and I had better things to do than to get beat up by Noah again and probably get suspended for the second week in a row. I hurried to the cafeteria to see Chance.

He was in his usual spot, toying with his food again. It was a quirky habit of his, but I thought it was kind of funny. I got my food and moved across the room and sat down.

"Hey Chance, guess what I just saw."

"A devil wearing Noah's face?" he replied.

"Not since last week," I retorted. "No, I just saw Noah and Jennifer making out down by the woodshop classroom."

"That's gross," he replied, though he didn't seem surprised.

"I mean, I knew they were sort of together, but I've only seen him with her a couple of times, and they've never been all over each other like that."

"Yeah, I've caught them at it once or twice," he said.

"Okay, is it just me, or is he really bad at it?" I asked. Chance laughed.

"It's not just you, he's one of those 'try to reach the tonsils' kind of kissers, from what I can see."

"How can anyone enjoy that?" I asked.

"What, you don't like it that way?" he replied, looking at me curiously. He was teasing, but he looked genuinely interested in getting me on the subject of kissing.

"Don't get any ideas, Romeo," I made a face at him. "I don't really know though, other than Maria in the third grade, I haven't kissed anyone but my mother. And Maria kissed me without any warning, in my defense. For that matter, so did Katie's mom." Chance stared at me, and I realized he didn't know about that either. He was clearly trying with tremendous effort to keep from open laughter.

"Dude, you made out with Katie's mom?" he asked in a carefully controlled voice.

"God no!" I retorted, starting to laugh myself. "I saw her at the hospital and she freaked out on me. Somebody told her I was the one who called. She kept calling me her daughter's little hero. Then she kissed me, full on the mouth. Poor lady almost lost a daughter, what was I supposed to do?"

"Tongue?" Chance asked with a sparkle in his intense gaze.

"Chance!" I laughed, reaching over to give him a playful shove on his shoulder. He broke, his laughter finally escaping. I laughed with him, enjoying the feeling and the sound.

"Hey," he finally said, "if you ever want to try out a real kiss, you just let me know." He winked at me.

"Cool down, man," I told him with a smile. "I've had enough kisses for the year, I think."

"Well okay, just thought I'd throw it out there. Let me know if you change your mind though," Chance said.

He didn't look hurt, which I was relieved by. He seemed okay with my not being into him, though he obviously still intended to flirt a little. I was okay with that, he wasn't over the top or anything.

"So I had an idea," I changed the subject after a few moments of silence. "I was thinking that maybe we should talk to Mrs. Bradley in the office and see if she knows anything about Dominic Hale's death that wasn't in the articles. She probably knows everyone in the school, and I'll bet she knows everything that goes on here."

"Okay," he replied, "but you're talking to her. She doesn't like me."

"I'm getting the impression that nobody does, Chance," he looked down and I hastily added, "except me, anyway." He looked back up and smiled.

"Hey, that reminds me," I said. I dug into my pocket and pulled out the bracelet. "I made this for you. Kind of a late birthday present I guess." I held it out to him. He stared at it for so long that I started to feel uncomfortable. "It's… it's just a friendship bracelet. It's cool if you don't want it, it's kind of lame, I know…"

"No, it's perfect," he said softly. He reached a hand out as if to take it, but hesitated before touching it. "This is going to sound really weird, but would you… would you maybe wear it for me?" I frowned, confused.

"I guess, but I was sort of hoping you would."

"I know, and it's not that I don't like it. I love it. Nobody's done anything like this for me since… well, since ever." His eyes had gained a sudden extra depth that made them hard to look away from. "You went to all the trouble to make it for me, and it's just perfect… but I can't really wear bracelets." He was looking at me like he was afraid I was going to be offended. I regarded him, then the bracelet, then tilted my head as I looked back at him.

"Is it your touching thing?"

"Yeah," he said, nodding. "I'm pretty particular about what I can touch. I was hoping maybe you'd wear it for me. It would mean a lot to me Ryan."

"Sure," I said, moving to tie the bracelet around my own wrist. "So what can you touch? Just so I know." Chance smiled wryly.

"So far? Just you, the chairs, and my lunch." He poked with his fork at the barely-identifiable mess of food on his tray.

"And your clothes, thank God" I pointed out. "And apparently basketball hoops."

"Right," he grinned at me. I was struggling with tying the knot one-handed, but I wasn't going to ask Chance for his help. I didn't want to risk setting off his touch issue. He didn't volunteer either.

"People are going to think I'm gay though," I said with a smile looking at the colors on the bracelet.

"I think Noah already thinks you are," Chance told me. "Besides, you're a social outcast already anyway, so why does it matter?"

"I don't know," I replied, "I might want a girlfriend someday." Chance smiled and nodded.

"Yeah, could happen. Well, we'll have to burn that bridge when we come to it," he replied.

"What?" I asked curiously. He shrugged.

"Just something my mom used to say," he told me. "I think it means that it's a problem we'll deal with when it actually becomes a problem." I nodded.

"Well?" I asked, holding the arm with the bracelet up to show it off to him. He grinned.

"Perfect. Now I'll know you're thinking about me when I see you wearing it."

"I'm always thinking about you Chance." I realized as soon as I said it that it sounded a bit... intimate, but it was too late to take it back and I recognized as the words left my mouth that they were completely true. He was always in my thoughts on some level.

The shine in his eyes made it worth it though. I smiled at him, and he reached out, touching my hand. I let him for a few moments before pulling away. I didn't want him getting the wrong idea.

"Come on," I said, "I can't eat this garbage today. Let's go bother Mrs. Bradley."

Chapter Fourteen

A Few Answers

"Hello, Mr. Jacobs. It's good t' have you back," Mrs. Bradley said with a smile as I walked into the office. I glanced back at her lack of greeting to Chance, but he was staying just outside the door. I glared at him and mouthed "coward". He shrugged sheepishly.

"Hi, Mrs. Bradley. I was wondering if maybe you could help me with a project."

"Sure thing, hun," she replied. "What can I do for ya?"

"I just wanted to know if you had any information on the death of Dominic Hale a few years ago." Her warm smile slipped.

"I don't think that's somethin' you should be focusin' on for a class, Mr. Jacobs."

A good point, I didn't have any classes where a subject like that would be an appropriate project. No reason not to be honest I guess.

"It's not for a class, it's sort of a personal project. With everything that's happened lately, I'm thinking there might be a connection between Dominic's death and Katie's…" I hesitated, but forced myself to say it, "Katie's attempted suicide." Mrs. Bradley regarded me critically.

"Ryan, considerin' th' trouble you got into last week, are you sure it's a good idea t' pursue somethin' like this? There're enough rumors goin' around about you, and Principal Avery is already tryin' t' figure out how you knew about Katie all th' way from home. If you start diggin' into it, it could mean more trouble for you." She sounded genuinely concerned, which I appreciated. This had to be done though, Chance's life, not to mention my own, might depend on it.

"I understand that, Mrs. Bradley," I told her. "It's important to me though, I really think something weird is going on, and I have to find out what." She stared hard at me for a moment, then sighed and nodded.

"Okay, but don't say I didn't warn you," she said. "I can't really tell you much m'self, other than what th' newspapers already said, but I can tell you that th' cafeteria staff thought it was mighty peculiar that Dominic had shut himself inside that oven.

"It doesn't have a handle on th' inside, see," she continued, "or anywhere t' grab it so it would be hard t' shut it tightly enough to latch from in there.

Truthfully, I'm not even sure how he did it." Well that was definitely an interesting bit of information!

"That helps a lot, Mrs. Bradley," I told her sincerely. "The police thought he could do it though?" She shrugged.

"I s'ppose so. I guess it's possible, but it sounds like a lot of trouble t' me. There's got t' be easier ways."

"That's what I thought too. Mrs. Bradley, do you think he did it himself?" I asked. She paused a long moment before answering.

"Ryan, Dominic was a very sweet boy. He wasn't well liked by his classmates though, an' was picked on a lot. I heard his fight with his parents when he... y' know, came out, was pretty bad."

"But...?" I pressed. She shook her head after another pause.

"I shouldn't say any more than that. It's not my place to go stirrin' up anythin'. I'll get m'self in trouble. I'll jus' say he was a good kid, very bright, and very troubled."

"Thank you, Mrs. Bradley."

"You're welcome." I turned to go. "Ryan?" I paused and turned back around. "What should I tell Principal Avery about your knowin' about Katie?"

"Tell him I dreamt it," I said. She raised a brow and I shrugged. "It's true. I don't know, maybe I'm psychic." I smiled at her. She sighed, but smiled back and nodded.

"All right. Take care, hun."

Outside in the hallway, Chance was waiting. He had been close enough to listen, and looked more than a little smug.

"I told you he couldn't have done it himself," Chance said.

"She didn't say that," I replied. "She said that it would have been hard, not impossible. And the cops obviously thought he could do it."

"No way," Chance replied. "You'd have to see that oven. I couldn't do it. I doubt you could, either."

"Actually I do want to get a look at the oven," I told him.

"Not much chance of that," he said. "There are always people in there during school hours, and for a few hours before and after. Unless you can sneak in here at night after the janitor leaves, it's not going to happen."

"That won't work either," I told him. "My dad picks me up and we go straight home. It takes us half an hour to get all the way here in the car. I'd never make it on foot," I told him. "I don't even have a bike. Besides, I can't break into the school." Chance sighed.

"Well, at least we got that much out of her," he said. "Maybe you can talk to the cafeteria staff?" He looked hopefully at me.

"Maybe I can talk to them?" I asked, not sure whether I should be annoyed. "Let me guess, they don't like you?" He shrugged and looked down.

"Well, they won't talk to me, so…"

"What the Hell did you do, Chance?" I asked him. He looked up at me in surprise. "What did you do that got everyone so upset? What happened to make it so that the school bully leaves you alone, and nobody, not even the school staff, will talk to you?"

"It's complicated," he replied.

"You've said that," I retorted, though my tone eased a little. "But seriously Chance, I'm starting to worry."

"Please don't worry," he said, his tone pleading. "I can't tell you yet Ryan. It'll… it'll ruin everything." He said that last like he was afraid that even saying that much might ruin everything. I took a long breath and sighed.

"At this rate, someone else is going to tell me before you do," I told him.

"I doubt it. Everyone's really touchy about me. Nobody really likes to talk about me, let alone talk to me. That's a big part of why nobody else really talks to you either, because you talk to me."

"When I told you I'd be friends with you that first day and you told me it would make me a social outcast," I said, "I really had no idea what I was getting myself into." I mentally kicked myself for saying that, he looked hurt.

"Do you regret it?" he asked softly. I smiled at him, and put a hand on his shoulder reassuringly.

"Not for a second. It just makes certain things

a little more… complicated," I said sincerely. He smiled back.

"Can we go talk to the cafeteria staff?" he asked hopefully.

"No, I have to get to class," I told him with an incredulous laugh. He just nodded. "Do your teachers talk to you?" I asked on impulse. He laughed.

"Not really, no."

"Do you ever get called on?"

"Nope." He grinned.

"Well, that's something anyway," I told him as I turned and headed down the hallway.

Chance never seemed in much rush to get to class. I'd never seen him with a backpack during school, only when I'd seen him before and after school. He couldn't possibly have been doing well with his grades.

He always got to school early and left late though, maybe he did his schoolwork first thing. His teachers probably didn't even yell at him when he was late to class.

Who knows how long he hung around the school after hours. He didn't seem comfortable with the idea of home and family, so maybe he stayed for quite a while. He obviously spent some time over the weekends here. Which was more than a little bit sad, I had to admit.

If I could get out here I'd hang out with him, just to give him something to do. I reminded myself to ask my dad to bring me out here on Sunday when he came into town for work.

I spent my class time trying hard to focus, but Chance kept slipping back into my mind. I was finding that it was becoming more and more difficult to sort myself out when it came to him.

I couldn't stop thinking about him, I got warm every time he touched me, and nothing brightened my day more than walking into the cafeteria and seeing his face light up when he spotted me. Something about the way he did that made it impossible not to smile back. It made me feel like I was the only person in his entire world. The way everyone treated him, maybe I was.

Maybe it was just that I enjoyed the attention and admiration he kept throwing my way. He was pretty good about not pushing the fact that he liked me but I could see it every time he looked at me, now that I knew to look for it. Who doesn't like a little adoration thrown their way now and then?

I kept fiddling with the bracelet. Everybody really was going to think I was gay, I thought as I looked at the rainbow pattern running down the middle of it. Was that such a bad thing? Chance was right, it's not like the girls were knocking down my door as it was.

I had started to think that maybe Jennifer might like me, but then I saw her and Noah in C hall today. I wasn't too upset by it, just a lot grossed out.

I didn't understand how she could be into a

slimy guy like that. He just didn't seem right in the head, although if her enjoyment of that church service had been any indication, she probably wasn't either.

And that kiss… I shuddered even thinking about it. Kisses shouldn't be an aggressive deep-exploration contest. God, maybe I was gay, I thought with a mental sigh. Real men didn't…

Real men… I thought about that choice of words for a long time; most of the way through English, in fact. I was beginning to suspect that my idea of real men was seriously skewed.

My father wasn't the butch, macho type, though he was masculine enough, but he had done everything he could to take care of me and my mom, even while she was really sick all the time.

Even after Mom had died, he'd always gone out of his way to try and look after me. I felt a pang of regret that I'd been as hard on him as I had been the last year. Longer, I knew. I'd started to shut him out for some time even before my mom had died. He had never really stopped trying though.

Chance certainly wasn't the butch, macho type either. I didn't see anything really effeminate about him though, except maybe his tendency for those little affectionate touches he'd slipped in like at lunch today.

He didn't do it a lot, but he sure seemed to enjoy it when he did. He also didn't walk or talk the way gay men in movies always did. Would it matter if he did? I didn't actually think it would. He was just another guy, really. He was polite, he was loyal, he was friendly, isn't that what a real man should be?

I tried to refocus on class, but it wasn't working very well. I was really going to have to push the homework hard this week, I knew. My grades when report cards came around were going to be really bad if I wasn't careful. I knew I had other things I was worried about that were more important, but I needed to keep my grades up. It was a lot harder to catch up than to keep up. Another thing my mom had taught me.

I made it through though, my classes felt like they were dragging on forever. I even managed to take a few notes that would help when homework time came around. It was amazing how fluid time seemed, the same amount of time feeling like an eternity one day, and flashing by in an instant another.

I got out to the front of the school and hadn't seen Chance. My dad wasn't here yet, so I sat on the low wall again out in front of the school. It was only a moment before a pair of hands closed across my eyes, their owner reaching around from behind me.

"Guess who," a playful voice said. I couldn't help but smile.

"If it isn't Chance, then this is a really awkward way to make a new friend," I replied. He laughed.

As he moved to sit beside me, he put his hand on my leg. Not high or anything, just casually on my leg, and only for a moment. He looked up, met my gaze, and smiled before removing his hand. It wasn't creepy or awkward, but there was something that felt a little intimate about it. I found myself smiling back.

"How was class?" he asked lightly.

"I should ask you the same thing. What classes do you take, anyway?" I retorted. He shrugged.

"The usual. Math, English, art, that kind of junk."

"You take art?" I asked, genuinely surprised. Chance looked at me like he was trying to decide if he should be offended. He apparently decided not to be.

"Yeah, I like art. I used to draw a lot. I haven't for years though," Chance said, sounding a little sad.

"Maybe you should. I'd love to see your work," I told him honestly. I shouldn't have been surprised, Chance was a sensitive enough guy that artistic ability would have seemed very natural in him. It just hadn't even occurred to me. Chance just shrugged noncommittally.

"Maybe. I haven't really felt it for a while, you know?" I didn't, but I kind of suspected that it all probably tied into whatever had happened with his parents a few years back.

"Yeah, makes sense," I nodded. A thought came to me then. "Hey, do you think maybe you could come over this weekend? Are you off grounding then?" Chance shook his head.

"No, not yet."

"Sorry, man," I replied, though I wasn't

surprised by his answer. "Maybe if you can come hang out here at the school on Sunday, I can get my dad to drop me off here on his way to work and we can hang out here instead. He's stuck working another Sunday shift." Chance looked over at me, surprised.

"You'd do that?" he asked. I laughed.

"Sure, what else am I going to do this weekend? Nobody else wants anything to do with me."

"You could go to church with Jennifer again," Chance suggested. I gave him a light shove.

"Maybe you should," I retorted, "somebody's got to save that soul of yours." Chance laughed at this.

"That's what I have you for," he replied with a grin. I was just about to ask what he meant by that when my dad pulled up.

"Gotta go," I said, standing up, "that's my dad."

"I remember," Chance replied.

I reached out and touched his shoulder with one hand. Seemed like the natural thing to do. He covered my hand with his for a moment, then let go. I turned and headed for the car. My dad was sitting, waiting patiently.

"Chance?" he asked, when I climbed into the car. I glanced back to where Chance still sat on the low brick wall.

"Yeah," I replied. My dad nodded and turned forward again. Chance gave a little wave. I waved back as my dad pulled the car away from the curb.

"Everything okay today?" he asked.

"Yeah," I said, about to leave it at that. I remembered our promise though, and continued. "I talked to Mrs. Bradley, the secretary." He glanced over at me before turning his eyes back to the road.

"About?" he prompted.

"About Dominic Hale," I told him.

"That's the boy who was killed a few years ago, right?"

"That's the one. I asked Mrs. Bradley about him. She says he was a good kid, and that she doesn't think he could have locked himself in that oven. She says there's nothing to grip on the inside of the door, and it would have been really difficult for him to lock it on himself from the inside," I finished with a smug look. My dad glanced back over at me again.

"Interesting. Difficult, but not impossible?"

"No," I grudgingly admitted, "not impossible, but very difficult. And what a painful way to go, right?"

"I have to admit I wouldn't want to go out that way," my dad said with a nod. "So you and Chance think he was killed, and you think he was killed because he was gay, right?"

"We think that's why Katie was attacked too, and that was set up to look like a suicide. I also think someone tried to kill Chance in the library, and tried to make it look like an accident."

"You mean the bookshelves," he asked.

"Yeah. And I didn't tell you this before, I

didn't want to scare you, but I saw someone last week parked outside our house in the middle of the night. They were driving a pickup truck. When they saw me watching them, they drove away, without their headlights on." My dad looked over at me intently for a moment.

"Why didn't you tell me that?" he asked.

"Are you kidding? And contribute to your theory that I'm going nuts?" He was quiet a long moment, then nodded.

"That's fair," he replied, his tone a bit sad. "I do wish you had told me that though, that's concerning. Too bad it was a pickup truck. That doesn't even begin to narrow it down." I couldn't help but laugh.

"That's what I thought, too," I said, "Way too many pickup trucks in this town." My dad smiled over at me.

"Okay, so what's the next step?" he asked.

"Well, Chance wants me to ask the cafeteria workers about the oven. I don't think we need to, Mrs. Bradley pretty much gave us what we needed there already, but he's pretty insistent. I wouldn't mind getting a look at the oven itself."

"You still think it's that bully?"

"Absolutely," I replied.

"Then who was driving the truck?" he asked. That stopped me.

"I… I don't know," I had to admit. "Maybe

it's not just Noah, maybe it's Noah and his father, the crazy preacher."

"Crazy preacher? From last Sunday?" he asked. I went on a rant about the sermon. We were almost home by the time I finished. My dad hadn't said a single word the whole time. When I finished, he took a long breath and let it out really slowly.

"It was always amazing to me that people could hate so much," he said, "and for such ridiculous reasons. 'Judge not, lest ye be judged yourself,' I think the Bible says on the subject. That always sounded pretty direct to me."

"Yeah," I replied simply, surprised that my father and I agreed so completely on something.

"The preacher was Noah's father, which you think explains part of why Noah is the way he is?" he asked.

"I think it explains pretty much everything about Noah, actually. I think he's a little fuzzy on the whole sin concept though. I caught him and Jennifer in the C hall looking like they were pretty interested in sin, if you know what I mean."

"I'm afraid I do," my dad replied. He sighed heavily. "Talk about screwed up priorities. Well do me a favor, and don't get yourself mixed up in anything you can't get back out of, okay? If someone is out trying to hurt people, I'd rather you be as far from that as possible."

"I have to look out for Chance, Dad."

"I know, but I have to look out for you, and I can't do it twenty four hours a day," he said, looking straight at me as he eased into the driveway. I thought about that for a moment, then nodded.

"Don't worry, Chance and I look out for each other. I wouldn't get involved in any of this to begin with, but we have to figure out what's going on, and try to keep anyone else from getting hurt."

"I get that," he said, "really I do. I even admire that. But if you find anything solid, any actual evidence, I want you to bring it to me, the principal, or if it's an emergency, the police. Do you hear me? Don't go doing anything stupid."

"No problem," I told him. I was just happy he wasn't questioning any more, and seemed legitimately concerned by the situation. He was taking me seriously.

I grabbed my backpack as he turned off the car and headed for the house. I had a lot of homework to do, and some serious studying to make up for an embarrassingly large amount of class time spent thinking about Chance. It was going to be a long evening.

Chapter Fifteen
Officer Friendly

Pain and heat. Pain from the bruise on my forehead that I was sure was just developing. Pain from the fire that was slowly, but tangibly, rising all around. Locked in the steel prison, burning alive as I peered through the tiny glass window, screaming noiselessly for someone to help me.

No one would help me. The devil was outside again, his smiling human mask a mockery to the species. The horns still protruded from the mask's forehead. The fierce, yellow eyes seemed to burn into me, their glee at my anguish evident. The mask had changed again.

It looked as though the Reverend Porter's face had been torn from his skull and placed over the face of the monster hiding behind it. I could see blood lining the edge of the mask where it had been torn from his skull and worn as a mask by the agents of Hell he so actively seemed to pursue. A long, forked tongue darted between the Reverend's bloody lips.

As quickly as it had appeared, the horrible face was gone. Moments later, a new face appeared. The heat was rising. I was still screaming, but I couldn't even hear myself anymore. Everything was silent. I pounded on the door, but no noise came back to me. Even the flames licking all around brought nothing to dispel the cacophonous silence. As the new face appeared, time seemed to slow. I shouted my pleas for help.

The new face drew close. For the first time, the new face was crystal clear. It was Chance, his face surrounded by the halo of wispy light. It still trailed off the face in the window like iridescent steam. As Chance's face stopped just before the window, he spoke. I couldn't hear the words. I couldn't hear anything. But I knew what Chance said.

"I'm sorry, Ryan. I can't help you." For the briefest of instants, his impossibly deep brown eyes glistened clearly with unshed tears.

Then the claws came, breaking through the face in my window as though my regretful visitor was made of nothing more substantial than the wispy light surrounding it. The perfect face broke apart like smoke in a breeze, glowing faintly for a moment before it was gone.

The devil wearing the Reverend's face reappeared. He was laughing. I couldn't hear it. I could feel it, grating against my bones as the flames consumed the tattered remains of my flesh. I silently screamed again, and the dream broke.

I sat up sharply in bed, gasping for air as I felt my heart trying valiantly to pound its way through my chest. I had to make this dream stop. I wasn't sure how many more times I could endure it.

It was interesting that it had changed again though. It was no longer Noah's face the devil wore, it was Reverend Porter's. Maybe that was because my dad's comment had brought up a good point and my subconscious hadn't yet figured out how to process it. Maybe I was just insane.

My dream about Katie had been true. That didn't mean this one was, or that it would be. This one kept changing though, so it couldn't be true. It was just weird that it had been exactly the same a dozen times and now had changed twice in a row. That worried me, though I couldn't quite pinpoint why.

I was covered in sweat again. It was a weird feeling, being covered in sweat, and freezing at the same time. It wasn't that cold, but I was shivering. I'd had the dream so many times, but it chilled me every time.

I stood up and began to move toward my bedroom door, heading for the bathroom, but I stopped. On impulse, I crouched down and snuck low over to the bedroom window. Something held me back from the ledge. Fear, I recognized, and not just from the dream. I was afraid of what I'd see when I looked. I was afraid of the truck I felt I might see if I lifted myself up enough to peek out the window. I had to know, though.

I eased myself up, my legs shaking slightly. I lifted myself just enough to look over the ledge out the front window. My already chilled heart grew even more icy. The truck was there. Still, dark, and menacing at the front of the yard.

The truck sat off to one side, partially hidden by some of the trees along the edge of the property. The cab was still in direct line of sight to the house though.

The angle was tricky, I couldn't make out if there was anyone in the cab. I strained my eyes looking to see if there was any movement. I couldn't see any. I don't know what was more terrifying; the thought that there was someone sitting still and silent in that truck watching my house, or the thought that there was nobody inside the truck at the moment.

I hadn't realized how much higher I had risen up while straining to see inside the cab or just how tense I was, until a flash of movement outside to my left startled me off balance. I yelped as I stumbled backward, falling to the floor.

After a moment's terrified hesitation, I decided I needed to know what it was more than I wanted to hide under the bed or run screaming to my father.

I scrambled back to the window and looked

out, ready to jump back again. A dark figure was hurrying into the truck. I heard the engine rev, no lights emanating from the vehicle as it took off and tore down the road.

I didn't hesitate this time, I ran straight to my father's room. I burst through the door and raced to his bedside, giving him a shake.

"Dad! Dad, wake up, the killer came back!" I shouted. My father, to his extreme credit, didn't moan and groan, didn't tell me it was just a bad dream, didn't tell me to go back to bed.

He sat bolt upright, took about a half a second to get his bearings then jumped out of bed. As I stumbled back out of his way, he grabbed a baseball bat from where it had been leaning up against the bedside table. With a look of determination, he held the bat firmly in one hand and looked down at me.

"Where?" he asked simply.

I was stunned. That bat always sat in the hall closet. He must have brought it in here after I'd talked to him about the first time that truck had been outside. I couldn't seem to wrap my head around the image of the man I hadn't seen in years.

This man before me was tall, strong, and determined to protect his family. He didn't look broken at all, he looked ready to take on the world. His expression softened just slightly.

"Ryan, where?" he repeated a bit more gently. I took a breath to clear my head, then spoke rapidly.

"Outside, in the truck! The truck just took off, but whoever it was, they weren't in it at first, they were along the tree line by the house! I think the killer saw me at the window and ran away! They got into the truck and just took off! No lights on, nothing!" I finally paused for breath, and my father moved.

"Stay here," he said firmly, and bolted out of the room. I noticed he grabbed his cell phone from the small desk by the door on the way out. I hesitated just a moment, then followed him. I knew he'd said to stay here, but no parent in their right mind would expect their teenage son to follow that particular instruction under these circumstances.

I caught up to him as he went out the front door. He had the bat up and ready in one hand, and the phone held to his ear with the other. I heard him talking to whoever was on the other line.

"...prowler snooping around outside my house... No, my son saw him, it's the second ti... No sir, he wasn't in the house... left in a truck... I don't know, you can ask him when you get here... okay, goodbye," my dad finished and hung up the phone.

Must have been the cops, I thought to myself. I admit, I was impressed. I'd seen a lot of movies where someone breaks into a home, or tries to, and the man just jumps up and charges in. he gets himself hurt or killed, never having bothered to call the cops.

My dad had charged in, but he'd called the cops already, and had only gone running into danger like that after I told him that the killer had left. He hadn't hesitated to go into potential danger, but he was at least being pretty smart about it, I thought.

He was wearing nothing but a pair of boxers like I was, so had nowhere to stash the phone. He held it in his hand, bat still up as he glanced side to side at the trees on either side of the yard. He made it to the road and looked up and down it, then down at the ground. He loaded up a flashlight app on his phone with a few touches on the screen and lit up the gravel lining the roadside.

Slowly he moved along the gravel by the road. What was he looking for, I wondered? Had to be looking for tire tracks or footprints or something, I decided. I couldn't help but find myself suddenly thinking more highly of my dad. On my word alone he'd charged after a prowler, and was now looking for clues in the yard.

"Find anything?" I asked from my place about fifteen feet behind him on the grass. He jumped, spun around, and raised the bat.

"Jesus, Ryan! Didn't I tell you to stay in the house?" he shouted, though he sounded more startled than upset.

"Yeah, but I told you the killer already left," I replied in my own defense.

"First, there could have been more than one of them," my dad scolded, "and second, how do you know it was the killer?"

"Sure Dad, I'll bet there are a lot of creepy dark figures stalking teenage boys in the middle of the night in this town," I retorted sarcastically. "Doesn't mean it has anything to do with my investigation of a murderer that has already tried to kill me once at school, tried to murder two others already in my school, and succeeded in killing another one two years ago. Hey I know, maybe this guy just wanted to bring us a welcome basket of cookies or fruit or something."

"Ryan," my dad said warningly. I bit back my further comments, realizing I was reverting to old habits again.

"Sorry Dad," I said a little sheepishly, "you're right. It just makes sense that whoever is stalking us here is the same person trying to hurt me at school. Too big a coincidence, otherwise." My dad nodded at this.

"You have a point, it would be a pretty big coincidence." He walked toward me, and I moved his way as well. "Except didn't you say it was Noah? I didn't think he'd be old enough to be driving a truck." I stopped at the reminder.

"He's not," I replied. "That definitely wasn't Noah anyway. Too tall. Couldn't tell about the build though, whoever it was had on a pretty big coat. I definitely think it was a guy though."

"How could you tell?"

"I don't know, just the way he moved, I guess. I didn't see much detail or anything," I told him.

"Too bad. A positive ID would go a long way at this point," my dad said thoughtfully. I grinned at him.

"A positive ID?" I asked, a little teasingly. My dad looked at me and grinned.

"I've been watching a lot of cop dramas on TV while you've been brooding in your room listening to your rock music," he told me. I don't know why I felt a little embarrassed by that, but I did.

"Oh," was all I could reply with. A bit of a breeze bit at my skin. "Let's go back inside and wait for the cops to show up," I suggested, "It's freezing out here." My father glanced at me.

"It's not really that col… Ryan, you're soaked! Is that sweat?" he asked. I nodded and he put a hand on my shoulder, guiding me back to the house. "Did the prowler scare you that badly?"

"No," I replied honestly, a little surprised. "He startled me, sure, but it was the dream before that that really scared me." My father nodded.

"The same one?" he asked.

"Yeah, but it was Reverend Porter's face the devil was wearing this time, not Noah's." I replied as we stepped inside. It was much warmer in here. My dad closed and locked the door.

"Maybe you should take a shower and get some clothes on before the police get here," my dad suggested, "I suspect you'll have enough time for a quick one. I nodded and headed to the bathroom.

As it happened, I would have had enough time for a long, leisurely soak in the tub, had I gone that route instead of the quick shower. It took more than half an hour for the cops to get there.

Half an hour during which I paced around the house, peering out the windows every few moments, trying to figure this all out after I finished my five minute shower. Their delay in response did not instill much confidence in me, or faith in their abilities to keep me and my dad safe.

By the time they arrived, I had worked myself into a late-night panic about what was going to happen the next time I went to sleep in that house. The killer's appearance at our house again hadn't scared me half as badly as my dream had, but by the time the cops got there I had managed to change those two around in my head pretty firmly.

The killer hadn't just been in the truck watching the house. He'd been moving around just outside. What was he doing? Was he trying to see inside? Figure out where we slept so he could plan our late-night murder? Or had he already done that and we'd slept right through that one? Maybe he was coming to finish the job tonight. It was going to be really hard to sleep the next night, I knew.

I saw the car pull up out front. One car. Not a group of police cruisers, lights and sirens blazing. Just one car, casually rolling up our drive like he was coming for a nice cup of tea or something. Inside was one officer. Just one.

I couldn't help but mentally write off the local police as a source of help. If the killer had actually murdered us right after my dad had called the cops, he'd have had time to casually watch us bleed out, pack up our bodies in the truck, and been several miles away before anyone had arrived to investigate.

Even worse, with only one patrolman and a single car, if the killer had wanted to, he could have murdered us both, and set an ambush for the officer. He could have killed all three of us, and it may have been hours before anyone came looking for the missing cop.

That would have left plenty of time to burn the house down to hide evidence, or do a nice bleach-intensive clean-up job before taking our bodies elsewhere for disposal. I shook my head. Maybe I had seen a few too many cop dramas on TV myself, I thought ruefully.

The knock on the door even sounded lazy, I thought bitterly. I moved to answer it. I'd pulled on a pair of basketball shorts and a t-shirt. My father had on a pair of sweats and a tank top as he came around the corner from the bedroom hallway.

Opening the door, the officer in front of me did nothing to dispel all previous assumptions I'd already made about him. He was incredibly fat, his uniform looking like it was under definite strain trying to contain his bulk, and looked like the only time he would ever run was if he had just been told the local donut shop was closing in ten minutes. He gave me a patronizing smile. I hated him instantly.

"Howdy there, son," he drawled. I wondered briefly if his accent was intentionally overdone, or if he really was this redneck.

"I'm not your son," I replied, irritated. The cop laughed.

"It's jes' a figur' o' speech, boy," he said. I opened my mouth to respond again, but my father intervened.

"Good evening officer, thank you for coming," he said.

"Mah pleasure, mister…" he paused expectantly.

"Jacobs," my father replied, holding out his hand. "Mark Jacobs."

"Mister Jacobs," the officer nodded as he shook my dad's hand, "what seems t' be th' trouble?"

"We just had a prowler," my dad told him.

"That so?" the officer asked, fishing a piece of candy out of his pocket and stuffing it into his mouth.

"Yes," my father replied. I could tell by his tone he was trying to keep from gaping incredulously at this clearly-incompetent lout.

"When'd this happ'n?" he asked.

"Half an hour ago. My son Ryan saw the man just outside the house. He must have seen my son at the window and realized he'd been seen. He ran to a truck he had parked out front."

"That so?" asked the man. My father clenched his jaw. I could see the muscle twitch.

"Yes," my father replied, still trying to sound friendly. I admired his patience.

"Well y' see, we have an awful lot o' trucks 'round these parts," the officer said. I stared. Was this joker trying to be a walking stereotype, or did it just come naturally to him, I wondered? I glanced at my dad. His expression had turned stony.

"Do you have a lot of prowlers, too?" my father asked. I almost smiled. The officer frowned slightly, as if trying to decide whether or not he'd just been insulted.

"I'm jes' sayin' sir, unless th' boy got a good look at th' feller, tryin' t get an ID from jes' th' truck is goin' t' be a might difficult." The man turned his squinty eyes at me. "Well son? Did y' see th' prowler good?"

"No, I didn't," I answered. "He was tall, but was wearing a big coat. I don't know what he looked like. He wasn't huge, but other than that I couldn't tell you."

"Shame," the cop said. "Well, without anythin' more t' go on, we can't do much fer y'all. I'll take a look outside, see if I can't find m'self some tracks er signs o' forced entry er somethin', but other than that I suggest y'all get yerself some better door locks, and give us a call if'n th' feller comes back."

My father and I both stared. The officer tipped his hat, and walked back out the door. My father and I continued to stare at the closed door the officer had just gone through.

"Wow," I said softly after a long moment.

"My thoughts exactly," my father replied. "I have never in all my life seen anything like that before."

"Me neither," I agreed. "What exactly was that, anyway?"

"That, son, is a total train-wreck."

My dad and I moved to the window, watched the incompetent cop poke around the yard for a few moments, get into his patrol car, and drive away. I shook my head in disgust.

"I'm going back to bed," I told my dad.

"Me too." As I moved away, he stopped me. "Ryan?"

"Yeah, Dad?" I asked.

"Thanks for coming to get me," he said.

"Thanks for believing me," I replied, just as sincerely. We shared a smile, then I headed back to bed.

Chapter Sixteen

Memory of a Dream

Saturday seemed to take forever. My dad had to work, and unfortunately I had studying and homework to do, so I couldn't really afford to take the time to go spend all day with Chance. Seeing him during lunch, and for a few minutes before and after school was great, but getting six straight hours to just hang out with him seemed to me like the best possible way to spend a day.

I'd have just about killed to be able to at least text with Chance or something all day, just to keep that connection with him. It seemed odd to me, someone not having a cell phone, but Chance's circumstances, like his income, weren't really something that would allow for those kinds of luxuries.

Funny that I'd never really thought about things like cell phones as luxuries. He probably didn't have any video games either. Or a change of clothes, for that matter. That last one really messed with my head. I couldn't believe that some state agency hadn't gotten involved with his family at this point. Although he didn't seem to be starving at all. He was in good shape and never seemed to eat a whole lot of his lunch.

I spent my day studying, doing odd jobs around the house, fine-tuning my room's wall decorations, homework, and I admit a large portion of time was spent playing video games.

By the time Sunday came around, I was practically jumping out of my skin with eagerness to go spend the day hanging out with Chance at the school. My dad had told me he was okay with it, as long as we didn't go anywhere else and that I was out front and waiting when he got off work.

Not a problem there, there wasn't really anywhere else to go. Chance's house was out of the question. He'd probably die of shame if I asked to see where he lived. Better to leave that one alone for the time being. Maybe someday he'd open up that part of his life to me. After all, we hadn't really known each other all that long, though to me it felt like I'd always known him.

My dad had seemed a little uncomfortable with the idea of me spending the day with Chance at the school, but I assured him we'd stay on the school grounds, and wouldn't enter the school or bother any of the grounds keeping or janitorial staff that might be working the weekend.

He didn't seem overly comforted by that promise, but he'd finally agreed. He seemed like he'd wanted to say something, but whatever it was, he kept it to himself.

I was in the car before my dad was ready, even though it was still pretty early. I hoped I wouldn't have to wait long before Chance showed up. I only had until three before my dad would be coming back to pick me up.

He climbed into the driver's seat and glanced over at me with a considering expression. Again however, he kept his thoughts to himself. We drove in silence almost the whole way.

It wasn't an uncomfortable silence though, we were both just lost in our own thoughts. It was quite a pleasant change from the awkward silences we'd both grown accustomed to with one another. As we pulled up in front of the school, my dad looked back down at me. He looked concerned.

"Ryan," he said, "I know you said you'd stay here with Chance, but I want to remind you that you yourself told me you think someone is after you. After the other night, I think there's definitely something going on. If anything happens that you think might be at all threatening or dangerous, call the police." He paused a long moment, then sighed. "On second thought, just call me."

I couldn't help but feel a little weird about the thought that the cops were useless. Maybe it was just that one officer, but he sure hadn't given me, or my father apparently, a good impression of the local police force. I had to remind myself that the cops had shown up quickly enough when I'd called them when Katie was in trouble. They couldn't be all that bad. Must have just gotten a real winner the other night.

"Don't worry Dad, you'll be the first I call. Chance and I will look out for each other," I reassured him. He sighed.

"I hope so. It's weird, feeling so nervous about leaving you in a public place. You'd think I would feel worse about leaving you at home, considering our visitor the other night."

"I'm definitely better off here, Dad. I told you, Chance will look out for me."

"Yeah," he said as he looked forward again. "Hey, if he doesn't show, or you just get bored, call me then too, I'll come get you."

"You've got it," I said with a smile. "He'll be here, though." He nodded and I got out of the car. He pulled away as I wandered around toward the back of the school. Last time I'd seen him here on a Sunday, he'd been by the basketball hoops, so I figured I'd wait over there.

I was more than a little surprised when I saw Chance sitting on the back steps of the school. He was spread out along the length of a step, head leaned up against the brick sidewall. His eyes were closed. He actually might have been sleeping.

I walked up to him, not trying to be quiet, but not really intentionally making any noise, either. I sat down on the step just below him, and looked up at him. He looked so peaceful. He always had a degree of calmness about him, even when he got excited, but this was different. I couldn't quite place it, though it may just have been the peace of a good sleep.

Why was he sleeping on the steps of the school, I suddenly wondered? I knew he had a home, I'd heard his mother talking to him. They lived somewhere. Maybe he'd just left his house really early and come here, and fallen back to sleep. That had to be it, I thought.

I don't know how long I watched him, but after a while I found myself reaching over to him. I gently touched his arm. I was a little worried he would startle at my touch, but he didn't. He smiled slowly at first, then opened his eyes. As his eyes focused on mine, his smile broadened.

"You came," he said, tone slightly surprised.

"I told you I would," I replied casually.

"Yeah, but you really came."

"I told you I would," I repeated with a laugh.

"But now you're stuck here. You know this place is boring, right?" he grinned.

"Oh sure, now you tell me." I rolled my eyes. "Seriously though, we can do whatever. We just can't leave school grounds."

"Can we break in and check out the cafeteria?"

he asked with a sparkle in his eyes. I couldn't help but laugh.

"No, Chance! It's illegal for starters, and I promised my dad we'd stay out of the school. I'm starting to worry about your moral compass, my friend." He just grinned at me.

"Well I'm already going to Hell. A little breaking and entering wouldn't make that situation any worse. Besides," he continued, "we wouldn't have to break anything. I know how to get in."

"I think I'm going to have to watch you even more closely than I thought," I told him, giving him a suspicious look.

It shouldn't surprise me that Chance knew a secret way into the school, but it did. He never struck me as the type to get into much mischief, but I guess if you spend that much time trying to get away from a rough home life, you might be inclined to get into a bit of trouble along the way. I shook my head.

"No dice, man. I promised my dad," I told him. He nodded.

"Understood," he said. I appreciated that he wasn't going to try to convince me to go against my promise. Yet another reason to like him, I thought, as if I needed any more. "No entering then. And no leaving the school grounds. Well, that certainly narrows our options."

"Yeah, sorry," I told him.

"Don't worry about it," he replied. He

hesitated a moment before continuing. "Does that mean no peeking in windows, either?"

"I didn't say anything about looking inside the school, just going inside the school," I said thoughtfully. "I don't really think that would hurt anything, right?"

"I wouldn't think so," Chance said. "Maybe we can get a view inside the cafeteria, check out that oven."

"Maybe," I replied. "You sure are focused on getting a look at that oven." Chance shrugged.

"I really just want you to look at it, now that you've said you wanted to see it. I've snuck in and checked it out already. I need to see if you come to the same conclusions I did."

"Makes sense. Okay, let's go check it out." Chance flashed me a bright smile. I couldn't help but notice how warm it made me feel. The sun was out and bright, and it was pretty warm, but this warmth went clear through me. I wished I knew how he did that.

I followed Chance around to the other side of the school where he pointed at a high window. It was ground floor, thankfully, but the narrow window sill was still six feet up. I frowned at him.

"Do I look like I play professional basketball to you?" I asked him. Chance grinned.

"I don't know, I haven't seen you jump yet."

"What?"

"Come on man, give it a shot!" he encouraged

with a laugh.

"Great," I muttered before turning back to the window. The sill looked narrow, but I might have enough grip there to lift myself up.

I wasn't worried about reaching the ledge, I could do that without jumping, though it was a bit above my head. I was worried about not having quite enough of a grip to lift myself up. Nothing to do but try, I thought.

I took a breath, grabbed the ledge, and jumped, trying to lift and lock myself into place. My feet angled in to catch the side of the brick building for traction, but it didn't help.

My eyes had just barely cleared the sill, giving me a great view of the back of the kitchen for a split second before my fingers slipped.

I went down at an odd angle, my feet having been up to grip on the wall, but Chance was ready for it, and grabbed me before I lost my balance as I came down. He stabilized me, and then held my arm for just a moment longer, before letting go. I smiled at him, both in gratitude for the help, and in appreciation for his not laughing at me for slipping.

"Thanks," I told him.

"No problem," he replied. "Going to give it another go?"

"No," I shook my head, "that sill is way too small to get a good hold on. Okay hot shot, why don't you come over here and help. Kneel down and I'll climb up on your shoulders."

Chance paused, as though this idea had never once occurred to him. He waited long enough without answering that I decided to tease him a bit.

"Hey, I'm not that fat!" I said as I gave him a playful shove. He laughed and shoved me back.

"Don't I know it. If you were any skinnier I might not even think you're cute," he chided. I tilted me head as I regarded him with a teasing smile.

"You think I'm cute?" I asked him playfully. His grin took on a mischievous cast.

"You're okay," he said.

"Uh huh," I said wryly, "Which is why you have fallen completely head over heels for me. Because I'm 'okay'."

"I like you for your endless charm and magnetic personality, not for your looks," he corrected me. I raised a brow as he said this, and he sighed. "Okay, I admit it. You're cute, too. The charm doesn't hurt though."

"What exactly makes a boy cute?" I asked him, genuinely curious. I'd never known anyone I could ask that question of before.

"I don't know, you mean to me?" he asked. I nodded and he considered a moment. "I guess for me it's the eyes mostly. I'm a sucker for a pretty pair of eyes. And your smile is great, very sincere. Makes your eyes sparkle." I smiled back at him, genuinely pleased by these remarks. I opened my mouth to reply, but he interrupted. "You've got a great butt, too." He added, with a sly quirk to his grin. I couldn't help it, I burst into laughter.

"All right, that's enough out of you," I told him when I'd caught my breath, though I couldn't deny to myself that I was pleased by that comment as well.

Odd that it didn't make me uncomfortable when he said it, not like it had when he'd first told me he liked me. Maybe I was getting used to the idea. Maybe I was just getting used to Chance. It felt kind of good knowing he liked me though. Probably just a shallow ego boost, I thought. I gave him a light shove toward the window.

"Get over there. I can't make it to the window without you." I told him. He sighed dramatically and went to the window.

"Always getting walked on by the cute boys. Story of my life," he said in an impressively tragic tone. I rolled my eyes, but couldn't help smiling. He knelt at the base of the window and I stepped up on his shoulders. I lifted myself up and looked through the window.

"You stable?" he called from below me.

"Yeah, no problem," I replied.

"Cool," Chance said to himself, sounding impressed and a little surprised. I decided to let that one slide.

The kitchen lights were all off, though plenty of light was coming in from the two small windows in the kitchen, and from the much bigger windows in the attached cafeteria to see by. It was empty, no surprise, and very clean. I felt marginally better about eating the school's lunches.

"Can you see the ovens?" Chance asked.

"Hold on, I'm scoping out the scene."

"No problem, take your time, don't mind me," Chance replied wryly.

"Keep your shirt on," I replied. Chance didn't take the bait. I found I was a little disappointed.

I looked over the ovens. There were two of them, side by side. Big, too. They looked about six feet tall and almost as big across. They looked ancient, too. The doors on them were big and heavy, made of old, but clean, metal.

Next to them stood a couple of multi-shelved rolling metal racks. I assumed they could be loaded with trays filled with rolls of bread or whatever and be rolled into the ovens.

The latches on the ovens were big pull handles, and the exterior locking mechanisms looked to be designed to lock whenever the doors were shut all the way.

That didn't bode well for the arguments against suicide. It looked like it would be possible to lock oneself into these ovens without much trouble, as long as there was something to grip on the inside. I tried to picture what the ovens looked like from the inside.

My eyes moved a little higher up. The viewing windows on the ovens looked thick, and were a light, uneven golden color, like a pan that had been oiled and baked one too many times. As I pictured the oven from the inside, I suddenly felt a wash of fear.

Those windows would look very familiar from the inside, I thought. I could picture them clearly, the view of the tall metal storage cabinets across from the ovens partially obstructed by a face. A devil's face. I almost fell backward off of Chance's shoulders as I scrambled to get down and away from the windows.

I no longer had any doubt that Chance was right. Dominic Hale had been murdered. I'd seen the inside of those ovens, all too many times. There was no handle, no locking mechanism, no release on the inside. Nothing to grip to pull the door shut, no way to get the door open again.

Chance picked up my reaction immediately and stood quickly, turning to face me.

"Ryan, are you okay?" he asked. I shook my head sharply.

"You're right, Chance," I gasped as I tried to catch my breath and still my racing heart. "Dominic was murdered."

"How do you know?" he asked, though he looked much more concerned about me than he was in my answer or even the affirmation that he was right.

"I've already seen the inside of those ovens, Chance. The one on the left, actually. I've been in it."

"What?" Chance asked, now confused and looking more worried than ever. "You can't have been."

"Not really, not yet. Remember when I dreamt about Katie being attacked? And it really happened?" Chance just nodded, but I could tell from his quickly paling expression that he knew where this was going and he didn't like it.

"I have this dream," I started, "where I get hit from behind and locked into a small metal room. It gets hot inside. Really hot. Feels like fire all around. The devil, the same one wearing Noah's face in my dream about Katie, is looking at me through that window, the one in the oven door."

"Ryan," Chance started, but seemed unable to get anything more out.

"Don't worry," I told him, sounding more confident than I felt, "I've only ever had the one dream that came true. And this one was different, kind of off. It didn't feel the same as the one where Katie was attacked. And it changes sometimes."

I didn't want to tell him that I'd seen him in this dream too, and that he'd refused to help me. That was even more proof that this dream couldn't come true though, Chance would always help me.

As I thought this, the memory of Chance standing and watching as Noah and his big, dumb henchmen roughed me up when I'd helped Katie the first time came through my mind. I shook it away. No,

Chance would help me. He had to help me.

"Okay," Chance replied, breaking me out of my thoughts, "but stay away from those ovens, okay? I don't want anything to happen to you. You've had dreams come true before…"

"Just one!" I protested. He nodded, conceding that point.

"You've had a dream come true before, I can't bear the thought of the same thing happening to you that happened to…" he choked off, interrupting himself. He looked about to cry. The tough guy in me took over and I steeled my own shaking nerves and stepped forward, putting my arms around him.

"Hey, don't worry," I told him as he clung to me, "nothing will happen to me. I've got you to watch my back, right?"

I felt him nod, his cheek just a bit below mine. A detached part of my mind noted that Chance was just a little bit shorter than I was. An odd thing to notice at the time, but it stuck in my thoughts for some reason. I hadn't ever noticed that before.

"See? With you and me together, we can take on anything. So I'll make you a deal. I'll stay away from the kitchen, if you promise to watch my back."

"I'll do everything I possibly can to help you," Chance said. Something about the way he said that didn't make me feel any better. Chance let go, pulling back, though he kept his hands on my arms. I let him, keeping my own hands on his shoulders.

"Besides," I told him as casually as I could manage, "the killer is targeting gay students. I'm not gay, so we're safe." Chance looked away.

I'd successfully distracted him, but with a little bit of hurt rather than the logical argument I was trying to make. I felt instantly guilty. I reached down to his cheek and wiped away the few tears that had managed to escape.

"I didn't mean it like that," I told him. He nodded.

"I know, I know. I'm just a big baby, I'll be okay."

"I didn't mean that either," I protested, starting to feel like I was falling into dangerous territory without a way out. Chance looked back up at me and smiled, reaching idly up to brush a strand of my longer hair back behind my ear.

"I know," he repeated, though this time it sounded like he meant it. "Come on, let's get away from here."

I followed as he led the way back around the school. I had to admit to myself that I was glad to be away from the windows by the kitchen. No way to fall into an oven from there, but I definitely didn't like being that close to them.

My fear of my dream had grown exponentially in the past few moments. Awareness of the reality had done some serious damage to the lies I'd been telling myself, that the dream couldn't possibly be real.

As we walked, Chance must have picked up my darkening mood. He reached over and gave me a gentle push. I glanced over at him, but he was looking as if nothing had happened. I gave him a gentle push back. He laughed lightly and looked over at me. I saw the look in his eyes at that moment and I knew without a doubt; Chance would help me.

Chapter Seventeen
Invitations and Awakenings

We made it over to one of the better trees on the school yard near the front road. Chance sat down, back against the trunk.

After his failure to take the bait on some of my earlier comments, I decided to play with Chance a bit more. I lay down and put my head on his leg as a pillow, giving him a bit of a daring smile. Chance looked surprised, but smiled. I hadn't intended to keep my head there, but found it was a surprisingly comfortable position and decided to stay that way.

Despite my comfort, images from my dream kept intruding. After a long moment, I spoke, both to break the memories and to change the subject to get my thoughts on other matters.

"How did you know you were gay?"

"Jesus Ryan, you don't do subtle, do you," Chance laughed.

"Sorry, that's probably an insensitive question," I apologized. He shook his head though.

"No, just a direct one. I don't mind, it just came out of nowhere."

"So how did you know?" I persisted. He thought for moment. I enjoyed the breeze and the shade, and his closeness while I waited for him to compose his thoughts.

"There was a boy in the sixth grade," he began.

"What?" I asked, interrupting him. "You mean I'm not the only man in your life?" He laughed, but reached over and touched my hair. I didn't mind. It was kind of comforting. Almost idly, he started playing with a lock of it.

"Everyone's got to have a first love, Ryan. If you'd moved here earlier, you might have been mine. This kid was something else though. Red hair, incredible green eyes. Great smile. Kind of stocky kid."

"Wow, I'm absolutely nothing like that," I said with a small laugh of my own.

"Great eyes, great smile. I told you I'm a sucker for those," Chance reminded me. "Besides, it's not about the body. It's not even really about the eyes or the smile. The eyes and the smile just show you something about the person.

"Sharp, focused eyes means they're smart, and paying attention to you when you talk. Depth in them means the person is more than just a pretty face, they've got something deeper in their personality.

"The smile is the same. A bright smile that lights up the whole face tells me the person has a passionate soul. If they do it a lot, it tells me they're a positive, happy person. When some people smile, like Noah, it doesn't light anything up. Even the eyes stay dead when Noah smiles. It's creepy, and not the least attractive."

"That actually makes a lot of sense," I said thoughtfully. I hadn't actually ever thought about it that closely, but clearly Chance had. I'd never really found anyone attractive enough to really analyze them like that. Chance seemed to be totally absorbed with people he liked though, if his reactions to me were any indication.

"Thanks, I thought so," he grinned. "As I was saying though, this kid was something else. Probably the happiest person I've ever met. Always smiling, always laughing. It was impossible not to be happy when he was around. Even the rougher kids didn't pick on him. Great guy."

"So what happened with him?" I asked, genuinely curious.

"He got sick and they moved to a bigger city to be near a specialty hospital."

"And…?" I prompted when he paused.

"I don't know. I never heard from him again," Chance said simply. He paused his playing with my hair, though he didn't remove his hand.

"He never wrote to you or called or anything?"

"He wouldn't have. I never spoke to him. I don't think he even knew my name." I stared at Chance in shock.

"You never spoke to him?" I asked.

"Nope."

"But you were in love with him?"

"Completely."

"That's about the saddest thing I've ever heard," I told him honestly. Chance shrugged.

"It was hard, when he left. Harder that I knew he was sick. I don't even know if he got better."

"You never looked him up or anything?"

"I was always afraid to," he admitted.

"I'll help you look him up tomorrow if you want," I offered, looking up at him. The sunlight breaking through the leaves left a patchwork of light dappling his features. It was a cool effect.

"I don't know," he said, "I'm not sure I want to know. What if he died? What if he's still there, still sick, and deteriorating as we speak? I don't know if I could handle that. I like to think he got better and is doing great in his new home. He probably has a girlfriend and everything."

"Was he gay?" I asked.

"Not a clue. Didn't seem like the type though." He had started playing with my hair again.

"Honestly, neither did you until you let that sensitive personality show."

"That's kind of a stereotype, actually. Not every gay male is a sensitive guy."

"It's true in your case," I pointed out.

"Coincidental," he assured me.

"Uh huh," I said, without sincerity.

"It is!" he argued, giving me a mock-glare.

"Uh huh," I repeated. He shoved me.

"That's it, city boy. It's time to show you just how sensitive I am."

He shoved me again, hard. I rolled off his leg, laughing, and he lunged at me. I caught him before he tackled me and rolled him to the side, trying to fight him off. He was laughing too, making it hard for either of us to really coordinate a good counter attack.

Pushing, shoving, grappling, we wrestled around in the grass. He was strong, I had to admit. Almost scary strong, when he really leaned into it. They sure bred these country boys tough, I thought as I grunted with the effort of keeping him from pinning me to the ground.

With a heave, he managed to sling me over and pin me firmly to the ground, flat on my back. I was laughing hard enough that I couldn't make myself resist any more. He put his knees on my shoulders and raised his fists high in triumph.

"And that's how we do it in the country, city boy!" he teased, letting out the most cowboy whoop I'd ever heard.

"Okay, okay! I give!" I said between gasps.

"Man you're a lot tougher than you look!"

"Hey!" he growled, leaning down. He shifted his knees back so he could grab the front of my shirt. He held a fist menacingly, though without any real sincerity. "Watch it, or I'll give you a black eye to match Noah's!" I leaned up as far as I could from my position and smiled.

"I'll bet you hit like a girl," I told him with a mischievous grin. I could tell from his expression that he was trying desperately to keep his serious face on and keep the laughter that was rolling beneath the surface from taking over. He shook his fist in my face.

"Keep pushing me buddy, and you'll find out," he warned. We both knew he wasn't serious. "Although," he said as he shifted position again. He slid lower, and lay himself down on top of me, belly to belly. He leaned in close, nose inches from mine. It didn't even occur to me to think that I should be uncomfortable with him that close to me.

"It's a pity you're not gay," he whispered.

"How do you know I'm not?" I asked him teasingly, though I was incredibly aware of his proximity and my suddenly racing heart.

His breath smelled sweet, and it was warm brushing across my face. His startlingly deep eyes seemed to burn into mine as their intensity grew. He leaned just a little closer and paused again. My heart was racing, my breath slowed almost to a stop. His lips paused a bare inch from mine.

"You're not sensitive enough," he whispered. Taken totally aback, I blinked in surprise. He pushed himself up to sit straddling me again.

"Dude, I think you actually would have let me do it," he laughed incredulously.

"Nah," I said, trying to recover, "I knew you didn't have the guts." Chance stared at me in shock.

"Seriously?" he asked. I laughed.

"No, but I knew you wouldn't have done it," I lied. "You know I'm not into guys." I was finding myself less sure of that the more I was around Chance. I couldn't deny, to myself at least, that I was a bit disappointed he hadn't done it.

"Yeah," he said, unconvincingly.

"Ryan?" a voice said from somewhere above my head. It sounded extremely hesitant, and distinctly female. Chance looked up and scrambled off of me. I sat up and turned around. Jennifer was standing there, in a delicate blue dress. She wasn't close, and may not have heard what we'd been talking about, but it wasn't impossible.

"Jennifer, hi," I said, trying to regain my composure. I stood and brushed myself off, glancing at Chance. He shrugged. I noticed her mother sitting in their truck parked on the curb a short distance away. "What are you doing here?"

"Mama an' I were headin' t' th' church. It's Sunday, so we've got a service. I saw you over here an' asked mama if we could stop. What are you doin' here?"

"Just hanging out with Chance," I told her, gesturing toward him. She didn't even look his way, though her expression grew uncomfortable. I grit my teeth. "Don't take this wrong, but why did you stop?" I asked, trying to be friendly, but afraid of where this was heading and annoyed at her reaction to Chance.

"Well you're welcome t' come with us t' church, but I know you won't," she amended hastily as she saw my jaw set. "That's not what I wanted to ask."

"Okay, cool. What did you want to ask me then?"

"Well, there's a dance next Saturday," she started. I frowned. I hadn't heard that, though I hadn't been paying much attention to school activities lately. Or ever, since I moved. "I was thinkin' maybe if you wanted, you an' I could go together."

You'd think by now I'd have gotten used to being stunned into silence, but apparently it still had a strong effect on me. It took a long moment before I could open my mouth to respond.

"Jennifer, I…" I paused and tried to focus my thoughts. "I'm flattered, but first of all, you barely know me; second of all, the last time we spoke I pretty much told you off; and third, aren't you with Noah?"

"No, I broke up with him. He's been… weird lately," she said. That was interesting, I thought to myself.

"Weird how?" I couldn't help but ask. She

shook her head dismissively.

"Just different," she hedged. "So do you think you might want to go with me?"

"Jennifer, it's really nice of you to ask me, it really is. With you and Noah though, I wouldn't want to get in the middle of that. He wants to kill me as it is. Besides, after the whole church thing, I don't know how comfortable I am going to the dance with you.

"You're really nice. Maybe one of the nicest girls I've ever met, but that church and everyone who goes there scares the life out of me," I admitted. She looked hurt. I couldn't blame her, but I wanted her to understand. "Thanks anyway, and I'll see you at school tomorrow. If you wanted to come talk with me or something you can. We can be friends if you want, just leave your God and that church out of it."

She nodded, but didn't say anything. She turned and hurried back to the truck. I think she might have been fighting back tears. The look her mother threw me before Jennifer climbed in and shut the door could have peeled paint.

I felt bad, and I'd done it as nicely as I could, but there was no way I could spend a whole evening with her. Especially since Noah would probably be there as well. That was an ass-kicking waiting to happen.

"Harsh, bro," Chance said. I looked at him. He was smiling.

"I know, but I couldn't have said yes."

"Why not?"

"You heard why not. Besides, I'm not really into her. She's pretty, and nice and all, but I don't think we click at all. Not that way. Not really my type."

"What is your type?" he asked, giving me a mischievous smirk.

"Not you," I said with a light shove.

"Oh, we're back to that again huh?" he asked. "Need another beat down?"

"Bring it on," I told him.

My cell phone rang. The ringtone was a sharp, hard rock riff. Easy to hear, and pretty cool, I thought. At the moment though, it served only to make Chance and I both jump. We both laughed as I pulled out my phone. It was my dad, which was weird.

"Hey Dad," I said into the phone

"Hi Ryan. Listen, I'm on my way over there."

"What? Why? I've only been here a couple of hours, you can't have finished work already."

"I know, I'm taking a break so I can come and get you. If you don't want to come, I understand, but I thought you'd be interested."

"Quit with the mystery, Dad!" I said in exasperation. "What's going on?"

"Your friend Katie just woke up and wants to see you."

Chapter Eighteen
Point Well Taken

"What's going on?" Chance asked as I hung up the phone.

"That was my dad," I told him. The look he gave me told me it was not a necessary clarification. "Katie woke up."

"Are you serious?" he asked incredulously. "That's great news!"

"Yeah, I'm glad she's okay." I replied.

"And…" Chance encouraged. Took me a moment for it to sink in.

"And she can tell us who tried to kill her!" I exclaimed. Chance grinned.

"Nice of you to join us," he teased. "So your dad is coming to pick you up?" He looked distinctly less happy about that part of the news.

"Yeah, he'll probably be here soon," I replied.

"Okay. I'll let you go, but only because it's a

great lead on our case."

"You make it sound like we're detectives," I told him, "and what do you mean 'let me go'?"

"Oh please, I could pin you down and hold you there all day long," he retorted. I had to admit he was probably right. He was definitely stronger than I was, despite being just a little bit shorter. "And of course we're detectives. We're searching for clues to solve a crime, aren't we?"

"Yeah, regular Hardy Boys here. Tell me one good bit of detective work we've done."

"We searched the internet for those articles on Dominic's death, you interrogated Mrs. Bradley, we inspected the murder weapon, sounds pretty detective-like to me."

"Interrogated is a bit strong, don't you think? And what murder weapon?" I asked.

"Hello, the oven!" he exclaimed.

"We barely got a look at it, genius!"

"True, but it was enough of a look to trigger that memory of your dream, where you'd seen it a lot closer up."

"Don't remind me." I shivered. "Good points though. We have done some good digging. And gathered other clues. We know Noah has been acting weird, but that someone other than Noah is snooping around my place at night. We know the killer is targeting gay students, and that Reverend Porter has been bashing them pretty hard in that joke he calls a church. We know that Katie is awake, and will certainly have more information for us."

At least she would be able to tell the cops it hadn't been a suicide. That might get them involved in digging for clues, though if ol' Officer Friendly were the investigating officer, I didn't think he'd be able to find water if he were standing on the bottom of a lake.

"Okay," Chance said, "so what are you going to ask her?"

"I'll ask who tried to kill her of course."

"And if she doesn't know the person?"

"I'll ask for descriptions, like hair, eyes, build, height, skin color, etc."

"Perfect. Ask her about voice, too. If he said anything, what he sounded like, that kind of thing. And what he was wearing. That might give us a clue too."

"Good idea," I said. The sound of crunching tires sounded on the gravel at the roadside behind us. My dad had been even closer than I'd thought. "Gotta go. I'll see you Monday and will fill you in on everything." I turned to head toward the car when a thought occurred to me.

"Hey Chance," I said as I turned back around.

"Yeah?" he asked.

"You going to the dance on Saturday?" Chance shrugged.

"Yeah, I'll be around."

"Can I go with you?" I asked.

"Ryan, are you asking me on a date?" he asked,

eyes twinkling.

"Get real," I retorted, "just friends, right?" Chance nodded and sighed.

"Yeah, just friends. Damn it. Fine, I can just meet you here."

"I can have my dad pick you up when he drops me off," I told him. He shook his head.

"That's okay, I don't live far." I nodded.

"Cool, I'll see you Monday. Man, I wish you had a phone so I could call you and fill you in right after. It's going to drive me crazy waiting to tell you."

"How do you think I'll feel?" he asked with a laugh. "Get going, Holmes! You've got a crime to solve!"

I turned and jogged to the car. My dad was watching me with an unreadable expression on his face. Climbing in, I worked on the seat belt. As it locked into place, my dad pulled out.

"Hey Dad," I said.

"Hey," he replied. "You guys have fun?"

"Yeah, it was cool getting to see him outside of school, even if it was only barely outside." I smiled at my dad. He smiled back.

"Sorry to cut it short, but I thought you'd want to come talk to Katie. She woke up this morning, but the cops wanted to interview her before they let anyone visit."

"The cops have been there already?"

"All morning, yeah."

"Did you hear anything?"

"No, they had the room all locked up. Just the two officers, Katie, and Anna."

"Anna?" I asked.

"Katie's mother." I bit back another irrational surge of anger at the reminder that my father had been spending time with this woman. She really was a nice woman, I reminded myself.

"Oh, right," I replied. "Chance thinks this will be a great chance to learn more about the killer."

"Probably will be," he replied. I had to smile. He was definitely keeping open. I appreciated that.

"Do you think it would be inappropriate of me to ask her questions about it?" I glanced over at him. He looked back for a moment, then back at the road.

"No, just try not to pry if she starts looking upset by it, okay? She's had a rough time of it lately, she sure doesn't need someone pushing any more than the cops already have."

"Got it," I replied. He had a good point. She'd already been over everything with the police once.

"Anna asked about you," he told me, "she was pretty excited when I told her I was going to pick you up to come see Katie."

"Really?"

"Yeah, she really thinks highly of you."

"She thinks I saved her daughter's life, of course she does," I replied.

"Didn't you?" he asked, looking back down at

me again.

"I guess so," I shrugged. "I just had to help if I could. I didn't even know it was real at the time. The dream was so vivid that I called 911 in a panic as soon as I woke up. I'm just glad she's okay."

"Thanks to you," he replied. "You're going to have to give Anna some leeway there, no way she isn't going to be a bit taken with you. Besides, you were so polite to her last time, it only reaffirmed her belief that you're a saint."

"Ugh," I replied. My dad laughed.

"Don't worry Ryan, just let her be fond of you. Nothing wrong with that."

"Yeah, I guess not. She's nice." We were quiet for a while as I thought. After a time, I spoke up, deciding to open up to him a bit more.

"Dad?"

"Hmm?"

"Do you think people choose to be gay?" He paused a long time before answering.

"No, Ryan. I don't think so," he told me. "I don't know exactly how it works, but I know straight people don't choose to be straight. I didn't. Why would it be different for anyone else? I think maybe it's partly genetics. Maybe partly circumstance. But I don't think anyone really consciously decides to be gay."

"Can it change?"

"Maybe," he answered, "if someone gets abused or hurt badly by someone they care about, it can sometimes make it hard for them to be with another person that reminds them of that person. I'm not sure that's entirely the same thing though. I don't know, I'm not an expert."

"I don't think anyone is," I answered. He laughed.

"I think you're dead on with that one. People love theories, but in the end there are so many variables that you can't make a single rule for every case. It just doesn't always apply. Every person is different, every person's attractions are different, every person's situation is different. It's important to remember that."

"Is it bad to be gay?"

"You're awfully focused on this," he said.

"Being around Chance has really made me try to look at things from his perspective. He's had it pretty rough. His mom is distant, his dad won't talk to him at all. He has no friends at school, even the teachers avoid talking to him. It's sad. They treat him like he's got some contagious disease. It's not fair."

"No, that's not fair," he agreed, "a lot of things in life aren't. I don't think being gay is bad, though. Love is love. Besides, if nobody is being hurt and everyone involved is consenting, why is it anyone else's business in the first place?"

"That's what I want to know," I agreed. "Why does everyone care so much? I mean, unless someone is actually in a relationship with you or is hitting on you or something, their interests don't affect other people at all. It affects me that Chance is gay only because he admitted that he likes me. Same with Jennifer." My dad looked over at me again.

"Jennifer likes you?"

"Yeah,"

"Did she say so?"

"Not in those words, but she asked me to the dance on Saturday. She broke up with Noah."

"Well that's interesting," he said.

"I thought so."

"Did you say yes?"

"I couldn't. She's nice and all, but her church is creepy. And she just broke up with someone who might possibly be a homicidal maniac."

"Good point. Probably safer to avoid that altogether."

"That's what I said. I'm going to go with Chance." My dad paused a moment.

"Like a date?" he asked. I laughed.

"That's what Chance said! No, not a date. Just friends. Two guys going stag to the dance," I reassured him.

"That's cool," he said with a nod. "Just so you know though, I'm fine with it even if it was a date."

"Good, then you won't mind giving me a lift to the dance," I said with a grin. He laughed.

"I can manage that, I think. What time?"

"I don't know, I'll have to check. I just found

out about the dance when Jennifer asked me."

"Okay. Just let me know. Hey, is it okay if I come in with you while you talk to Katie? I'd like to hear what she has to say."

"Sure Dad," I replied. I was pretty eager to hear what she had to say as well.

"So Jennifer likes you?" he asked, switching back to a previous subject abruptly. I looked his way.

"Yeah," I replied, waiting.

"And Chance likes you?"

"Yeah," I said again.

"Has Chance ever tried to… you know, put the moves on you?"

I laughed at his choice of words, but inside my mind immediately went to the very close call we'd just had. I hated to admit it, but Chance had been the one to pull back on that one, not me. It raised some very uncomfortable questions in my mind. Questions I didn't really intend to share with my dad.

"Not really. He jokes about it a bit, but he's never tried anything." Again, I felt suddenly disappointed by that. I shook the feeling off.

"What would you do if he did?" he asked.

"Are you asking me if I'm gay again?" I asked him directly. He shrugged.

"Sort of. I mean, you already said you weren't, you just seem really interested in the subject."

"I told you, being around Chance makes me see a lot of it through his eyes. It's been really hard for him, not having anyone to connect with even just on a friends level. The hicks out here are death on anything outside their creepy little Christian norm."

"Christians aren't creepy," my dad said, giving me a sidelong glance.

"Not all of them, sure. The ones out here sure are though," I replied. My father didn't respond to that last comment, instead focusing on pushing his point that little bit further.

"I just want to make sure that you understand that the people out here you have had experiences with isn't symptomatic of Christianity as a whole. I've known some very nice Christians who were just great people all around. Of course they don't go to the church your school mates all seem to attend, so maybe that has something to do with it.

"A lot of the time someone with authority just slips into the right position and uses a lot of natural charisma to slowly poison the people around them. You can't just jump in and start spouting that kind of hate though, it takes years to ease people up to it. Like the frog in the pot," he said.

"The what?" I asked, curious.

"The frog. You know, the old story about if you drop a frog in a pot of boiling water he'll jump right out, but if you put him in a pot of lukewarm water and slowly heat it, he'll sit in there until he cooks. Hate is a lot like that. It sneaks into you in a lot of tiny little unnoticed ways, slowly building on itself until one day, before you know it, you're spouting the same kind of hateful garbage that you yourself condemned just a few years before. I'd bet that if they got rid of that preacher, things around there would calm down a lot over the next several years."

I thought about that. It made sense, really. Most things were like that. They seemed drastic if someone jumped right into the deep end with it, but if something was eased into your life, your thoughts, it could gradually take over. It would explain a lot about the people around here.

Poor Jennifer was probably raised in that church, giving her constant bombardment of that from the time she was really little. Come to think of it, it was remarkable she was as nice as she was at all, with that kind of garbage being fed to her from birth.

I was convinced that hatred wasn't a natural state. After that sermon, I was more convinced than ever. People are naturally a bit selfish, it's built into our survival mechanism, but they weren't naturally hateful. That has to be taught. Unfortunately there were a lot of people teaching it.

"Yeah, that makes sense," I told him. He nodded. "Good and bad in every group, right?"

"Exactly. On the other side of things, not everybody who is gay is a nice person wanting only to be allowed to love who they love. People each have to be taken on their own merits. Being Christian doesn't make you a good or bad person. Neither does being gay. The only thing that makes you a bad person is seeking to do harm to others. I think it's really that simple." He looked down at me to be sure I was paying attention. I nodded thoughtfully. He smiled, satisfied he'd gotten his point across. After a moment, I sighed.

"I just wish people would quit looking for reasons to suck." My dad broke into startled laughter.

"A bit more crass a way to put it than I'd have chosen, but I get what you mean. Hatred and love are unique in the world, in that they're the only two things you'll always get back more of than you give away. Funny how many people seem to choose the hatred." I wished I could argue with that, but I couldn't.

"Hey, can we stop in the gift shop and get Katie something?" I asked on impulse. My dad smiled.

"Sure, Ryan. Whatever you like." I sat back, lost in thought until we pulled into the hospital parking lot. He left me alone to my thoughts. Naturally, they were of Chance.

Chapter Nineteen

Half Answers

We made it up to her room after a brief stop at the gift shop. The same nice lady from before let us right through with a smile for my dad, and a wink for me.

The door was open, so we walked straight in, though my dad knocked on the door lightly as we passed through. There was a curtain drawn partially across the entryway, but I could see Katie's mom.

"Mark!" she exclaimed as she saw my dad walk through the door. She stood and moved over to him, giving him a quick hug. I bit my tongue, but was a little relieved that it seemed to be just a casually friendly hug.

"Hello Anna. How is she?" my dad asked her.

"A bit tired, but she's okay. Doing great, thank God." She looked down to me then and gave me another huge smile. She leaned over and hugged me as well, though not with the same bosom-smashing intensity she'd used the last time. She did lean down and kiss my cheek though. Weird that her hugging my father bugged me, but her kissing me didn't. It was nice, very comfortable.

"Hi," I said with a smile.

"Definitely good to see you. Katie's tired from talking with the officers this morning, but she made me promise to let her talk to you when you came," she told me.

"I won't keep her too long," I promised. "I did want to ask her what happened though. Is that okay?"

"I don't think I could stop her from telling you. Come on Ryan, she's excited to see you." Anna pulled the curtain back and ushered us in. Katie sat in the bed, looking pretty rough, but with a big smile on her face as she saw me.

"Hi Katie," I told her, suddenly feeling very awkward. I'd only ever even seen this girl once before, while she was conscious at least, and she'd run off within moments of my arrival.

"Hi," she rasped. She sounded worse than she looked. Her short hanging must have damaged her vocal cords too, I thought. Hopefully not permanently. I looked back at my dad, who gestured me forward. I moved to the chair by her bed and sat down.

"I'm glad you're doing better," I told her, feeling very lame. She smiled though.

"Thanks to you," she rasped. Funny, she sounded a lot like her mother when she said that. Not in voice of course, but definitely in tone. I looked away, embarrassed.

"It's okay," I said. Chance flashed through my mind. I had a job to do. I looked back at her. "Listen Katie, I did have some questions though. Is it okay if I ask you about the attack?" She nodded. "Cool. I'll try to keep it yes or no, so you don't have to talk too much, okay?" She smiled gratefully.

"It was an attack," I stated, more than asked. Katie nodded. "You did not attempt suicide." She shook her head sharply, then winced. I winced with her. I thought for a moment about how I wanted to approach this.

"Do you know who it was?" I asked. She shook her head more gently. That narrowed things a bit. She'd know most people around here. I was sure she'd recognize Noah or Reverend Porter. I frowned.

"Can you describe the person? A man?" She nodded. "Adult?" She nodded again. "Heavy set?" Katie hesitated.

"Hard to tell. He wore a robe," she said after a moment. It sounded painful. I held firm and didn't wince. I didn't want her to think I was pitying her or anything. I remembered people doing that with my mom. Used to drive her crazy. She never said so, but I could see it.

"And his face?" She shivered suddenly.

"The devil," she rasped. A cold chill crept along my spine as well.

"What?" I asked.

"He wore a mask," she clarified, "looked like the devil." Well that was interesting. In my dreams, the devil wore a human mask. It seemed that in reality, the human wore a devil mask. That certainly reinforced my theory of it being Reverend Porter. He struck me as the type to just love the irony of dressing up like the devil to go and send people to Hell.

"Hair?" I asked. She shook her head.

"He had a hood," she explained.

"Boots?" I guessed. She nodded. Figures. "Brown ones?" She shook her head. "Black?" She nodded. Well, that was something anyway.

"Did he talk?" She nodded. "Did he sound local?" She nodded again. "Accent and all?" She nodded. Good, that supported Reverend Porter too. And most of the rest of town, I had to remind myself. "What did he say?"

"He said I was going to Hell for my sins, and that God's justice was my reward for my evil," she got out. I gave her an apologetic look for the long answer that one needed, but she smiled her encouragement and reassurance. It really was just like my dream. The devil strung her up, condemned her for her sins, and tried to hang her.

"Was there anything that might have given you a clue who it was?" I asked, feeling almost desperate. We didn't really have much to go on, though I felt vindicated that I had been right all along. I was thrilled my dad was behind me hearing all of this. It had to give me a sizeable dose of credibility in his eyes. She shook her head sadly.

"I was scared," she said simply. I nodded.

"That's cool, I understand. Don't worry about it. They'll catch him, and until then, you've got a lot of people here looking out for you. You've got nothing to worry about," I reassured her. She looked up at me, worry on her soft features.

She was pretty too, I thought. A different kind of pretty than Jennifer. It was softer, less intense, though definitely still pretty. After a moment I admitted to myself that I wasn't attracted to Katie either. Probably a good thing, since Katie was gay anyway. I still wasn't building a good argument for my actually being straight though. Pretty bad when you're having trouble convincing yourself, I mentally grumbled.

"I'm worried about you," Katie said, surprising me out of my thoughts.

"Me? Why?" I asked, genuinely surprised. Katie took a deep, shaky breath. This was going to be a long one. I braced myself so I wouldn't show how much I felt for her being in pain.

"I heard Noah telling his buddies that there was a special place in Hell for you, that you had something special coming because you were a special kind of sinner," she told me, then coughed. I handed her the glass of water on the table beside me. She drank and nodded her thanks.

"What the Hell does that mean?" I asked, annoyed. I wasn't gay, I wasn't a devil-worshipper, what special kind of sins was I committing?

"Because you talk to… to your friend." She said, glancing away.

What was that about, I wondered? Katie was gay too, what did she have against Chance? This definitely told me there was something else, something darker, that Chance wasn't sharing with me. Something to make even his fellow oppressed turn against him.

"Chance? He's gay, I'm not. What's my being friends with Chance got to do with anything?"

"You shouldn't talk to him, Ryan," she rasped. Her voice was getting worse. I realized I was overworking it. I was torn between concern for her and anger that she was against Chance too.

"I wish I knew what everyone's deal with him was," I said. She opened her mouth, but I interrupted her. "Don't tell me, I don't actually want to hear it. He's a good friend, whatever anyone else might think." She was quiet a moment, regarding me, then nodded.

"I'm sorry. He's your friend, and that should be all anyone cares about," she said. Finally, I thought.

"Thanks," I told her sincerely. She nodded.

"Ryan?" my dad interrupted. I looked back at him. "I'm going to step outside with Anna for a moment, I wanted to talk with her about something. Are you good here for a minute?" he asked.

"Yeah," I said, though I wasn't sure what I'd do with Katie while he was gone. I couldn't exactly have a real conversation with her in this state. The two adults stepped out and I turned back to Katie.

"You know why Noah…" she started, but broke into coughing again. I handed her the water again.

"Hold on," I told her, and began digging through the drawers on the end table. Luckily, I found what I wanted. "Here," I said, handing her the notepad and pen. She smiled brightly and scribbled quickly on the first line. She showed it to me.

"Brilliant!" she'd written.

"Thank you, I have my moments." I smiled at her. She was writing again.

"You know why Noah tried to hurt me?" she asked.

"Yeah," I answered. "That dude has a real thing against gay people." She nodded and began writing again.

"Does it bother you that I'm gay?" she asked.

"No," I replied honestly. "Should it?" She shook her head. "Doesn't bother me at all. After all, that's one less girl I have to fend off." I gave her a playful smile. She started to laugh, but winced. I winced too. "Sorry," I said sheepishly.

"My fault," she wrote. *"Thanks for helping me. Both times. I shouldn't have run away the first time."*

"You definitely should have run," I corrected her, "those guys were determined to hurt anyone around. They'd have gone back to you after they were done with me if you'd stuck around. You couldn't have helped."

"You did," she replied.

"Yeah," I said, "stupid huh?" She shook her head and wrote some more.

"Brave. Noble. Good."

"You're starting to sound like your mother," I laughed. Katie grinned.

"Thank you, she's a great lady."

"She does seem pretty cool," I admitted.

"I think she likes your dad. A lot." I hesitated before answering this one.

"I think so too. I think my dad likes her too." I looked down. Katie was quiet a moment again before writing.

"You're not cool with that." It was a statement, not a question. I sighed.

"Can I trust you?" I asked. She crossed her heart and held her two fingers up.

"I just lost my mom a year ago." Katie's expression fell. She went to write but I stopped her. "Don't say you're sorry. I get so sick of hearing that." She nodded but started writing again anyway.

"That sucks. You're thinking if your dad likes another woman, it'd be like cheating on her." I thought about that.

"Kind of, yeah. I mean, he should still love my mom. He shouldn't be looking somewhere else."

"Do you think his loving someone else takes away from

his love for your mom?"

"You can't love more than one person like that," I replied. "You shouldn't."

"You'd rather he stayed lonely?"

"I didn't say that!" I protested. "Besides, he shouldn't be lonely, he has me!"

"Would you be lonely without Chance?"

"Yeah, he's my best friend," I answered, then saw where she was going with that. I waited for her to write it though.

"Your dad can't be everyone for you, and you can't be everyone for him. He loves you, and I'm sure he still loves your mom as much as he ever did. But he's lonely. He needs more than just you can give him. If he wants to date again, you should let him."

"It's only been a year though!" I argued.

"When's the deadline?" she asked. I stopped and thought about that. She had a point.

"I don't know," I replied honestly, "it just feels too soon."

"For you," she answered. *"He's ready and needs to move on. You can grieve as long as you need to. Let him grieve as long as he needs to."*

"Okay, knock it off," I told her half-heartedly. "You're starting to sound smarter than me. I'm going to develop a complex." She cough-laughed again. I winced. "Sorry. You're right though. I need to let him move on when he needs to." I sighed. "It's just hard for me. Could be worse though. At least your mom is cool." Katie nodded. She paused a moment, then wrote again.

"Do you like Chance?"

"Sure, he's my best friend." She took the pad and drew one single, dark line.

"Do you like Chance?"

"No, I'm not gay," I said, sounding a bit overly defensive even to my own ears.

"Do you like Jennifer?"

"No," I answered, "she's pretty, but her whole church thing freaks me out. She asked me to the dance though." Katie grimaced.

"Jerk." Katie wrote.

"Why?" I asked, surprised.

"I like Jennifer," she replied.

"Seriously?" I asked, genuinely surprised. Katie nodded. "Well, like I said, she's pretty. It would never work out between you though, seeing as her God apparently hates you. And me, for whatever reason." Katie nodded again.

"I know, but knowing it won't work doesn't stop me from wishing."

"She's your first crush, huh?" I asked, though I was pretty sure I knew the answer. Katie nodded. "First one's tough, I hear," I told her.

"No crushes?" she asked, raising a brow.

"Not really," I said, but noted with concern that Chance's face had come up when she'd asked about my crushes.

"Sad," she replied simply. I shrugged.

"Too much going on for crushes, I have a mystery to solve," I said with a half-smile.

"Like the Hardy Boys," she joked. I laughed.

"Exactly!" She smiled, and our parents walked back in.

"Hey Ryan, I have to get back to my shift," my dad said. "Can you maybe stay here with Anna and Katie?" I glanced at Katie and her mom. They both smiled at me.

"Sure Dad," I replied, "it'll give me a chance to get to know them better."

"I have cards," Katie's mom said, "we'll talk and play the afternoon away. Careful though, Katie cheats." Katie made a face at her mom. My dad laughed and nodded, then ducked out the door.

"We can get some food sent up from the cafeteria downstairs," she said to me. I nodded, though I wasn't all that hungry. I was already thinking about getting back to Chance in the morning to tell him what I'd learned. I shuffled my feet and kicked the small bag we'd brought up from the gift shop. I'd totally forgotten about it.

"Oh hey, my dad and I got this for you," I told her, lifting the bag up into her lap. "Just to keep you smiling while you get better," I said, though I felt a bit foolish as soon as it was out of my mouth.

She reached into the bag and pulled out the small white bear. It had the hospital logo on the chest.

Lame, but it was the cuddliest thing in the tiny shop.

Katie's face lit up though. She reached over and grabbed me, pulling me into a hug. Gently, she kissed my cheek. Must be a family thing, I thought with a laugh.

"Come on now!" I protested laughingly. "It's not that great!" Katie settled the bear comfortably into her lap and smiled at me. Katie's mom did too. I felt distinctly awkward. "You said something about cards?" I asked, desperate to get the attention off of me. Katie's mom laughed and dug into her purse.

Maybe Chance would get more out of the few clues Katie gave me than I could find in them. I'd have to wait until tomorrow to find out. I couldn't wait to see Chance to tell him what I'd learned though.

I was kidding myself, I abruptly realized. I just couldn't wait until tomorrow to see Chance. With a sigh, I turned to the cards Katie's mom was dealing. This was going to be problematic.

Chapter Twenty
Begins and Ends With Sleep

Pain and heat. Pain from the bruise on my forehead that I was sure was just developing. Pain from the fire that was slowly, but tangibly, rising all around. Locked in the steel prison, burning alive as I peered through the tiny glass window of the oven I now recognized all too well, screaming noiselessly for someone to help me.

No one would help me. The devil was outside again, his smiling human mask a mockery to the species. The horns still protruded from the mask's forehead. The fierce, yellow eyes seemed to burn into me, their glee at my anguish evident. The mask had changed again. It looked melted, deformed.

The features were impossible to identify, as if it were made of rubber once more, but had been exposed to just a little too much heat. Heat from the fires around me or heat from the devil I didn't know. I could see blood lining the drooping edges of the mask, the forked tongue darting between melted lips. Parts of the mask were sagging so much that the devil's face was starting to become visible.

I almost felt like I recognized the face of the devil itself, but as quickly as it had appeared, the horrible face was gone. Moments later, a new face appeared.

The heat was rising. I was still screaming, but I couldn't even hear myself anymore. Everything was silent. I pounded on the door, but no noise came back to me. Even the flames licking all around brought nothing to dispel the cacophonous silence. As the new face appeared, time seemed to slow. I shouted my pleas for help.

The new face drew close. This face was crystal clear, no halo of light, no traces of the wispy iridescent light around it. He looked solid and real. I knew without doubt, it was Chance's face. Hope leapt in my chest. As Chance's face stopped just before the window, it spoke. I couldn't hear the words. I couldn't hear anything. But I knew what the voice said, I heard it clearly in my mind.

"I'm sorry, Ryan. I can't help you," is what it said. The voice in my mind belonged to Chance. For the briefest of instants, his impossibly deep brown eyes glistened clearly with unshed tears from the otherwise calm face. Then he started laughing. He laughed, with an almost manic enthusiasm.

Then the claws came, breaking through the form in my window as though my regretful visitor was made of nothing more substantial than smoke in a breeze, swirling for a moment before it broke apart and was gone.

The devil wearing the melted face reappeared. He was laughing. I couldn't hear it. I could feel it, grating against my bones as the flames consumed the tattered remains of my flesh. I silently screamed again, and the dream broke.

I sat bolt upright in bed, sweat stinging my eyes. Damn it, I was getting really sick of that. I let out a sharp breath in frustration, trying to clear my mind. I swear that dream is getting more intense, I thought to myself.

I glanced at the clock. It was later than it felt like. Only another hour or so before I was going to have to get up for school anyway. I sighed. No chance of going back to sleep before then, I might as well just get up.

My inner monologue grumbled in annoyance as I stood from the covers, shivering only slightly in the cool, though not cold, air of the bedroom. I'd cracked my window slightly, the weather having been a bit warmer the night before. I was regretting it now though.

I snuck to the window, certain that the killer would be just outside. I'd lowered the blinds this time, in the whole house in fact, to prevent our recurring prowler from spying. I leaned to one side of the window and pulled the blinds back just slightly.

Sure enough, the truck was just pulling away. I tried to keep my teeth from chattering, and not from the cold. Whoever it was, I was starting to think his presence was causing the nightmares.

Who the hell was that, and why did he just snoop around? Why didn't he come in and get it over with? Why didn't he bust in the window or a door and just come at us. My dad would fight. He wasn't as helpless as the middle-schoolers the killer preferred to pick on. Maybe he'd even win. Maybe.

Turning away from the window I considered waking my father but decided against it. I'd tell him in the morning. Nothing could be done now anyway except call in Officer Friendly, the most useless cop on the force. For all I knew, that guy was cooperating with the killer. They probably went to church together. Bunch of sick bastards.

Crossing the hallway to the bathroom, I started the shower running, then stepped in front of the mirror. For the briefest of instants, my face in the mirror looked like the unidentified one in my first few dreams had, luminescent and trailing wispy fragments of vaporous light.

I caught myself before the full shout I wanted to make escaped, though I was annoyed with myself for the distinctly un-manly yelp that made it through my lips.

I looked back at the mirror. I looked normal. Or as normal as a person who had just awakened from yet another bad nightmare could. My skin was pale, my cheeks flushed, my eyes sagged, and I was covered in sweat. My hair was plastered to my forehead and cheeks. I'd probably been thrashing around a bit in my sleep, I realized.

Reminding myself that dreams were just electrical impulses in my brain didn't help. It got more real every time. I was afraid this one actually was real, I just didn't have all the details right.

If it were real though, it meant the killer was going to lock me in the school cafeteria oven and roast me alive just like poor Dominic had been two years before. I caught myself wondering if being hanged to death in a closet would be worse, or roasting in the oven. I had to admit that hanging probably hurt less, though I'd heard death by suffocation was terrible too.

Shaking my head to clear it of the morbid thoughts, I turned toward the shower. The water was steaming, it had at least warmed up fairly quickly this time to my relief. I dropped my boxers and stepped into the tub, pulling the curtain around behind me.

The hot water felt perfect, warming my body and my mind, rinsing off the sweat and the chill. I wasn't sure what I was going to do. I was convinced the dream was prophetic, but it still didn't tell me who was going to try and kill me or when, or why Chance couldn't help me.

Maybe it was symbolic, I thought. Maybe Chance wanted to help, but for whatever reason wasn't there when this happened. Not likely, that kid seemed to spend more time at the school than at home, and I couldn't imagine being at school without Chance there.

Could be that he'd been knocked unconscious or something and wasn't able to do anything to help. Or had been tied up and couldn't reach the door to let me out. It was possible he'd already been killed by that point, but I refused to consider the possibility. If I died it would more than suck, but I'd trade my own life in a heartbeat to save Chance. I hoped he knew that. The crazy punk would probably try to sacrifice his own to save mine too, I thought.

I shoved the memories of his manic laughter in my dream, and of his standing by while Noah and his minions roughed me up out of my mind. That wouldn't happened again, I told myself. He was just scared. If my life were really in danger, he'd do anything to help me.

Stepping out of the shower, I toweled off quickly, heading back across the hall to my room and got ready for school.

My dad took the news about like I expected.

"Ryan, why didn't you wake me?" he asked, sounding frustrated and concerned. His eyes were on the road as we drove to my school.

"It wouldn't have helped," I told him, "You'd only have been able to call the cops, they'd have sent that same useless jerk they sent last time, we'd end up late for school and work, and nothing would be done. This way you got an extra hour of sleep."

"You're probably right, but I still wish you'd come in to wake me up. This is getting out of hand, Ryan. We need to sort this out one way or another. I think tomorrow I'll get some new locks from the store on the way to pick you up too, just in case. I wonder if this town has a security system monitoring facility. I should get something installed."

"Don't get too carried away," I told him. I didn't want to point out that if things happened similarly to how they did in my dream, I wasn't in danger at home, just at school. If I told him that, he might not let me go to school now that he believed that I was actually in danger.

"Just trying to take care of my own. You be sure to go straight to Principal Avery if anything suspicious happens, okay? Then call me."

"Sure thing, Dad," I replied with a reassuring smile. We were quiet the rest of the drive. Chance was waiting on the low wall out front when we pulled up. He grinned as he saw me. I couldn't help but return the smile, though an image of him laughing as I burned to death tried to push to the front of my mind. I shoved it back again.

"Have a good day," my dad said as I climbed

out of the car.

"You too. I'll help you set up the new locks tonight," I told him. He smiled.

"Thanks, I'd appreciate that," he said. I nodded and shut the door, turning to Chance as my father pulled away from the curb.

"Hey bud," I told him as I approached. He grinned again.

"So?" he asked.

"So what?" I retorted.

"What did she say?" he asked in dramatic exasperation. I laughed.

"Not much, I'm afraid. I was right, someone did try to kill her. It wasn't suicide."

"I knew that already," he replied. "What did the killer look like?"

"Like the devil."

"What?"

"He was wearing a devil mask and a heavy black robe with a hood. She couldn't even really identify his size right, let alone any features we could identify him with."

"Damn," Chance said in irritation. I nodded and started heading for the school. Chance fell into step beside me.

"Yeah. He said pretty much the same stuff he said in my dream too, all that 'God hates you' bull. What a crock. I'm pretty sure if God hates anything, it's self-righteous, prejudiced assholes."

"Right?" Chance laughed. "Seriously, how they can go on about an all-loving God and in the same breath say he hates anyone I'll never know."

"Me neither. I gave up trying to understand it. I don't understand religion to begin with, but that's just over-the-top insane."

We entered the school, actively ignored by almost everyone. The overhead lights flickered faintly. I gave them a scowl. "Are they ever going to fix those lights? Every hallway in the building, the library, and the cafeteria? They need to just rewire the buildings. At least the classrooms don't do that."

"This town is too cheap to approve anything that drastic. Like you said, they probably won't lift a finger to fix it until something shorts out and the school burns down," Chance said, looking up at the flickering lights.

"Well that's reassuring," I said drily. Chance laughed lightly.

"Don't worry, I'd rescue you," he said with a wink. "If I were lucky, you'd need mouth to mouth."

"Okay, perv boy," I glared playfully at him, "try any nonsense like that and I'll kick your teeth in."

"Sure, just like yesterday?" he retorted. I shoved him lightly. He laughed again. I made it most of the way across the entry hall when I noticed the whispers. I always heard whispers when I was in this dump, Chance and I were apparently good gossip, but this was different.

It sounded more hostile, more aggressive. I listened a bit more closely and heard several unpleasant euphemisms for homosexuals used more than once, though I couldn't, or didn't want to, hear the full comments. Chance noticed my attention and frowned.

"Just ignore it, Ryan," Chance said softly.

I was angry. I intended to ignore it though. My picking more fights wasn't going to help me with anything. I wouldn't leave it completely alone. My social life was already shot, so I knew I had nothing at all to lose. I reached over and took Chance's hand in mine. I noticed several sets of eyes glance down at the movement, then quickly away.

"Jerks," I muttered. I glanced at Chance when he didn't reply. He was looking down at our hands curiously, with a definite tinge of surprise on his face. He looked back up at me questioningly. "Something to talk about," I said quietly to him.

"That's cool," he said as casually as he could, though I could hear the slight waver in his voice, and could feel the way he held my hand. He was having another emotionally sensitive moment. I squeezed his hand reassuringly and kept walking toward my class.

We were given a pretty wide berth as we walked. I made it to my class door and looked over at Chance again. We hadn't spoken again since the entry hall.

"This is my stop. I'll catch you at lunch

though, okay?" I told him.

"Ryan?" he asked. He was obviously going to say something hard for him. I waited, giving him time. "Thanks. For standing up for me, I mean. Nobody has ever really stood up for me. Even my parents never stood up for me."

"Don't worry about it," I told him casually, "that's what friends are for, right? We help each other out."

I couldn't help but feel that I was trying to both reassure myself and remind him that when the time came, he needed to help me if he could. I hoped he could.

He nodded, but didn't reply. I was afraid he would cry if I made him talk about it more, and class would start any minute so I let him off the hook. "Class time. I'll see you at lunch."

I could feel his eyes on me the whole way to my seat, but he was gone by the time I sat and looked back at the doorway.

The professor wasn't there as I looked around, but Noah was. He had stood up and walked toward me while I was looking back at the doorway. He shoved me hard, knocking me completely out of my seat and onto the floor. I half expected the class to laugh, but they didn't. It was very quiet.

I scrambled to my feet as fast as I could, and glared at him. He stepped over my chair toward me, a vicious smile on his face.

"Hey fag," he said coldly.

"Classy," I replied.

"Just callin' it like I see it," he shrugged as if it weren't of any importance. "I heard you an' yer devil boyfriend were havin' a bit of fun on th' schoolyard yesterday. I told you consortin' with th' devil is a sin, right?" Figures, Jennifer told him about me wrestling around with Chance.

"Pretty sure that only counts if you're actually 'consorting' with the devil. There's no consorting going on, though frankly he'd be a better choice than any of the loonies around this place," I said. Noah's expression darkened.

"What are you sayin' 'bout my girlfriend?" he said threateningly.

"I thought she dumped you," I replied. He lurched forward. I flinched back, and he laughed.

"Not a chance. She's mine, an' always will be."

"Yeah, that doesn't sound creepy at all," I retorted. I was apparently feeling brave, I thought. Or suicidal.

"Listen homo, my father says that sinners like you," he started to say as he leaned in menacingly.

"Your father," I interrupted, "is a complete frickin' psycho." Suicidal was apparently the better description for my feelings that morning.

I didn't even see it coming. Noah's fist caught me square on the temple. I caught a glimpse of the other students as I dropped, my vision darkening rapidly. Their expressions, to my surprise, were horrified, not amused or excited. There was hope for this town yet, I thought before everything finished going black. I don't remember hitting the floor.

Chapter Twenty One
Another Suspension

The first thing I felt when I started to regain consciousness was the headache. I felt like I'd been hit by a truck. I didn't appreciate the painful reminder that I'd gotten really lucky the first time I'd gone toe to toe with Noah. As much as I hated to admit it, I realized that chances were his own goons had probably saved me from a much more serious beating last time.

The second thing I felt was the ice pack pressed firmly against the side of my face, and the sting of it contacting the point of impact. I winced as the pain hit me fully hand in hand with my full consciousness. I may have groaned, though I wasn't sure, because suddenly I felt people's attention on me.

Voices spoke, though I couldn't quite identify either the speaker or the words themselves. Could have been Greek for all I could tell. Very slowly, they began to coalesce into something resembling understandable.

"Ryan? Ryan, talk to me buddy. Hey, Ryan. You okay?" the first voice coaxed.

"Give him a moment, Mr. Jacobs, he may have a concussion," the second voice said, though not harshly. Great. A concussion. Well there went the rest of my already manly reputation. I'd been dropped like a sack of rice with one shot, and now might have a concussion.

"I know, I know. I just have to make sure he's okay."

"I understand that, Mr. Jacobs. Just give him a moment."

"I'm fine Dad," I said carefully, and instantly regretted it. It made my skull ache.

"Ryan?" he asked.

"I said I'm fine," I said as I opened my eyes. I was getting irritated, though not with my dad. I was angry with myself for letting Noah slip one by me like that; angry with myself for provoking someone I knew was violent. I'd foolishly thought a classroom full of witnesses would be enough deterrent, but clearly that hadn't been the case. I moved to sit.

"Not yet," the second voice said.

I turned my gaze toward that second voice. As my eyes adjusted, I could see it was a large woman in a white coat. She looked like a doctor, though glancing around I could see out the window in the small white room that I was still at school.

The school nurse, I assumed. I hadn't even

realized this school had one. The way things had been going, I was on a guaranteed course to learn this little fact sooner than later though. My dad moved in front of my gaze, looking closely at me.

"Ryan, how's your vision? Is everything clear, or is it a little blurry?"

"Shouldn't you leave the medical diagnosis to the professionals?" I asked, though I gave him a small smile to let him know I was teasing. "You're not a doctor. Not even a nurse." He gave me a small smile, but I could tell he was still very concerned.

"He's not, but I am," stated the large woman. She clearly took her role as the school nurse very seriously. She clicked on a small pen light and shone it in my eye, using her other hand to pry up my eyelid. I tried to pull back, but she was having none of it. She moved to the other eye.

"Any dizziness?"

"No, ma'am," I replied.

"Nausea?"

"No, ma'am."

"Are you sleepy?"

"Not really."

"Ringing in your ears?"

"No."

"Well he doesn't show any initial signs of concussion," she said, leaning back, "but keep an eye on him for the next few days. And I wouldn't let him go to sleep at least until late this evening."

That seemed like a pretty quick diagnosis to me, but my father didn't say anything so I didn't either. I wondered where she'd gotten her degree.

"Can you stand?" my dad asked. I nodded, taking over holding the ice pack from him. I moved to stand, slowly and carefully, just in case. I felt okay though, aside from the headache. No dizziness or balance issues when I made it to my feet. My dad was looking at me questioningly. I gave him a reassuring smile. "Okay Ryan, let's go home."

"What? No!" I protested. "I've missed half the days of school at least since we moved here!"

"Well, it's been a rough month."

"It's been a rough year, but we keep going. Seriously dad, I don't want to go home. I want to stay at school."

In truth, I just didn't want to miss more time with Chance. I didn't much care about anything else anymore. He was all I really had. As I looked into my dad's concerned eyes, I mentally corrected myself. He and my dad were all I had.

"I don't know Ryan, you got knocked unconscious…" he started.

"Don't remind me," I interrupted. "I'm falling behind in my classes as it is though. My education is suffering, along with my attendance record," I joked. "You don't want that, do you?" I hoped he understood my meaning. I was a bit concerned with my grades at this point, but we both knew there were more important things going on. My dad looked uncertain, but glanced at the nurse. She shrugged.

"It's up to you, Mr. Jacobs. The teachers in his classes can be notified to keep an eye on him for you and we can call you right away if there are any changes, but if you're more comfortable taking him home, by all means." He looked back at me, sighed and nodded.

"Okay Spo- Ryan," he corrected. He hadn't slipped like that for a while. I really had worried him.

I was a little surprised that I felt bad about that, though I guess I shouldn't have been. We'd been opening up a lot more lately, connecting better. I really didn't want to worry him any more than I had to. Some worry was built into having a teenage son though, I thought to myself, mentally quoting a TV commercial I'd caught once. I smiled at him.

"Thanks Dad. I promise we'll call you if I start feeling more than just the headache."

"You'd better," he told me as we walked out of the nurse's office.

"I'll be fine though, as long as I can keep clear of Noah."

"That'll be easy," my dad replied, "he got suspended." I stopped in my tracks.

"He... what?" I was stunned. Of course, he'd hit me in front of twenty witnesses, but I just sort of assumed that guys like that always got off clean.

"He got suspended," my dad replied with a small smile. "Principal Avery dragged him into the office before I got here. He was screaming at the kid for quite a long time. I'm kind of impressed."

"Me too," I said, slightly in awe. Turns out things did go right once in a great while. I started walking again, out into the office proper. Mrs. Bradley was there at her desk, as usual. Principal Avery's door was closed. I couldn't tell if he was in there or not. She looked up and gave me a sympathetic smile.

"Nice t' see you up an' about, Ryan," she said.

"Thanks," I replied. "Nice to be up and about." As we walked past I whispered to my dad, "Geez Dad, how long was I out?"

"Long enough for them to call me, have me get here, and listen to your principal educating your boxing partner."

"Ouch," I replied. He nodded.

We made it to the front doors of the school when he paused and turned to me. He gently pulled my icepack-wielding hand back from my face, and brushed my hair back from my temple. It was wet from the condensation, but he managed it without touching my face itself much. I appreciated the effort. He analyzed my temple for a moment, then nodded.

"Could have been worse. I think he caught you far enough back that you might not even get a black eye. Most of the bruising will probably be covered by your hair anyway. You should probably get a haircut soon," he told me. I rolled my eyes.

"Yeah, that's gonna happen," I retorted. He

grinned at me, patted my shoulder and turned to go. "Dad?" He paused and looked back. "Thanks. For coming, and for letting me stay." He smiled and nodded.

"You're welcome. Say hello to Chance for me," he said, his smile genuine. I returned it, very pleasantly surprised. After the start to my morning, my father's effort to extend a bit of friendliness Chance's way meant a lot to me. More than he probably understood.

I watched him drive away from the front window, then turned to go to class. Chance was right behind me. I jumped, made another less-than-manly sound, and almost dropped my ice pack. I shoved him back in annoyance.

"Damn it, Chance! Don't do that!" I scolded him, wondering if my probable mild concussion and the probable mild heart attack I'd just had would combine to cause complete system failure. He laughed, though I could tell he was worried.

"Sorry man," he said, sounding less than sincere. "Hey, are you okay? I couldn't go back and see you."

"Don't you have class?" I asked him. He shrugged.

"It doesn't matter. I heard what happened and came to wait for you."

"Dude, you're going to end up living in a cardboard box, flipping burgers for a living at this rate.

Aren't you worried about your GPA?"

"No, not really," he said. I was somewhat horrified to realize he meant that.

"What are you going to do with your life?" I asked, baffled.

"Well clearly you're okay," he replied sarcastically. I laughed lightly, wincing at the jarring sensation that went through my skull.

"Sorry Chance. I'm fine, thank you for your concern. No concussion, just a mild heart attack, thanks to some dumbass who likes to sneak up on people." He laughed.

"I said I was sorry."

"Uh huh. So what are you going to do with the rest of your life?" I asked again.

He'd gotten me genuinely curious. I didn't exactly have my whole life planned out, but my mother had made it very clear to me that maintaining good middle- and high school grades was critical to getting into a good school, which was a huge contributing factor to later professional success. Besides, I'd promised her I'd do my absolute best. I intended to. Chance shrugged.

"I don't know, I was thinking I'd find some brilliant, gorgeous, professionally successful sugar daddy. Say, what are you doing for the rest of your life?" he asked with a quirk to his smile and sparkle in his eye. I couldn't help but smile.

"Working hard for a living to support my

beautiful wife," I retorted.

"Supermodel, huh?" he asked.

"Damn right," I replied.

"She'll never love you the way I do," he quipped.

"That's okay. Whether she loves me for my huge bank account or my riveting good looks, it doesn't matter. She'll want me."

"Will you want her?" he asked, a bit more seriously. I paused a moment, considering how sarcastic to be with him. I caught the look in his eyes though, and decided to be honest.

"Nah," I replied, "she'd probably just want to spend all her time at the salon and out shopping, spending my hard-earned money."

"Well that's good. If it helps, I don't love you for your looks, either."

"Yeah, that's comforting. Well you can't love me for my money either, I've got less than twenty bucks in the ol' piggy bank."

"Twenty bucks more than I've got," Chance retorted.

He had a point. I felt guilty at the reminder of his obviously less wealthy position. We weren't rich by any means, but at least I had more than one change of clothes. It suddenly struck me that he'd been saying love a lot this conversation. I wasn't sure how I felt about that.

"Do you hear that?" he asked suddenly,

breaking me from that dangerous thought process.

"What?" I asked, straining to hear whatever it was he'd heard.

"I'm pretty sure that's the sound of your GPA falling below a C average…"

"Don't make me go all Noah on you," I laughed. He grinned.

"Sorry, I couldn't resist," he said, voice ripe with insincerity. "Seriously though, you should probably get to class. You miss a lot of those."

"You're one to talk. I really should go though, these stupid lights aren't helping my headache," I said glaring up at the flickering fluorescents, as if they stuttered intentionally to spite me. "What period is it?"

"Third."

"Man," I replied. "This is going to be a rough week."

"No it isn't, Noah's gone," he said with a triumphant smile.

"The killer may not be," I replied. Chance's smile slipped. He gave me a nod to show me he understood the subtle warning to keep his guard up. I reached out and squeezed his upper arm briefly, then turned away. I stopped and looked back at him.

"Oh hey, my dad said to tell you hello," I told him. Chance stared, obviously at a total loss for words. It took a long moment before he could find anything to say.

"He did? Like seriously?" he sounded like I'd

just told him I'd seen Elvis' ghost tap dancing on Mrs. Bradley's desk. I couldn't help but grin.

"Yeah, he did. See? People don't all suck. Later," I said as I turned away again.

The look on his face at that moment was one I'd never forget. It was full of astonishment, awe, wonder, and an almost desperate hope that filled me with sadness for him and whatever it was about this world that pressed down on him so brutally. Someday, he'd tell me what it was.

Chapter Twenty Two
The Closet

The week was a breeze, despite my warning to Chance. People seemed content to ignore me rather than mock and whisper behind my back. I'm sure they still were, but at least they kept it hidden enough I didn't see it everywhere I went. I wondered what had caused them to ease off, especially after how they'd been Monday morning.

Additionally, I didn't have the dream a single time, or any other nightmares for that matter. No midnight visitors as far as I knew since I was sleeping so well. No attempts on my life either, which was always a good thing. My dad had even been given Katie's cell number and I'd texted with her a bit, to help keep her company.

Her mother had called the school and asked them to send her work home with me. I gave them to my dad, who brought them in when he went to work.

Katie's texts were funny, she had a quirky sense of humor. I liked her, though despite Chance's light teasing on the subject I didn't like her as anything beyond friends. Not that she'd have been interested anyway, since I didn't happen to be female.

I did think she and I could get to be really close friends though. We shared a lot of interests. Just another good point to a great week. I couldn't remember the last time I'd had such a good week. I felt almost normal.

I studied at home, talked with my dad about nothing in particular, from school to baseball to his job, and spent every moment I could at school with Chance, laughing, joking, even a bit of plotting our next move in our murder investigation.

The eventual conclusion was that we were probably going to have to set a trap of some kind. We seemed unable to come to an agreement on what kind of trap we needed to set for the killer though.

We also decided that I needed to go get a closer look at the ovens. Chance wasn't at all keen on the idea, and frankly neither was I, but I was hoping that my getting closer to the oven might trigger something in whatever psychic trait I seemed to have developed lately, giving me more clues to work with. I remembered from a show I'd watched years before on television that psychics could sometimes pull images or memories off of inanimate objects.

If I was really lucky, I might get a glimpse

inside my mind of who the actual killer was when Dominic Hale was murdered. It was so much easier to solve a murder when you knew who the killer was, I mentally joked. Seriously though, it would be easier to find evidence to link the crime to the killer if we knew who to look for links to.

I wouldn't have a chance to get a closer look at the oven unless we could sneak away during the dance, though. We both thought that was our best bet. It'd take some luck, and a bit of spy skill we both had the bravado to tell the other we possessed in large quantities. We both knew it was nonsense of course, though we really did think we could pull this off without too much trouble. We only needed a few minutes uninterrupted in the kitchen.

Friday afternoon I climbed into the car to go home with my dad with very mixed feelings. On the one hand, I was ending the best week of school I'd had since I moved to this hillbilly heaven, longer than that if I was being honest with myself. I was also walking away from Chance, who sat watching me from where we'd just said goodbye on the low stone wall.

On the other hand, school was done for the week, and the next day was the dance. I was excited. I couldn't quite pin down why, and kept telling myself that it was because we'd get another chance to make some progress on the murder.

I knew better though. I was very excited to spend some social time with Chance. I wondered briefly if he would try to get me to dance with him. He probably would joke about it. I doubted I'd say yes if he asked, but I also doubted he'd push it so far as to actually ask me.

My phone buzzed. I glanced down at it. I had a text from Katie. I scanned it quickly and smiled.

Going to the dance, stud? she asked.

Yeah, with your mom, I texted back.

Figures. I wouldn't put it past her. I'm pretty sure she worships the ground you walk on.

I thought she was Jewish, I replied.

Ha ha, very funny. Seriously though, you going? She continued.

Yeah, I am. I'm meeting Chance there.

Is he your date?

He wishes, I replied, chuckling to myself. My dad glanced at me, smiled slightly, and looked back to the road.

Do me a favor, tell me what Jennifer wears.

Are you kidding me? I asked.

Just do it, would ya? You have your impossible crush, I have mine.

What's that supposed to mean? I asked, not sure if I should be offended.

Oh please, anyone who's heard you talk about Chance for more than two seconds knows you're into him.

I'm not gay! I protested.

Bullshit, she retorted. I couldn't think of what to say to her next. I wanted to tell her how crazy she was, that she couldn't be more wrong, but the more I tried to phrase my arguments the more hollow it sounded even to my own ears.

I liked Chance. A lot. But I wasn't into him. I mean, it's not like I wanted to get it on with the guy. I remembered back to when he'd been threatening to kiss me on the school yard the weekend before. I had been scared he would do it.

Not scared, I corrected myself, nervous. I wasn't grossed out by it, I wasn't scared of it, I was just nervous. As anyone would be with their first kiss, I realized uncomfortably.

I thought about him, a lot. All the time in fact. I enjoyed spending time with my dad, and messaging with Katie, but I wanted to be with Chance every second of every day.

I liked when he gave me those little touches. I liked that he was careful not to push it too far, respectful of my boundaries. I loved his smile, and his laugh. I even loved his flirting. Not only did it not bother me that he wore the same clothes every day, I had actually grown to think of it as another of his quirky charms.

The thought of him being hurt, like he was when his mother had come to the school yard and talked to him on his birthday, made my heart tighten up painfully and a knot grow in my stomach. I wanted to take care of him. I wanted him to take care of me, too.

Running my fingers along the rainbow bracelet still on my wrist I couldn't argue it any more. I'd been dancing around the idea for weeks now. All the walls I had built to deny the fact to myself slipped. Katie was right. I was in love with Chance.

Damn you, I texted to her finally. It took her a long moment to reply.

I'm sorry.

Don't be. You're right.

I know, but I'm sorry I pushed it on you like that. It's just so hard to see someone like me denying it to everyone, especially themselves. All we've got is ourselves. Denying who we are is emotional suicide.

Thanks. Do you think it's really that obvious?

Painfully, she replied, *I'll bet everyone who knows you knows it already. You were the last one to realize it, I think.*

How could I reply to that? She had a point. I knew I'd been denying it to myself. I knew I'd been trying to convince myself that Chance was just my best friend.

He was that, but he was so much more than that to me as well. Now that I was looking, I could see it. She was right, it was painfully obvious. Amazing what we could deny to ourselves, I thought.

I glanced at my dad. He'd caught the shift in my mood and was quietly driving, obviously willing to give me my space. I knew he'd be willing to listen though. And right now I needed to say it out loud.

"Dad?"

"Yeah?" he replied expectantly.

"I want to tell you something."

"Anything you like," he said. I took a deep breath.

"I think I might like Chance."

"I know," my dad said.

"No, like I think I might *like* Chance."

"I know," he said again, this time with a smile. I made a mental note to kick Katie later.

"You do?" I asked stupidly, since he'd already said he did.

"Yes Ryan, I do. The first time you started talking about Chance I suspected. I knew for sure the second time you brought him up."

"That soon?" I asked in surprise. "How did you know?"

"Not too hard to figure it out if you're paying attention. When you say the name of someone you love, it sounds different. I'm not sure I could explain how, but it sounds different. You take more care with it, I guess. Taste it more, if that makes sense."

"That's weird, but it actually does kind of make sense," I replied thoughtfully. Did I say his name differently? I didn't know, nobody else really said his name unless they had to. "Does it bother you?" I finally asked him.

"Ryan, I've told you two things before that make that a silly question. First, I told you that love is love. If everyone is consenting, nobody is being hurt. If nobody is being hurt, it isn't wrong. To me, nothing else really matters.

"And second?" I asked, feeling certain that I was actually hearing that first one for the first time.

"And second," he continued, "I've told you that I love you."

"That's it?"

"What else is there? I love you, Ryan. You're my son, and mean more to me than anything else in the world. Who you love means a lot less to me than whether or not you love. Besides, you can't condemn someone for something they didn't choose. That's ridiculous."

"Thanks, Dad," I said sincerely. "So you're cool with Chance?"

"Seeing you happy is all I've ever wanted for you, Ryan. Watching you since Chance came into your life, you're happier. A lot happier. Why he's in your life, I don't know, but he is. Things have been scary around here for a lot of reasons, but watching you since you met Chance, I'm a lot less worried for you personally than I used to be. Took a little while for me to get to that point, but there it is."

"Can I tell him you said that?"

"Sure," my dad said with a laugh.

"Can we have him come over sometime?"

"If you like."

"Will you talk to him?"

"Not sure if we'd make a very good

conversation, but I'd be willing to give it a try."

"Dad, what is it about him that everyone hates so much?" I asked. He hesitated and glanced down at me as we pulled into the driveway.

"Do you really want me to tell you why he makes people uneasy?" I thought about it.

"No, not really. I don't think it matters. And he'll tell me when he's ready. It's his secret."

"Fair enough," he replied and climbed out of the car. I grabbed my bag and followed suit.

"Dad?" I asked as we walked.

"Yeah?"

"Do you think being gay is a sin?"

"Of course not."

"Why not?"

"You don't choose who you fall in love with. Life would be a lot easier if you could, but you can't. Like I said, it's stupid to condemn someone for something they didn't choose.

"Besides," he continued, "I can't imagine any truly loving God would damn someone for loving someone else. Falling in love is a beautiful thing, and there's no way a benevolent God has a problem with that. Any god who saves prime real estate in Hell for people who fall in love is a god I don't want anything to do with, and certainly doesn't deserve my worship."

I pondered this. He made perfect sense to me. One thing bothered me after all of that though. I tossed my bag on the table by the front door and leaned against the back of the couch.

"Dad, why don't we go to church? You sound pretty comfortable with the idea of God. I thought for a while that maybe you were just mad at Him for letting Mom die." He was quiet for long enough that I wondered if I'd upset him.

"I don't really think that's how it works," he replied eventually. "It's complicated, but the short answer is that I got tired of people trying to tell me what God's plan was with her death. Awfully arrogant to assume to know something like that, huh?

"I just got to really resent being told why God let it happen, or made it happen, depending on who was talking. Some people said He was calling His angel home, others said I was being punished for my sins, some said that she was the sinner being punished. I just got sick of hearing it all."

"Would it bother you if I went to one? Like every week?" I asked.

I wasn't asking because I had any intention of doing so. If anything, my recent experiences had made me pretty down on the whole concept of organized religion. I was mostly just curious at this point. My dad was turning out to be a much deeper guy than I had first assumed and I found myself genuinely wanting to know what he thought and felt.

"Not a bit. If you found one you liked I'd even drive you there, as long as that church made you want to be a better person."

"Cool."

"Why, have one in mind?"

"No way. Just wanted to see how open you were." He smiled and nodded.

"Ryan," he began after a moment in a serious tone, clearly changing subjects, "one of these days you're going to find out why Chance upsets people. It's going to upset you too, though in a different way. I just want you to remember that when you find out the truth that you can come talk to me about anything, or nothing. I'm here for you whatever you need, okay?"

"Thanks Dad," I said. I considered him for a moment, wishing I understood what he meant, then nodded and turned away, grabbing my bag and heading for my room.

Chapter Twenty Three
The Dance

Pain and heat. Pain from the bruise on my forehead that I was sure was just developing. Pain from the heat that was slowly, but tangibly, rising all around. I recognized it now as not truly being fire, though the distinction made little difference.

I was still locked in the steel prison, burning alive as I peered through the tiny glass window of the oven I was now painfully familiar with, screaming noiselessly for someone to help me.

No one would help me. The devil was outside again, his smiling human mask a mockery to the species. The horns still protruded from the mask's forehead. The fierce, yellow eyes seemed to burn into me, their glee at my anguish evident. The mask had changed again.

It was melted, deformed, even more than the last time. It was nearly liquid, large globs of the rubbery features dripping from the chin and pointed cheekbones. Bright red skin showed through in several places.

The features were still impossible to identify, but the devil below seemed more and more familiar to me as the human mask melted. I could see blood lining the drooping edges of the mask, the forked tongue darting between melted lips.

I had almost placed the identity of the devil. I knew this person. Recognized who it was. An instant before the name came to my mind, the horrible face was gone, the sense of recognition and awareness of the devil's true identity vanishing with it. Moments later, a new face appeared.

The heat was rising. I was still screaming, but I couldn't hear myself anymore. Everything was silent. I pounded on the door, but no noise came back to me. Even the flames licking all around brought nothing to dispel the cacophonous silence. As the new face appeared, time seemed to slow. I shouted my pleas for help.

The new face drew close. This face was crystal clear, no halo of light, no traces of the wispy iridescent light around it. He looked solid and real. I knew without doubt, it was Chance's face. Hope leapt in my chest. As Chance's face stopped just before the window, it spoke. I couldn't hear the words. I couldn't hear anything. But I knew what the voice said, I felt them in my bones.

"I'm sorry, Ryan. I can't help you," is what it said. For the briefest of instants, his impossibly deep brown eyes glistened clearly with unshed tears from the otherwise calm face. Then he started laughing again. He laughed, with an almost manic enthusiasm.

Then the claws came, breaking through the form in my window as though my regretful visitor was made of nothing more substantial than smoke in a breeze, swirling for a moment before it broke apart and was gone.

The devil wearing the melted face reappeared. He was laughing, like Chance had been a moment before. I couldn't hear it. I could feel it, grating against my bones as the heat consumed the tattered remains of my flesh. I silently screamed again, and the dream broke.

I sat bolt upright, the slight chill in the air of the room feeling icy on my sweat-covered skin. I ran my hands through my hair to get the damp strands out of my eyes and took a long, shaky breath. My hands were shaking.

I stood up a moment later, making my way to the window. Sure enough, there was the truck. The driver was nowhere to be seen. I realized the dreams only seemed to come when he was around. Every time I awoke from the nightmare, he was there, lurking in the truck, in the yard, in the... where the Hell was he now? I had regained enough of my awareness to realize that if the driver wasn't in the truck, he was outside in the yard somewhere. Or in the house.

I moved quickly to the doorway and listened as hard as I could. There, was that the creak of the floorboard? This house was old, made all kinds of noises. My dad always said it was "settling". You'd think after ninety years the place would have finished settling in by now. I couldn't be sure that's all this was though.

I peeked around the half open door, but saw nothing but shadows. I swore half of them seemed to be moving, taunting me to come out into the open. My shivering had intensified, and it wasn't from cold.

Was that shadow moving closer? No, that one was from a tree outside the front window. I shook my head. I was scaring the life out of myself. Except, that shadow actually was moving closer. Not fast, but fast enough.

I made a split-second decision and raced out into the hallway, ducking back down away from the approaching shadow to my dad's room. Opening the door, I saw immediately that my dad wasn't in there. The blankets were all mussed, and the bedside lamp was on, but he wasn't in there. I spun around to face the dark hallway.

"Ryan?" asked a voice from the approaching shadow. It was my dad's voice. He came close enough to move into the light and I saw the glass of water in his hand. He saw my expression and his look of mild confusion turned to concern. "What's wrong?"

"He's here, Dad," I whispered. I was relieved that he immediately knew what I was talking about. He ducked past me into the room and grabbed the baseball bat, setting the glass down.

"In the truck?" he asked quietly. I shook my head. His grip tightened on the bat.

"He's not inside the house," he reassured me. "There's not really anywhere to hide and I could see into every room on the way between here and the kitchen. Don't worry Ryan, he's still outside. Stay here, call the police. Close the door behind me." He moved out into the hallway, and we both heard the truck engine rev outside.

"Damn it," my dad cursed, and raced for the front door. I ran to my bedroom window, a closer vantage point than the front door.

I made it to the window just in time to see the truck race out of sight, and see my dad halfway across the yard, running toward it. I was impressed, he'd made it clear out the front door and halfway across the yard before I'd made it to my window. He hadn't been quite fast enough though. When he came back in, he was muttering under his breath.

"Did you call the cops?" he asked when he saw me by the window. I shook my head sheepishly. He just nodded and went into his room for his phone.

It took almost an hour for the cop to show up. It was the same fat, useless guy again. He spent another five minutes telling us there wasn't anything he could do before he left again.

"When I take you to your dance today," my dad said when the officer was gone, "I'm heading into town to buy some security cameras and an alarm system. I think the locks we put in last week will help, but I want to be sure." I just nodded.

He reached out and put his hand on my shoulder, giving me a reassuring squeeze. I smiled half-heartedly, then headed for a shower. No more sleep for me tonight. At least the dance was today, I thought as I turned on the water. Something about that thought didn't comfort me like I thought it would, though.

I scrubbed hard, partly to clean off the sweat, partly to cleanse the feeling of violation I felt at the continued nighttime visits from what I was convinced was a psychopathic killer, and partly because it was the dance, and I wanted to look good. For Chance, I admitted to myself. Worse than any girl, I chided myself. I didn't stop though.

As I relaxed a bit under the heat of the shower, I decided I was going to tell Chance that I liked him. I was going to tell him tonight, at the dance. Kind of sappy, maybe a little romantic, but now that I had admitted to myself I was into him I couldn't deny that I really was very attracted to him.

I thought about him all day, which wasn't unusual. It was odd though, reassessing all those little moments, all the looks, all the touches, everything about him under that new light.

It was remarkable I'd been able to deny it to myself for that long, and it was no wonder everyone else already knew it. Katie was right, it had been painfully obvious to everyone but me.

The day seemed to go on forever. I played video games for most of it, hoping to pass the time. I had a hard time focusing though. Not only could I not get Chance out of my mind, I also couldn't get the dream out of my mind.

Remembering him laughing at me while I burned like that terrified me. He wouldn't do that. When it happened he would be trying frantically to help, not refusing to help and then laughing. He had to.

'When it happened', I had thought. I was forced to admit that I no longer had any doubts about the dream. The devil was an exaggeration, representing the devil mask worn by the killer, hiding under a normal face. But there was a real killer. I recognized the oven, I knew that was real.

Katie's attack had happened exactly like I'd dreamt it as well. At some point, some day, I would be hit over the head and shoved into that oven. I would be in danger for my life, and Chance would be my only help.

That was where I knew the dream had to be wrong though. Chance would help me. Chance would never let me die like that. Chance would help me, he would be there for me.

Chance loved me. He'd never made any

pretense about that, though he'd never actually said it. And I could see it, every time he looked at me. You couldn't stand by and watch while someone you loved was hurt when you could do something about it. In the dream, he was right there. He would help me.

I spent more time getting ready that evening than I had probably ever spent on my appearance before. It was tricky though.

I knew Chance would be wearing his gray shirt and jeans, so I didn't want to show up looking all dressed up. I wanted to look casual, so he wouldn't feel so out of place, but I wanted to look good too.

I took a bit more care styling my hair than usual, a bit more time picking out which shirt and pants I'd wear. In the end, I was passably satisfied. I looked nicely casual, but nice. When my dad came in to ask if I was ready to go, he looked a little surprised.

"No shirt and tie? I thought this was a formal?" he asked.

"It is," I replied, "but Chance doesn't own anything formal, and I don't want him to feel out of place." My father considered this for a longer moment than I felt was necessary, but finally nodded.

"Fair enough. You ready then?" I nodded as well and followed him out to the car. We drove mostly in silence, with me lost in thought and my dad respecting my need to figure things out. I knew he'd talk it over with me if I wanted, and I appreciated that more than I thought he knew. When we got to the school, my dad spoke before I could open the door and get out though.

"Hey Ryan? Be careful, okay? Stay around other people, and if anything weird or suspicious happens, you call me immediately, are we clear? I'll be in town for about an hour or so, then I'll come hang out right outside the school. I can be inside in moments if you need me."

Wow, I thought. That last visit from our nighttime stalker had really freaked him out.

"I will Dad, don't worry. Chance will look out for me, and there's going to be a ton of people all over the place. Nowhere for anything dangerous to happen." He nodded, but didn't look convinced.

"Just call me if you're at all scared or feel threatened, okay?" he said. I didn't mention that Noah would be there, so it was pretty likely I'd be threatened at least once.

I didn't think Noah was the killer though. Not unless he'd gotten good at stealing trucks, and looked a lot bigger in the dark. He probably would look bigger in the dark, I mused. More from intimidation factor than actual size though. Some things just got scarier in the dark.

"I will, Dad," I reassured him, "thanks."

He nodded, and drove off as I closed the door. By the way he drove off, I suspected he was planning on making it to the hardware store and back in much less than an hour. I'd have to tell him later that I was comforted by his sticking close by to look out for me. I really did appreciate it, and after the dream the night before I was definitely feeling a bit uneasy.

I turned around to face the school. A couple of other kids were walking in as well, the school backlit by the sun slowly setting behind it. Rather picturesque, I thought. Then I saw Chance.

He was sitting off to one side of the front doors, and had obviously been waiting for me. He was smiling brightly at me. I felt that warmth rush over me again. I walked over to him.

"You made it, huh?" he asked.

"Yeah, not like I had anything better to do on a Saturday evening," I replied. He reached up and touched a lock of my hair alongside my forehead. I'd styled it forward a bit more, to hide the bruise on my temple.

"Looks good, man," he said. I smiled.

"Thanks. It looks awful though."

"I meant the hair," he said with a smirk.

"Yours too," I retorted, "I see you took extra care to style it up."

"Well, not much you can do with hair this short. I hate gel, so it's not like I can spike it or anything. It just sort of sits there. Nothing like yours. Maybe you'll let me braid it sometime."

"You love it and you know it," I told him. He laughed lightly. "Come on," I told him, turning him toward the front of the school and giving him a light push. He protested, but walked toward the school. I moved along beside him and we walked into the flickering hallway.

There were a few young couples around, dressed in slightly nicer dresses and shirts than usual. A couple of the boys wore ties. Formal meant something different to a middle school than to a high school. They were all moving toward the gym, where a table had been set up and two of the teachers were taking tickets.

"Did we have to buy tickets beforehand?" I asked, surprised. "I didn't even think to ask."

"You can buy at the door," he said. "I could walk right in, they wouldn't care. They'd just ignore me like usual. Did you bring any money?"

"I'll buy you a ticket," I told him. I had my twenty bucks in my wallet. I usually had my wallet with me, just in case. The sign below the table said they were only five dollars, so I had plenty.

"Don't do that," Chance protested, "save yourself the five bucks. They really won't care."

"I do," I told him and walked toward the table.

The teachers were two that I didn't have any classes with. They glanced up, saw us coming, and exchanged a glance. Figures, I thought. The teachers were just as bad as everyone else.

"I need two tickets," I told the one holding the roll of cheap carnival tickets. She raised an eyebrow. "Please," I added. She shrugged, and tore off two tickets as I handed my twenty to the other teacher, sitting in front of the small cash box. She took my twenty and handed me back a pair of fives.

"Hold onto those," said the teacher who handed me the tickets, "we're having a raffle at the end of the night."

"Cool," I replied. "What are the prizes?"

"Some gift cards to some of the stores in the mall." This town had a mall? How was I just now hearing about this?

"Thank you," I told her and walked with Chance into the gym.

"You didn't have to do that," he said.

"Yes, I did," I replied.

"Thanks."

The gym was crowded. I had obviously been one of the last to arrive, though I'd come in a bit early by my watch. It was decorated with streamers and balloons, and they had music playing over the PA system. Too cheap for a DJ, I thought wryly. I was truthfully surprised they'd sprung for the balloons.

Along the far wall, under the basketball hoop, a row of low tables held snack foods and a couple varieties of drinks. The lights had been dimmed a little, though they still flickered slightly.

A few of the couples were dancing, but as I expected most of the couples had segregated out, leaving groups of girls here, boys there, chatting with their friends. A few groups were mixed, but not many.

Cowards, I thought.

"Wow, this is actually a lot more than I was expecting," I told him.

"Yeah, this town doesn't have much going on for entertainment, so they take the few excuses they have fairly seriously."

"What's the excuse for this dance?" I asked, curious. I hadn't thought to ask that before either.

"Fiftieth anniversary of the founding of this school," Chance told me.

"Seriously?" I was honestly surprised. I had thought this place was far older than that.

"Crazy, right? I can't believe nobody burned this place down in that long," Chance said with a laugh. I laughed with him.

"Come on, let's check out the food," I said, heading that way. He fell into step beside me. Several teachers were scattered around, chaperones for the dance I assumed, and one of mine was by the punch bowl.

"Hello, Mr. Jacobs," he said as we approached.

"Hi, Mr. Allen," I replied with a friendly smile.

"Good to see you here. I wasn't sure if you were going to make it," he said. Curious that he'd thought about it at all, I thought to myself.

"Yeah, thought I'd try to join in some of the local social scene."

"Glad to hear that. Good job this week," he said. I frowned.

"I'm sorry?"

"With your work. You started strong when you came here, but have been steadily declining since then. Until last week, that is. You've done very well this last week. Top grade work, in fact."

"Thank you," I replied. "Things at home got a bit less stressful this week, I had more time to focus." He nodded knowingly, as though I'd just explained a lot of things.

"I understand. Well, I appreciate the extra effort. You've got a lot of potential, Mr. Jacobs. You're a bright boy, but a lot of folks here are concerned about you."

"I know, Mr. Allen. I'm sorry. I really am just fine though, and I'll try to keep the grades up." He smiled slightly at that, the first smile I think I'd ever seen from the normally very serious man.

"I hope that you do. Always a shame seeing good potential wasted, and you're one of the only students in that whole class who actually pays attention, most days."

"Their loss," I replied, trying to be friendly. His small smile broadened slightly.

"It is that, Mr. Jacobs. It is that," he said, raising a glass of lemonade in salute before turning and walking off.

"Strange dude," Chance said. I smiled at him, but shrugged.

"Nice enough. Just takes his work seriously. I

can't really blame him, he's got a tough job."

"Oh man, please tell me you're not going soft on the teachers," Chance laughed.

"They're not so bad," I protested, "just trying to do their jobs just like anyone else. Besides, you've got to cut some slack to anyone that has to put up with jerks like Noah on a daily basis." Chance pondered that a moment.

"That's a really good point," he acknowledged.

"Thank you. And speak of the devil," I said, getting a chill as I said it, instantly regretting my choice of words. Chance followed my gaze.

"Are they kidding?" Chance exclaimed. Noah and Jennifer walked in, hand in hand.

"What the hell? She told me she'd dumped him!" I replied, equally confused. Chance shook his head.

"Some people just don't learn. Sad that it's true what they say; nice guys do finish last, and that's probably because the girls are all attracted to the assholes. What's with that?"

"What do you care? You like the guys anyway," I replied. He grinned at me.

"Just one of them," he said.

"Noah? Dude, your taste sucks," I teased.

"Don't make me kiss you to prove a point."

"Please don't," I laughed, though inside my stomach did a little flip.

"Point made then," he said with a smug look.

Noah and Jennifer made their way straight to the dance floor and turned toward each other. As Noah put his arms around her, his hand immediately went low. Chance and I simultaneously made faces.

"I wouldn't have expected she'd let him go that far," I said.

"She might, but Mrs. Bradley won't," Chance said. I looked where he pointed. Mrs. Bradley, in another flower-print dress that seemed oddly to work well with her larger figure, was storming their way with a dark look.

"Ten bucks on Mrs. Bradley," I told him. Chance laughed.

"No bet, that lady could probably take down any guy in this school, student or teacher."

"You may be right," I said. She was a little big, though by no means huge, but at the moment she seemed more solid than soft.

Watching her move like that I could easily see her taking down the average guy. I hadn't seen that in her before. She'd always seemed so soft and friendly. With that look on her face though, I actually wondered what she'd look like in a dark alley. I didn't like the image that came to mind.

Mrs. Bradley reached the couple and yanked Noah around, hard. I couldn't hear them from across the gym and over the music, but the scolding she was giving was clearly a sharp one. Even Noah seemed to wilt a little under that tirade.

When she was done, she turned and walked about ten paces away, then turned back and watched him pointedly, arms crossed. Noah resumed dancing with Jennifer, looking frequently over at Mrs. Bradley, but keeping his hands well above the waistline. Chance and I were both laughing, hard.

"I've never seen anyone put Noah in his place like that before! I'm starting to actually like that woman!" Chance exclaimed.

"Mrs. Bradley? I always liked her," I replied. "Nothing but nice to me."

"Yeah well, at least she talks to you," he replied. I nodded, losing my good humor at the reminder that Chance still had some serious stuff going on in his life.

I considered him for a moment as he watched Noah and Jennifer dancing. I considered telling him how I felt, but it wasn't time yet. Too many other people around, and the moment was wrong.

We had moved toward the chairs along the side of the gym when Jennifer caught up with me.

"Ryan?" she called. I turned around.

"Hi Jennifer," I said.

"I'm glad you came," she said.

"Thanks," I replied, not sure how else to answer that. "I thought you and Noah broke up?"

"My mama made me get back together with him," she replied, looking embarrassed.

"Wait… what?" I asked, completely baffled.

"She says marryin' th' son of Reverend Porter can only improve our station. They own a big ranch on th' east side of town. I don't know if ya knew that. She also says it'll bring us closer t' God."

"Marrying the guy with the groping hands and the quick right hook is considered a good move in this town? And since when do our parents get to pick who we date? If my father ever told me who to date, I'd tell him where to shove it," I replied, stunned. "But he wouldn't. Do you know why? Because he cares about my happiness, not his 'station'."

"Noah's not so bad," she said a little defensively, "just a little forward."

"A little forward? Jennifer, that jerk is a rapist waiting to happen. A wife beater at the very least," I replied. That might have been a little extreme, but it sure looked that way from where I was standing.

"Ryan, I really worry 'bout you," she said. "You seem so nice, I don't understand how ya can be so against th' good folk of this town. Is it yer friend that's pullin' you away from God?" I glanced at Chance in disbelief. He shrugged.

"Jennifer, I think you're seriously misguided about which people are the good people in this town," I told her. "Chance is the only one in this town, who's been nothing but nice to me. All those 'good people' you're talking about constantly verbally and physically attack me and Chance. You really do seem like a nice person, Jennifer. How can you keep hanging out with and listening to people who do nothing but spread hate and violence? Don't take this wrong, but I seriously think you're missing the whole point of a Christian church."

"It's not about that," she protested, but I interrupted.

"Yes, it is! 'God hates fags' is hateful, and hurtful," I ranted. "Telling people they're burning in Hell and that God will bring His justice down on them for their perceived evils is hateful, and hurtful. That asshole Noah going around beating people up, including innocent girls, for something they have no control of is beyond hateful, it's evil. I really wish you could see that.

"Walk away from it, Jennifer," I continued in a pleading tone. I truly hoped she would do exactly that. "Walk away from Noah, from that damned church, from all of that nonsense filling your head. I dare you to really read that Bible of yours and then come back and honestly tell me that you think your Christ would be all happy and cool with anyone, let alone a church in his name, spreading hatred and prejudice. I dare you. I want to be friends with you Jennifer, but not if you're still neck deep in that filth."

I could tell I'd struck a nerve in there somewhere. She looked very upset, and not at all certain. I wondered if she'd ever stopped and asked herself before if what she was being taught was right, if what she was being taught really was meant to help her become a better person, a better soul.

I suspected she had, and that I'd just fed her doubts. I felt a little bad about that, but all I really wanted was for her to understand what she, and those 'good people' were doing to others. She opened her mouth, but I interrupted her again.

"I can't talk about this anymore. Come talk to me another time about this if you want, as long as you're willing to really talk and not just parrot back the nonsense they shout at your sermons." I turned and walked away, leaving her standing there, stunned. Chance followed me out into the side hallway.

"Wow," he said simply.

"Sorry," I told him. "Every time I talk to her, it's like she's trying to save me. I appreciate the thought, I really do, but I seriously think she needs saving a whole lot more than you or I do."

"I don't know about that," he replied with a shrug, eyes downcast. "Some of us might need more saving than others." He looked up at me. "You're a good person though. I have no doubt if there's a Heaven, you've got a spot reserved."

"Uh huh. I'll be sure to save you seat," I laughed. He shrugged again, eyes locked on mine. I was once again pulled into the depth of them. So intense, so focused. My heart fluttered. I had just about steeled myself to tell him when he spoke.

"Ryan? I think this is a great chance to go look for clues."

"On a two year old murder?" I asked. "What on earth do you think we'd find?" He shrugged.

"I don't know, we just didn't do anything with it last week, and I figure we could get a really good look at that oven like we talked about. Nobody's back there." I got a chill.

"No!" I said, more sharply than I intended. Chance blinked in surprise. "Sorry man, I had my dream again last night. That oven kind of freaks me out right now."

"Oh man, I'm so sorry," Chance replied, putting a hand on my arm.

"It's cool, just please let's not go back to the kitchen, okay?"

"Definitely not," he replied.

"So what else have we got?" I asked, wanting to find a good compromise.

"I don't know Ryan, that oven is the only evidence probably still around," he said.

"Well, we already pretty much figured out it couldn't have been latched from the inside," I told him.

"Yeah, I guess we did," he replied, though he didn't sound entirely convinced.

"We also figured out it isn't Noah, since he couldn't be driving the truck that keeps staking out my place."

"True," he grudgingly admitted.

"Hey, maybe we could check out the closet in the library where Katie was attacked!" I said. Chance brightened.

"That's a good idea, maybe the cops missed something, since they were thinking it was a suicide."

"Do you think they came back and checked for evidence after Katie woke up and told them what had happened?" I asked.

"I don't know," Chance said, "maybe. I didn't see them though."

"Probably not. The cops out here seem like a bunch of morons," I grumbled, half to myself. "Besides, I might be able to get a vision or see something about what really happened if we check out that closet. Come on, let's go check it out." I turned to walk down the hall and froze. Chance almost bumped into me, I stopped so fast.

"What?" he asked, instantly recognizing something was wrong.

"Do you see that?" I asked, pointing out one of the few windows along the side of the hallway. Chance looked.

"I see some cars and a couple of trucks," he replied, not following. "What do you see?"

"That's the truck, Chance."

"*The* truck?" he asked, suddenly subdued.

"Yeah. I have to text my dad. That means the killer is here, right now."

"Oh man, Ryan, we have to get back into the gym, where everyone else is around," Chance tugged at my arm.

"Yeah," I replied, but I'd pulled out my phone and started texting my dad. I hit send and looked up. Chance stood by the closed gym door, waiting. I moved to open the door, but it didn't budge. It had locked from the inside.

"This door always does that," Chance told me. "They usually just prop it open during the day. We have to go back around. Can we run? I'm getting nervous."

"Sure," I said, trying to sound confident, but I was suddenly worried. We were in a poorly lit hallway, locked out of the gym, all alone, with the killer's truck in plain view. In the darkness outside, it was silhouetted by the distant lights just like it always was in front of my house, backlit by the moon. It was definitely the same truck. It was also empty.

We turned and ran down the hall, heading for the hallway crossing that would let us move back to the front of the gym. Chance was right behind me. As we reached the crossing and turned, we stopped short. The fire doors were closed. Certain they were locked, I tried them anyway. They didn't move. The fire doors on all the other directions were closed too.

"We have to go back," I told him.

"What if the killer is back there?" Chance asked. He sounded as afraid as I felt.

"No choice, come on," I said, making my way back to the hallway. I paused, looking down the length of it. Nobody was in the hall. "All clear, see?"

"Okay, okay," Chance replied, though he didn't sound convinced. We ran down the hall, Chance right behind me again. "Ryan?" he asked behind me.

"Yeah?" I asked over my shoulder.

"The only way back around from here is through the cafeteria." My heart sank.

"Please tell me you're joking," I panted. I was getting out of shape, I realized. Too long without baseball. I used to practice almost every day. It had been months now, though.

"Sorry, man. We can just run through. We don't have to stop."

"Fine, but we do it fast," I told him. I was glad he was afraid too. I didn't want to feel like a coward, but I was getting more frightened by the moment.

We passed several doorways, some of them open. I was sure we were going to get ambushed from behind one of them, but nothing happened. We made it to the cafeteria, but those doors were locked too. I looked to the end of the hall.

The kitchen doors were the only ones left. The kitchen had doors on both sides too, so if those were unlocked we could make it across to the other side and into the front hall again. That meant crossing through the kitchen though.

I braced myself and moved to the doors. They opened. I was almost more upset that they opened than I would have been had they been closed. Without waiting a moment longer, knowing I'd chicken out if I hesitated, I opened the door and ran in.

"Ryan!" Chance shouted from behind me an instant before pain exploded in the back of my head. I felt my forehead hit the floor an instant before my world once again went dark.

Chapter Twenty Four
Fires of Hell

Pain and heat. Pain from the bruise on my forehead that I was sure was just developing, and the lump on the back of my head I knew was also developing. That part was new. Pain from the heat that was slowly, but tangibly, rising all around.

It took me a long moment to understand that this time it was different. Everything felt sharper, and my vision was fuzzier. My vision cleared slowly, allowing me to look around. Metal walls surrounded me, like they always did in this dream. Only this time, it wasn't a dream.

Panic struck me like a freight train, my breathing suddenly coming far too fast, my heart racing in my chest. I bolted to me feet and instantly felt dizzy, almost falling again before I caught myself against one of the metal walls. It was very warm.

I pulled away and spun to where I knew the

small glass window would be. Dizziness washed over me again. I needed to move more slowly. The oven was smaller than it had been in my dreams. There wasn't enough room to move around much. Tall enough and deep enough for one of the metal racks the kitchen staff loaded with rolls or mini pizzas in the mornings, and not much more.

The window was edged in a murky yellowish-brown residue from countless baking sessions. The middle was still mostly clear though. Clear enough to see the devil's face staring in at me, gruesome smile twisting already horrifying features. The eyes behind the devil's face were human though. Dark, intense, and human.

The devil's face was a mask, I realized as my clarity of thought slowly returned. I'd known it would be, but somehow it still seemed odd after seeing the human mask on the devil's face so many times. A tongue darted out from the slit in the mouth of the devil mask. The tongue was human as well.

I pushed on the door. It didn't budge. I had known it wouldn't, but something inside me had to try it anyway. I slammed a fist against the window and shouted out for my release.

The person behind the mask laughed. I could hear it, unlike in my dream, though it was faint and very muffled. It was also the most chilling sound I had ever heard, grating across my nerves. The laughing devil was taking genuine glee in my situation. It was not a sane sound.

I slammed repeatedly against the door, pounding on the glass with all my strength. Aside from creating a dull, resonating thud, my efforts had no effect. The devil outside the window watched me closely, reveling in my helplessness. The evil creature winked at me once before it vanished from the window, moving out of sight. The heat in the oven was rising uncomfortably fast.

I pushed on the door, frantically looking for some catch, some clasp, some kind of release to let myself out. I thought things like this had to have an emergency release on the inside, but this oven was old enough that it seemed to have no such safety feature. The door was closed, latched, and locked all from the outside.

A new face appeared in the window. I recognized it instantly. Partly because I'd been expecting it, partly because I saw that face every time I closed my eyes these days. Chance looked through the window, face perfect and soft, expression filled with horror, fear, and to my own growing fear, resignation. I banged on the door again.

"Chance!" I cried. "Is he still out there?" Chance didn't respond.

"Open the door, Chance!" I called frantically.

Chance didn't move. He shook his head slowly, sadly. I stared in shock, nausea building in my stomach.

"I'm sorry," his lips moved, "I am so sorry. I can't help you, Ryan." I felt sweat trickling down my back. Despite the rising heat, ice seemed to be crawling along my spine.

"Chance!" I shouted, more angrily. "What are you doing? Open the damned door!" He again slowly shook his head.

"Dominic," he said. I froze.

"What?" I asked, too confused to react.

"My name is Dominic," he replied. I struggled to understand. Chance moved forward toward the door. From the center of the door, a hand appeared, passing through the metal as if the door weren't there. Or as if the hand weren't there.

I staggered backward, away from the hand as it rose toward me. I jerked away as my back touched the hot metal wall. The arm followed slowly behind as Chance, or Dominic, continued to move forward. His face reached the glass and passed right through. In another moment, Chance stood inside the oven.

"I don't..." I began, unable to find the words.

"I'm so sorry, Ryan. I told you I couldn't touch things." The air was starting to feel thinner, and I was getting more light-headed as the heat rose.

"But you... I... you touch me," I protested, trying frantically to get my mind wrapped around what he was trying to tell me.

Chance reached up and touched my cheek. I flinched back, hitting my head on the back wall right where I'd been struck before. My vision swam and I started to fall. Chance caught me, feeling as warm and solid as ever.

"Ryan!" Chance shouted. I could hear the concern in his voice. My vision returned, slowly, and I stood with his help.

"Dominic?" I asked, mind a blur.

"Dominic," he agreed. "Ryan, hang on. Someone has to come by soon. Don't let go, just hang on."

"How can I touch you?" I asked.

"I don't know, Ryan. I really don't. But you can. Only you can." I fought to regain enough focus to figure out a way out of here. My mind wouldn't let go of the revelation though. Chance was Dominic Hale. Chance was killed two years ago, in this oven. Chance was dead.

All the clues I'd had over the past few weeks swam back to me in a jumble. In retrospect, I should have known something was more than just odd about the way people reacted to Chance. Or, not to Chance I realized, but to my talking with and about Chance.

I suddenly understood why everyone was so bothered out by my friendship with him, why my dad had taken me to a shrink, why Noah thought I was consorting with the devil, as he put it. Nobody else could see or touch him. To them, he wasn't there. I was just some screwed up kid who had an imaginary friend. A schizophrenic or something. My vision was getting darker, and I couldn't seem to refocus it.

"Chance?" I asked.

"What?" he asked, still helping to support me. I wasn't at all sure how that even worked.

"I want to tell you something before…"

"Stop that, Ryan," Chance said sharply. I could hear tears in his voice. Looking up at him, I could see them, running down his cheeks. I wasn't sure how that worked, either. "You're going to be okay. You have to hang on until someone gets here to let you out."

"It's okay, Chance," I said. Some part of my mind had already resigned itself. Too much had happened, things were too out of control. I had known this was coming, had known it for weeks. At the end of the dream, I always died. "Let me tell you this though."

"Okay Ryan," he said softly. His voice broke slightly as he said my name. It did sound different, the way he said it. I forced a deep breath of the stiflingly hot air. I had to get this out before I no longer could.

"Chance, you're my best friend," I whispered.

"I know that," he said.

"But you're more than that," I went on, forcing myself to speak louder. I needed him to hear this. "I love you, Chance. I think I have since the first time I saw you." He was quiet a long moment.

"Ryan, this is a really lousy time to tell me that," he said, voice breaking. I laughed weakly.

"Sorry," I told him, "I wanted to tell you tonight. I didn't mean for it to be in…" My own voice broke, and I was having a hard time getting it back. I'd forgotten what I was about to say anyway. The lights outside in the kitchen were flickering. I could see them filtering through the yellowed glass of the oven. For some reason, the flickering seemed comforting to me.

"Ryan!" Chance shouted again. "Don't let go of me, please don't let go! Someone is coming. Someone has to be coming!"

"Nobody is coming," I told him painfully, my throat feeling as dry as a desert. "Hey, maybe this means I'll be a ghost too and we can still be together," I said with a smile.

"No!" Chance cried. My knees gave out. Chance didn't seem able to support me, so he just eased me down. He didn't let go of me though. I tried to speak again, but I couldn't seem to form the words. It was so hot. So hot I couldn't breathe. My clothes were soaked with sweat.

I could hear Chance screaming my name, but it seemed so far away, so muted and dull. The last thing I saw was the fluorescent light I could see through the small window flickering madly. Finally, it flared blindingly bright once and exploded, showering sparks down from the light fixture. They seemed to slow as they fell, and then there was nothing.

Chapter Twenty Five
Chance for Salvation

I awoke slowly, as though climbing back from someplace dark. I could hear ringing in the distance, like alarm bells or something. There was also a soft hiss I couldn't identify. Gradually, I realized someone was touching me.

"Ryan?" a voice asked. I had a hard time identifying it at first. "Ryan?" the voice repeated. I recognized Chance this time. He was cradling my head, gently stroking my hair. I could still hear tears in his voice.

"Can't a guy get some rest around here?" I asked groggily. Chance laughed, a relieved, slightly manic laugh.

"Don't scare me like that, Ryan!" he exclaimed.

"I wouldn't if I could help it. What happened? Am I dead too?" I asked, my thoughts slowly returning to clarity.

"I don't know what happened, but you're not dead," Chance said. I noticed he was totally untouched by sweat. It was still warm in here, I recognized we were still inside the oven and the door was still closed, but it was no longer stifling or painful. I, on the other hand, was drenched with sweat. "The oven shut off. I think I might have overloaded the breakers."

I moved to stand. Chance seemed reluctant to encourage that move, but after a moment helped me stand.

"How did you do that?" I asked, genuinely curious.

"I don't know that either," he replied with a shrug. I pushed on the door, though I felt weak enough I probably couldn't have moved it even if it weren't latched. Still latched, though.

The kitchen outside was dark, and only the emergency lights gave me anything to see by. I could tell the emergency sprayers in the ceiling had triggered, and were misting down water all over everything.

"Any time I'm emotionally riled up, the lights flicker. They always have," he explained.

"They always flicker," I replied.

"Only when I'm around," he argued. I thought about it. He was right, I realized. The classrooms never flickered, and I never saw him in there.

"But they always flicker when you're around."

"When I'm around you, yeah. You kind of get

my emotions riled up, Ryan," he said with a smile.

"So I was about to die, you freaked out, blew up the lights, fried the breakers, and set off the fire extinguishers and the alarm?" I could hear the ringing more clearly now, and it was definitely a fire alarm.

"Actually when the lights exploded they set a few things on fire," he said. I stared at him, then shook my head slowly. My vision wavered, but I didn't black out again. I was grateful for that, I was getting tired of blacking out.

"That's… kind of awesome, Chance. But this is really weird, man."

"You're telling me? I spent two years stuck in this dump, with nobody seeing me, hearing me, feeling me. It's extremely painful when people walk through me or I touch most solid objects," he said.

I nodded as I searched carefully for a way to pry the door open or release the catch from the inside. That explained why he didn't let anyone touch him. He probably didn't let anything touch him either.

"Wait, but you touch the chairs in the cafeteria, and you eat lunch," I said, trying to understand. I paused and looked over at him.

"Look, I don't know how it works," he explained, "I can walk on the ground, but I can also just be wherever I want to be, as long as it's on school grounds. I can sit in chairs, but I can't move them. Every day at lunch, I find myself in the cafeteria holding a tray of whatever garbage they're serving that day. I can touch it, I can use the fork on the tray, but I can't eat anything. It's really annoying."

I paused as I thought about it. He was right about that, too. He always sat in a seat that was slightly pulled back, always stood up without moving the chair back, always played with his food, but I couldn't recall actually seeing him eat any of it. It always looked partially eaten.

"Ryan," he said, interrupting my thoughts, "Can we figure out how to get out of here? That killer is still out there, and once he figures out the power going out means the oven shut off, he might come back to finish the job.

"What am I supposed to do?" I asked as I banged on the door, trying to jar it open. "I can't open this door from the inside any more than you could. Too bad you can't walk through the door and go find help…" I trailed off as the sound of the latch unlocking from the other side echoed through the door. I stepped back and stared as the door opened.

Jennifer stood on the other side. Her perfectly styled hair was dripping wet, plastered to her scalp, and her dress was completely ruined. She looked absolutely perfect. She looked at me for a long moment, overhead extinguishers raining down on her. I stepped forward and wrapped my arms around her. She hesitated, then hugged me back.

"Thank you," I told her as I pulled away. "How did you know we were here?"

"Th' power went out," she explained, "an' I couldn't find you anywhere. I came looking. I heard th' thumpin' from th' oven when I came through th' kitchen."

"Thank you," I said again with a smile, "You're a great friend." The cold water pouring down over me felt amazing, but I knew we had to move. "We have to go though. Someone knocked me out and shoved me in there. Whoever it is might be coming back."

"What?" she asked, looking suddenly scared, and more than a little confused.

"I'll explain later," I told her, grabbing her hand. "For now, we have to move." She thankfully didn't argue, and instead came along with me.

Chance came up on my other side. I gave him a smile, which he returned. I looked forward again in time for a heavy black figure to slam into us. Jennifer fell to the ground. I would have as well, but two big, very strong hands grabbed me by the neck and squeezed.

I immediately started thrashing, hands going to the vice-like grip at my throat and trying to pry them back. I might as well have been trying to bend prison bars. These hands were solid, and frighteningly strong. In another few moments, they might well snap my neck.

"Why won't you just die!" a deep, angry voice shouted from the devil's face inches from my own. I kicked out at the devil, but it seemed to have no effect.

"We don't need you fags in our school, or our town, or our world. There's no place for you in God's kingdom!" The hands tightened and my vision swam. Not again, I thought. His powerful arms lifted me off the ground.

I changed tactics and reached out, clawing at the devil's mask. I could hear Jennifer screaming, And Chance was yelling again. I wished he could help. I had little hope for Jennifer though, she was far too timid to fight back. I hoped someone came by to help though, or Jennifer and I were both dead.

The mask was slick with the water that continued to spray down on us. One finger hooked the eyehole of the mask and I yanked back. The mask came off, revealing my attacker. It was almost unrecognizable, twisted into a gruesome caricature of hatred. I knew that face though. Principal Avery.

A man entrusted with the caretaking of the school and its students, and he'd killed at least one, and tried to kill at least two more. Who knew how many more he'd gotten away with over the years. He wasn't a young man.

I clawed at his face. He stretched his arms out, moving backward. His arms were much longer than mine, so I couldn't reach anything but his hands, and I could no more move them than I could move a mountain.

"I will kill you, sinner," he growled darkly. "I

will send you to God's justice. You and every devil like you. I don't care how long it takes."

I looked as far to the side as the devil's grip would allow looking for some kind of weapon in reach when a dark, and apparently heavy object collided with the side of his head with a dull, but solid, thud.

Principal Avery cried out and stumbled to the side, letting me go. I fell to the ground in a heap, gasping for air.

On the ground in front of me was a heavy industrial stapler. It probably weighed several pounds. I looked to see who my savior had been and was even more shocked than I was at the revelation of who my attacker had been.

Mrs. Bradley was charging across the kitchen at a full run. It would have been almost comical were it not for the severity of the situation. I was amazed how fast she could move.

Principal Avery had stumbled and caught himself on one of the counters. As he straightened, he held a large carving knife in one hand. Mrs. Bradley didn't slow a bit.

He swung, but she had gotten too close and grabbed his wrist in both of her hands. He pushed hard, but her two arms were too much for his one. Shifting stance slightly, he got his other hand up and pushed. The knife crept closer to Mrs. Bradley's face.

I tried to stand, but between the oven and the stranglehold, I was having trouble clearing my head and getting upright. I had to help though.

Principal Avery released the knife with one hand and swung, hitting Mrs. Bradley hard across the side of her head. She grunted and stumbled slightly, but she neither went down, nor let go of the knife hand.

Another figure raced past me, grabbing Principal Avery's other hand before it could strike Mrs. Bradley again. The pair of them wrestled with the frighteningly strong, large man. As the new figure shifted around, I recognized my father.

He and Mrs. Bradley struggled with Principal Avery, who seemed to have horrific amounts of strength and rage to draw on. He shoved Mrs. Bradley back and took a swing at my father, connecting with him solidly in the side of his gut.

My father almost folded over the blow, stumbling slightly, but he also held his ground and kept his hold. Mrs. Bradley was back on him as well, barely keeping the knife from my father's neck.

Principal Avery might eventually have won however, even against the pair of them, if the others hadn't arrived. Three teachers, including Mr. Allen, and two firefighters in full regalia. Quickly understanding the situation, they all ran to help.

It took only moments for the seven of them to bring Principal Avery face down on the ground and pinned tightly with his arms behind his back. Principal Avery was screaming obscenities and hatred, vowing to kill us all. My dad came straight to me, while Mrs.

Bradley went to Jennifer.

"Ryan, are you okay?" he asked. I nodded, still gasping for air.

"Yeah Dad," I croaked, "I'm good. Good timing." He smiled, looking intensely relieved.

Chance appeared over my dad's shoulder, giving me a look of such intensity that I couldn't look away. He came around my dad to place a hand on my arm, careful not to touch my father.

One of the other teachers was on the phone with the police. I could hear him explaining what little he understood of the situation. The overhead sprinklers shut off abruptly, leaving us all soaked, shaking, and alive. Almost all of us, anyway.

"What happened?" my dad asked. I told him, leaving out only the parts involving Chance. When I was done, my dad had tears in his eyes.

I felt the tears well in my own eyes, and I grabbed onto my father like he was the last life raft in a tumultuous ocean of fear and pain. In a way, he was. With that release, the walls holding back years of pain and heartache of my own all broke as well.

Chapter Twenty Six

Crossing

I don't know how long I cried, holding him, him cradling me like a baby as he stroked my hair, but the police and a couple of paramedics were there when I finally got myself under control and eased away from him. The cops had already handcuffed Principal Avery and were hauling him away.

"I love you, Dad," I told him, for the first time in years.

"I love you too," he replied simply. He'd said that often before, but it struck me as I looked at him how much he really meant it. We had lost so much, been through so much, but he was there for me, and always would be. I finally understood that I was all he really had.

One of the paramedics said something to my dad, who nodded and eased back a bit to give the man some room. The paramedic began looking at my neck.

I winced when he touched it. It was going to bruise. So was my head, probably front and back. I had a killer headache as well, but I found my thoughts had begun again to slip back to Chance.

He was there, hovering close by as he waited for everything to calm down. I could tell he wanted to talk with me, but this wasn't the time. It took some doing before the paramedics agreed I didn't need an ambulance to the hospital, and that it would be okay if my dad drove me there as long as we went right away.

My dad even convinced the cops to wait until I had been checked out at the hospital before taking my statement. Thankfully neither officer was the useless slob who kept coming out to our place after reporting our nocturnal stalker.

I stood, my father and Chance both helping me to my feet. I marveled at Chance's touch, and that my father couldn't see him. But I felt his strength, his warmth, and his concern. I saw the look in his eyes as he watched me and I felt his love, as well.

I felt other eyes on me. I looked over, and Mrs. Bradley was watching me, also looking concerned. I eased away from my dad and Chance and found to my satisfaction that I could stand and walk on my own, I just had to be careful. I went over to Mrs. Bradley.

"Mr. Jacobs," she began. I hugged her. She embraced me without hesitation. I'd discovered that these country women were good huggers.

"Thanks, Mrs. Bradley," I told her when I let

go. "You are one tough country girl." She laughed, a delighted, bright, melodic sound.

"Why thank you, Ryan," she replied. "I grew up with four older brothers, an' by god if I didn't toughen up jus' fine."

"And good timing, too," I said with a smile. She smiled back and nodded.

"I did a quick head count after th' fire alarm evacuation and realized we were short a couple of students, had t' make sure everyone was all right."

"And the stapler?" I asked, curious. She laughed heartily at that one.

"I came in th' side door there, saw what was happenin', an' that stapler was on th' table by the door. First thing at hand, so I let 'er fly!"

"Darn good shot. Thanks again, Mrs. Bradley. I'm going to make sure everyone in the school knows not to mess with you. I have to go get myself checked out by the doctor though. I'll see you on Monday at school?"

"I'll be here," she replied. I moved back to my dad.

"Dad?" I asked.

"Yeah?" he replied.

"Can I have a minute alone with Chance?" I glanced Chance's direction, so my dad would know where he was. My dad glanced that way as well, but now that I was watching for it I could see he didn't focus on Chance, just sort of scanned the general area.

"Sure," he replied. "Don't take too long, I think those officers are eager to get your testimony."

I nodded and walked to Chance. Unconcerned with everyone else's reaction to this, I took his hand and walked with him back out into the empty hallway.

When we'd gotten a bit of distance so I could be sure we wouldn't be overheard, I stopped him. He turned around to face me.

"Listen, Chance, or Dominic, or whatever," I started, "I'm honestly not quite sure how to deal with this. I understand a lot more now, but I don't know why you didn't tell me earlier." It made sense he'd used a fake name, if he was going to have me help him solve the murder of Dominic, but I couldn't believe he hadn't told me about this.

"Chance," he clarified. "And are you kidding? 'Hey buddy, my name is really Dominic, and I was murdered two years ago. Want to help me catch the killer? Oh and by the way if you keep talking to me everyone's going to think you're nuts.' Yeah, that'd go over well." I could see his point, but I was still a bit hurt he hadn't told me.

"True, I guess. So when your mom came to talk to you, she wasn't really talking with you?"

"No, she comes by a couple of times a year and talks about how sorry she is, how it was all her fault, that kind of stuff. I'd kill to be able to tell her it wasn't her fault." I didn't remember the exact words of the conversation, but I did recall that she kept interrupting him.

"I'm sorry," I told him honestly. I couldn't imagine how hard it would be to have the people you loved blame themselves for your death and not be able to help them at all. Chance nodded.

"Thanks. It is what it is, though. They're stuck with the guilt, and I'm stuck hanging out as a ghost."

"Why are you a ghost?" I asked. "Is that what happens for everyone?"

"I haven't the slightest," he replied. "I've never met another ghost that I know of, though maybe they're all stuck where they died, too. I can't leave school grounds at all. Maybe it's the whole 'unfinished business' cliché."

"What would yours have been?"

"Solving my murder, I would think. You helped me bust that open though. Thanks for that."

"Wait, but that would mean you would be going to the other side, or crossing over or something right now. Right?"

"Yeah," he replied thoughtfully, "that's a good point. Maybe I am just stuck here forever. Hey, do me a favor though, would you?"

"Anything," I said.

"When you give the cops your testimony, can you make sure they connect Principal Avery with my death too?"

"Definitely," I promised. "Principal Avery, can you believe that?"

"Figures," Chance replied, shaking his head. "The guy always was a self-righteous ass."

"I'd have bet money it was Reverend Porter," I told him. "Maybe even with Noah's help."

"Me too. I'd even considered some of the teachers as possibilities. I don't know why I never thought of Principal Avery."

A faint light shone through the hall window onto Chance. Odd, I thought. It was still early evening, and the sun had set. I glanced that way, but saw nothing. No light, no glow, nothing. I looked back at Chance, and there it was. Like traces of sunlight.

"Chance?" I asked softly. He had followed my gaze, and now looked down at himself. The light was only on one side of him, for all the world like sunlight coming in through the window.

"Ryan? I feel a little strange." I felt that panic rising again.

"Don't, Chance," I begged. "Not yet." The light was gradually brightening.

"I don't know, Ryan. This is really weird. It feels really good though. Warm. I don't remember feeling warm, except when I touch you." At that, I reached out and touched his hand.

"You can't leave me with this bunch of rednecks!" I joked, though a knot was building in my throat. Chance laughed, though a little sadly.

"Sorry man, I can see it now though." The light had started to feel warm to me as well. I still saw no source for it, but Chance kept glancing in the direction the light seemed to be coming from. Whatever he could see, I couldn't.

"Chance," I started, having to take a deep breath to keep my voice steady, "what am I going to do without you?"

"Live a long, happy life. Find some cute boy and settle down," he said with a smile. "I needed you a lot more than you needed me."

"That's not true," I protested. As I felt the warmth of the light reflecting off of Chance, I felt a feeling of peace wash over me. He was right, it felt amazing. "What do you think is over there?" I asked softly. Chance shrugged.

"I don't know, I can't see it that clearly yet. Heaven maybe. Maybe just another life. I don't know. Looks too nice, feels too nice to be Hell. "

"I guess Principal Avery and Reverend Porter were wrong," I said with as much of a smile as I could muster. "Looks like God doesn't hate you."

"Means there's hope for you too, huh?" Chance grinned, giving me a playful shove. I laughed, but it broke midway and turned into something just short of a sob. Chance's grin slid into a look of such tenderness I almost broke.

"Ryan, I have to go," he said sadly, though he looked with hope toward the unseen source of the light.

"I know," I told him. "You deserve better than

this. I hope it is Heaven, or something like that."

"I think it's something like that," he said as he looked back at me. "Can you feel it?" He closed his eyes and looked to be basking in the warmth. I actually could feel it, as if his connection to whatever was beyond stretched through him to me as well. I couldn't deny him this.

"Go, Chance." He opened his eyes and looked at me. "And if you see my mom over there, tell her I love her."

"I will. If you promise to do the same for me."

"I will."

"Ryan?" he asked, reaching a hand up to gently touch my face. He stepped forward, bringing himself right up to me. "I love you, Ryan." I felt the tears slip, warmth running down my already wet cheeks.

"I love you too, Chance."

He leaned forward, closing his eyes. I did the same, until the soft warmth of his lips touched mine. It could have lasted a second, or even a thousand years. For me, in that moment, time was infinite.

It was at once electric and calming. It was soft, but intense. It was gentle, but full of the fierceness of his love for me. It was perfect. I more than simply knew that he loved me in that moment. I felt it, deep in every fiber of my being.

When we broke, his intense, brown eyes, inches from my own, locked on mine. In that instant, I knew he'd be with me forever, even if I couldn't see him. He turned his head again, looking back toward whatever it was that awaited him. He looked back at me, his goodbye wordless but clear. I squeezed his hand, and let him go.

He turned and took a couple of steps toward the window, then looked back at me once more. He grinned, one last look at that smile I loved so much.

"Hey Ryan," he said, "no rush, man. I'll save you a seat." And with that he turned and stepped into thin air, vanishing with traces of wispy, iridescent light that seemed so familiar to me.

I stared at the empty spot for a long moment, gathering myself before turning to head back to my father. He was standing, a short distance down the hall, tears streaming down his face. I got one look at his awestruck expression and knew that he'd seen Chance.

I ran to him, and grabbed him tightly. He held me tighter than he ever had before. His hands shook, and I could feel his heartbeat pounding. Both of our worlds shaken, in the same instant. Neither of us would ever be the same.

Epilogue
Lessons

It was only a couple of weeks until Principal Avery's trial. Things moved at a different pace out here in the country, I'd learned. Some things moved slowly, almost agonizingly slow for someone like me, so used to the fast pace of the city, but when there was business to be done the folks around here rallied and worked and got things done in incredible time.

Mrs. Bradley, my father, even Jennifer had all testified. I had to as well, retelling the story to the jury. I aimed my words at the jury, rather than the lawyers. I wanted them to see in my eyes the truth of what I was saying. I left out Chance of course, though I did talk about what I'd learned about Dominic Hale's death. I had already told the police what I knew and Dominic's murder had been added to his charges, just like I'd promised Chance.

In the end, he was found guilty of two

attempted murders, and one murder in the first degree. He had even been found in contempt of court when he started screaming about God's justice at the judge. Principal Avery would be going to the state penitentiary for long enough that even with good behavior he'd almost certainly die decades before his sentence expired.

Whatever place Chance had gone on to, I felt sure it was for the souls full of love. I believed, now more than ever, that whatever divine power existed we would be taken care of after this life in the same manner we took care of our fellows in this life.

As the trial was concluded, I waited outside the courtroom for Chance's parents. They'd been pointed out to me by Jennifer while we sat, waiting for our turn to testify. My father sat on a bench nearby, content to wait for me.

They came out, holding each other for support. I could only guess that this trial had brought back a lot of old pain, but finally some closure for them as well. I approached the couple.

"Excuse me, Mr. and Mrs. Hale?" They stopped, looking at me curiously.

"Hello," Mrs. Hale said, dabbing at her eyes with a handkerchief, "I want to thank you for helping to prove that my son didn't kill himself. I knew he couldn't have. I always knew it."

"He wouldn't have," I agreed, "he was too strong for that. I had something I wanted to tell you too."

"Go 'head, son," Mr. Hale said to me. He looked like a nice, but broken man. He reminded me very much of my father, not so long ago. He also had the local accent, which Mrs. Hale didn't. That explained why Chance's accent was so subtle.

"I wanted to tell you that Chance wasn't alone." At that, his parents looked surprised and exchanged a glance.

"Ya called him Chance?" Mr. Hale asked.

"Yes, sir. He preferred it," I told him. "I just wanted you two to know that he wasn't alone, he had at least one good friend. He told me a lot of things, but the most important thing he ever told me was that he loved you both a lot and didn't blame either of you for anything." Mrs. Hale had started to quietly cry. Mr. Hale looked close to tears himself.

"He wasn't angry?" Mr. Hale asked. I shook my head.

"No, sir. Just sad that things had happened the way they did. He regretted fighting with you, but wanted you to know that he was who he was, and that deep down he knew you loved him too."

Mrs. Hale moved forward and hugged me. This was getting to be a habit with the women around this town. Oddly, I didn't mind. The people here were so genuine about their feelings, so open, for good or bad. I found I really liked that.

"Can I ask you a question though?" I asked,

once she'd let me go.

"Of course," Mrs. Hale replied.

"Where did the nickname Chance come from? He never told me." Mr. Hale smiled. It was a sad, but very fond smile.

"After we got married, we tried fer years t' have a child," he said. "We wanted one so badly, but it jus' didn't happen. We saved fer years an' finally had enough t' pay for in vitro fertilization, but we could only afford one chance. It worked, an' Dominic was born. When he was little, I always used t' call him my lucky chance. It sorta stuck. I always called him Chance. I didn't know anybody else did, though."

"I think," I said, venturing an educated guess, "that it was his way of staying connected to you, after the fight. Sort of his way of reminding himself that you loved him, and that he loved you. Anyway, I don't want to take up too much of your time. I just wanted to let you know that he talked about you both fondly, and that he loved you."

"Thank you, son," Mr. Hale said, reaching out and touching my head, "fer everythin'."

I nodded, and they walked away, still holding one another. I turned back to my father. Katie and her mother were sitting on the bench beside him. They were clearly waiting for me as well. Jennifer got to me first though, running up from behind.

"Ryan!" she called. I waited. "Ryan, I wanted t' tell you, I stopped goin' t' church. I started readin' an' listenin' an' realized you were right, 'bout everythin'. My mama was furious, but I won't let 'er make me go. I'm sorry for how I treated you."

"Don't worry about it, Jennifer," I told her, "you were trying to do what you thought was right. I really do appreciate the concern. Friends?" I asked.

She smiled and hugged me, kissing me lightly on the cheek. I smiled back at her. She started to turn and walk away, but she spotted Katie, gave a small, friendly wave, and then hurried on her way. I turned back to the bench. Katie was staring, stunned, at Jennifer's retreating back. I walked over, with a little laugh.

Katie's mom and my father were holding hands, and smiling at me. I returned the smile. They both deserved happiness, and if they found it together, I didn't think my mom would be upset about it at all.

"She kissed you," Katie said fiercely in my ear as the four of us walked toward the parking lot. My father had promised us all a nice lunch after a couple of rough days of trial. I laughed and whispered back to her.

"Just on the cheek, and not like that. We're friends. Besides, she waved at you, did you see that? Maybe there's hope for you two yet."

"Not likely," Katie replied, "but it's nice that she's at least being friendly. I'll take it." She was quiet another moment, then said in a more serious tone, "You holding up okay without Chance?"

I'd told her about him. I figured I'd rather she knew that I wasn't just schizophrenic or something, if we were going to be friends. To my great relief, she'd believed me. I nodded.

"Yeah, I think so." It had taken the weeks leading up to the trial to get me to the point I could say that. I was a wreck for a while after he'd gone. I was only okay now because I knew he was somewhere he was finally able to be happy, and that I'd see him again. "I miss him, a lot. But I can still kind of feel him, it's weird. Comforting, but still a bit strange. I know he's happy, and where he needs to be. I can almost hear him laughing sometimes." Katie nodded. "Besides, I still have a friend to rely on, right?"

"Hell, if your dad keeps smooth-talking my mom the way he has been, I might end up your sister," she whispered with a playful grin. I laughed.

"That'd be cool, I never had a sister."

"Me neither," she retorted. It took me a moment to understand what she meant.

"Hey!" I protested with a laugh, giving her a light shove. She laughed and we climbed into the car.

I thought about Chance as we drove, like I did every second of every day. I didn't think I'd ever stop, truthfully. I did miss him, but I was okay. Chance would want me to be.

I didn't understand much about what had really happened. Had God called him home? Was there a God? How had Chance been trapped here, unseen by anyone but me? I didn't know. I probably never would.

There was something after this life, and it was beautiful. It was the perfect place for a beautiful soul like Chance.

What it was, I tended to think of as Heaven, though I didn't really have another frame of reference for comparison so that might not be an adequate description. All I knew was that there was something, and it was worth living for.

Why I could see Chance and no one else could, I'll probably never know. Maybe we were soul mates, if there is such a thing. Maybe it was a fluke. I've never seen another spirit since, not that I know of anyway, so it could have been anything.

It didn't really matter though. Either way, my life would never be the same. I wouldn't want it to be. I learned so many things from him in such a short time, but it all amounts to the same thing. In the end, he taught me that everyone deserves to love and be loved. All they need is a Chance.

About the Author

Christopher Bailey lives in Washington with his amazing wife with their first child. Working professionally with families for more than twelve years has given him a unique outsider's perspective on many of the personal struggles individuals of all demographics go through in our society.

Inspired by his frustrations with a society so full of prejudice and hate, his second novel 'Without Chance' was a way for him to express his support and encouragement to the many young folks struggling with their sexuality and the pressures put on them by our society to conform to an arbitrary 'norm'.

A firm believer that 'love is love', he hopes this book might help at least one such young person come to realize that they too deserve to love and be accepted by not only their friends and family, but by society as a whole.

COMING SOON

STARJUMPER LEGACY

BOOK TWO

THE VANISHING SUN

CHRISTOPHER BAILEY

NOVEMBER 2014